THE RETURN

DULCE MARIA CARDOSO

THE RETURN

Translated from the Portuguese by
Ángel Gurría-Quintana

MACLEHOSE PRESS
QUERCUS · LONDON

First published in the Portuguese language as *O retorno* by Edições tinta-da-china Ltd, Lisbon, in 2011

First published in Great Britain in 2016 by
MacLehose Press
An imprint of Quercus Publishing Ltd
Carmelite House
50 Victoria Embankment
London EC4Y 0DZ

An Hachette UK company

This book has been selected to receive financial assistance from English PEN's PEN Translates
programme, supported by Arts Council England. English PEN exists to promote literature and
our understanding of it, to uphold writers' freedoms around the world, to campaign against the
persecution and imprisonment of writers for stating their views, and to promote the friendly
co-operation of writers and the free exchange of ideas.
www.englishpen.org

Supported by
**ARTS COUNCIL
ENGLAND**

FREEDOM
TO **WRITE**
FREEDOM
TO **READ**

A CIP catalogue record for this book is available
from the British Library.

ISBN (HB) 978 0 85705 432 6
ISBN (Ebook) 978 0 85705 435 7

10 9 8 7 6 5 4 3 2 1

Designed and typeset in Scala by Libanus Press, Marlborough
Printed and bound in Great Britain by Clays Ltd, St Ives plc

Translator's Preface

On April 25, 1974, a military rebellion triggered the downfall of the *Estado Novo*, the dictatorship that had ruled over Portugal for almost fifty years. The socialist government installed after the "Carnation Revolution" had three declared objectives: democracy, development, decolonisation.

Portugal's grip on its African colonies was unravelling. Under pressure at home, and after defeats abroad, the new regime granted most of its "overseas provinces" their freedom.

In the turbulent run-up to formal statehood, half a million Portuguese citizens were forced to flee their homes and farms in Angola, Cape Verde, Guinea-Bissau and Mozambique. In the weeks before Angola's independence, up to four thousand of these evacuees landed daily in Lisbon and Porto as Angola prepared for its formal independence.

Because labels such as "colonists" or "settlers" were too politically charged, too redolent of past colonial sins, they were referred to instead as *os retornados*, the returned – even though many were born on African soil, and had never before set foot in Portugal. Dulce Maria Cardoso, who was eleven years old at the time, was among them.

The new arrivals felt unwelcome in a "Motherland" they had once idealised. They felt shunned by a population that considered them tainted through their involvement in Portugal's disastrous colonial venture. Their possessions languished in crates and containers piled up near the ports. They carried with them the memories of African landscapes, and the music of African languages. Their plight shamed a country, and changed it forever.

Drawing loosely on memories of the author's own childhood and adolescence, *The Return* tells the story of one of those uprooted families, and its efforts to make itself at home in an upturned world.

ÁNGEL GURRÍA-QUINTANA
Cambridge, 2016

For the uprooted
For Luís, my ground

But there are cherries in the Motherland. Big, glossy cherries that the girls wear like earrings. Pretty girls like only those from the Motherland can be. The girls here don't know what cherries are like, they say they are like the *pitanga* fruit. Even if they are, I've never seen them wearing *pitangas* as earrings and laughing with each other the way the girls from the Motherland do in photographs.

Mother tells Father to help himself to the roast. The food will go bad, she says, this heat ruins everything, just a few hours and the meat starts going off, when I put it in the fridge it becomes as dry as a shoe sole. Mother is talking as if we weren't going to take an aeroplane to the Motherland tonight, as if tomorrow we'd be able to eat the leftover roast in a sandwich, during the long break at school. Leave me alone, woman. As he pushes away the platter Father knocks over the bread basket. Mother picks it up and arranges the bread rolls with the same care with which she arranges her pills every morning before taking them. Father wasn't like this before it all began. By all I mean the gunfire ringing out around the neighbourhood. And our four half-packed suitcases in the living room.

We sit in a silence so solemn that the breeze sounds unusually loud. Mother helps herself from the meat platter with the restrained gestures she used when we had visitors. When she puts the platter back on the table her hand lingers over the tablecloth with the dahlias. Now there is no-one to visit us but even before it all started visitors were rare. My sister says, I still remember the day when that cockerel, the porcelain cockerel on the marble countertop, fell on the ground and broke its comb. We like to revisit insignificant anecdotes because we are beginning to forget them. And we haven't even left home. The aeroplane leaves a little before midnight but we have to be there earlier. Uncle Zé will drive us to the airport. Father will come later. After he puts down Pirata and sets fire to the house and the trucks. I don't believe Father will put down Pirata. I don't believe Father will set fire to the house and the trucks either. He probably says it so we won't think that they will be laughing at us. By they I mean the blacks. In the meantime, Father has bought petrol cans and stored them in the shed. Maybe it's true, maybe Father will go through with putting down Pirata and will set fire to everything. Pirata could stay with Uncle Zé who is not going away because he wants to help the black people build a nation. Father laughs every time Uncle Zé talks about the glorious nation that will rise by the will of a people oppressed for five centuries. Even if Uncle Zé promised to take care of Pirata it would be no use, Father thinks the only thing Uncle Zé is good at is bringing shame on his family. And maybe he's right.

Despite this being the last day we spend here, nothing seems very different. We have lunch sitting at the kitchen table, Mother's food is still bland, we're hot and the moisture of the dry season, or *cacimbo*, makes us sweat. The only difference is that we are quieter. We used to speak about Father's work, about school, about the neighbours, about the vacuum cleaner Mother saw in magazines and longed for, about the air-conditioning system that Father had promised, about the BaByliss to straighten my sister's curls, about a new bicycle for me. Father always promised we'd have everything the following year and almost never kept his promises. We knew the score but we were happy with Father's promises, I think we were content with the idea that the future would always be better. Before the gunfire began the future was always better. But it's not like that anymore and that's why we have nothing to talk about. And we have no plans. Father doesn't go to work, there is no school and the neighbours have all gone away. There will be no air conditioning, no vacuum cleaner, no BaByliss, no new bicycle. Not even a house. We are silent most of the time. Our trip to the Motherland is an even more difficult subject than Mother's illness. We never talk about Mother's illness either. At most we refer to the bag full of medicines on the kitchen counter. Whenever one of us has to prepare anything, we say, careful with the medicine. Same with the gunfire. If one of us goes near the window, careful with the gunfire. But we soon fall silent. Mother's illness and this war that makes us leave for the Motherland are similar in the silences they bring about.

Father coughs as he lights another cigarette. His teeth are yellow and the house smells of tobacco even when Father is away. I always saw him smoke A.C. cigarettes. Gegé, after returning once from a holiday in the Motherland, said that they didn't have any A.C. cigarettes there. If that's true, I don't know how Father will cope. I'm certain it's the last thing on Father's mind now and I don't know why I even think about it, why I waste my time thinking about uninteresting things when there are so many important things I should be thinking about instead. But I have no control over my thoughts. Perhaps my mind is not too different from Mother's, she is always getting lost in the middle of conversations. Every now and then Mother asks Father to smoke less but Father doesn't take her seriously, he knows that after some time Mother will forget her request the way she forgets almost everything. The neighbours used to get annoyed by Mother's absent-mindedness, if Dona Glória were not the way she is we'd have had to take offence at some of the things she does. But Mother is how she is and the neighbours couldn't hold a grudge against her, even if they had wanted to. But it was not only her absent-mindedness. The neighbours also thought that Mother did not take good care of me and my sister, whenever they saw us playing in rain puddles or running behind the T.I.F.A.'s fumigation truck they would say, pity those children growing up so wretchedly. The black children ran behind the truck, opening their mouths to gulp down the spray that killed malaria, but the white children never did this, the neighbours knew that the spray was dangerous and forbade their children from doing that just as they forbade them from splashing in puddles because of the roundworms. Dona Glória, those black people are different from us and nothing in this hellhole does them any harm, but we have to take care of our own, the neighbours warned.

It's because of this country that Mother is the way she is. For Mother there were always two countries, this one, the country that made her ill, and the Motherland, where everything is different and where she was also different. Father never talks about the Motherland, Mother has two countries but Father does not. A man belongs to the place that feeds him unless he has an ungrateful heart, that is what Father replied when he was asked if he missed the Motherland. A man must follow work like a cart follows the oxen. And he must have a grateful heart. Father only got as far as second grade but there is nothing he doesn't know about the book of life which, according to Father, teaches us the most. Lee and Gegé used to make fun of Father when he started talking about the book of life and I tried not to be embarrassed. It's in parents' nature to do and say things that embarrass their children. Or in children's nature to be embarrassed by their parents.

Everyone has gone away. My friends, the neighbours, the

teachers, the shop owners, the mechanic, the barber, everyone. We should no longer be here either. My sister accuses Father of not caring what happens to us and if it were up to Mother we would have gone away a long time ago, even before Senhor Manuel. I don't think it's true that Father doesn't care what happens to us although I don't understand why we haven't left when something bad could happen to us at any moment. The Portuguese soldiers hardly come this way anymore and the few that do have long hair and untidy uniforms, their shirts unbuttoned and their boots unlaced. They go skidding into curves on their jeeps and they drink Cuca beer like they're newly demobbed. Father calls the Portuguese soldiers lousy traitors but for Uncle Zé they are anti-Fascist and anti-colonial heroes. If Mother and my sister are not around my father says to Uncle Zé, instead of anti-fascists and anti-colonialists they should be anti-whores, anti-beer and anti-*liamba*, and an argument flares up between the two.

I don't know how Uncle Zé can continue to stand up for the Portuguese soldiers after what happened to him. Perhaps things happened differently in his mind, people can easily change their minds about what happened even when their minds are not as feeble as Mother's. It was only this morning, in my own mind, that today stopped being today. Mother was making rice pudding and, for a brief moment, this day became like any other earlier Sunday, one of those Sundays before there was any gunfire. The smell of rice cooking, the half-opened kitchen blind, the spots of sunlight on the green kitchen tiles, the buzzing of flies against the window's thin netting, Pirata wagging her tail as she waited to lick the pot lid, everything was just like one of those Sunday mornings. My sister thinks it's disgusting when Pirata licks the pot lids, so gross. She pulls the same face when my hands are dirty with bicycle oil but she doesn't mind the avocado and olive oil mush that she puts into her hair to straighten out the curls, a revolting green mush that makes her look like an alien from Mars. I don't know if I'll ever understand girls.

Mother poured the rice pudding into pink glass bowls and wanted to write our initials with powdered cinnamon but her hand was shaking. She blamed the pills and tried again, the cinnamon powder dropping from between her thumb and index finger to make our misshaped initials and even that was the same, our initials were never properly shaped on those Sunday mornings when we came back from the beach and rinsed ourselves off with a hose by the water tank. Pirata slipping on the water as it ran into the flower beds, the beach towels hanging on the soursop tree, Mother calling from the kitchen, careful with the flower beds, remember that salt water kills the roses. Mother doesn't like the sun or the salt water. She likes roses. Mother's flower beds have roses of all colours that Mother rarely cuts, the neighbours paid no attention to what Mother said and simply shook their heads, Dona Glória is so odd, what's wrong with cutting the flowers, they look so beautiful in a vase. Don't let the salt water kill the roses, Mother said, but even though we tried our best to wash it away there were always a few small specks glinting in the flower beds. The salt always killed off some of the roses.

Mother licked the cinnamon off her fingers as if it were a delicacy and went to the sewing room to retrieve a tablecloth from the suitcase where she kept her linens. The morning was still like any other Sunday morning. So much so that I felt like going out into the back garden for a sneaky cigarette. I was certain that everything was going to be the way it was before and that in the other gardens the neighbours would be lighting up barbeques and slathering olive oil onto the meat using cabbage leaves and the neighbours' children would be swinging on car tyres that hung from trees and licking the ice lollies they had just made. But Mother returned with the tablecloth, the one with the dahlias, and started crying once more, I'll never see my linen again, I'll never see this tablecloth again. And once again our morning became our last morning here, the gardens are empty, the barbeque grills are filled with old rain, the tyres hanging still from the trees like inquisitive eyes suspended in the air. Our last morning. So quiet despite the gunfire. Not even the gunfire can undo the silence of our departure, tomorrow we will no longer be here. Even if we like telling ourselves that we will be back soon, we know we will never be here again. Angola is finished. Our Angola is finished.

Pirata raises her head and then lays it back on my foot. The black spot around her right eye is the only spot on her short and bristly white coat. Pirata always welcomes us by jumping up and down, the way all dogs do, and has her ears folded back, as if someone had creased them forcefully. Father puts his lighter on the tablecloth with the dahlias, it's a Ronson Varaflame, we bought it at Mr Maia's jewellery shop when Father turned forty-nine. Mr Maia must also be in the Motherland. Father knows I smoke but I have never smoked around him, you need to be respectful, when you turn eighteen you can do whatever you want. I don't really like smoking but girls prefer boys who smoke. Girls also prefer boys who have motorcycles but Father will never give me a motorcycle, I need to knock some sense into you, just look at how a motorcycle left my shin. The scar is ugly as hell, the skin all bunched up around the bone, but it won't make me change my mind, the first thing I'll buy when I earn some money is a motorcycle. The girls in the Motherland must also like boys with motorcycles, girls are the same everywhere, at least where these things are concerned.

I'm feeding Pirata the leftover meat, says Mother, as if Pirata did not eat our leftovers every day. My sister pulls off the elastic band that holds her hair in a ponytail and puts it around her wrist, at least Pirata won't complain about the meat being bland, says my sister as she bunches up her hair, her gestures well practised, the elastic sliding off her wrist and onto her spread fingers, twice around the bunched-up hair, my sister never manages to get the smaller curls, the layer of curls closely attached to the dark skin of the nape of her neck, blonde curls, they are pretty but my sister hates them, you have black girls' hair, the neighbourhood children used to say to wind her up, except that black girls don't have blonde hair, girls take everything too seriously, it's as if they want to take offence.

Apologise to your mother, Maria de Lurdes, Father orders. The electric fan starts screeching, Father gives it a good whack and the emerald-green blades go back to their usual whirr. Apologise to your mother, Maria de Lurdes, when Father is cross he calls my sister Maria de Lurdes but the rest of the time she is Milucha. At least she tried the food, Mother almost always defends us. Father gets cross, how can I educate them if you always take their side, he bangs his fist on the table, the cutlery clinks on the plates, clink clink, Mother blinks, it sounds as though it might be a happy sound, like a clinking of glasses at a party, parties in the Motherland must sound just like that, clink clink, parties are similar everywhere, Mother gets up from the table, clink clink, trips on her high heels, skinny legs, the pills diminish her appetite, the neighbours are no longer around to laugh at Mother's clothes, clink clink, the neighbours packed into tight dresses copied from *Burda* magazine that exposed their thighs and their fat knees, let's eat the rice pudding, says Mother putting the bowls in front of us, clink clink, she sits down again, lips invisible beneath the pink lipstick, eyes sombre beneath the blue powder she puts on her eyelids, the neighbours used to comment on it, Dona Glória certainly uses a lot of make-up, the neighbours with their plain washed-out faces and the layers of lacquer applied at Dona Mercedes' salon and which made their foreheads so high they looked like extra-terrestrials, the neighbours with their poisonous tongues, Dona Glória is too old to have long hair, it will give people the wrong idea, surely Dona Glória doesn't want people speaking ill of her, clink clink. In front of me, the bowl of rice pudding with an R badly written in cinnamon powder, R for Rui, L for Lurdes, M for Mário and G for Glória. Clink clink.

Father lights another cigarette and stubs it out immediately on the ashtray with the Cuca logo, he grumbles, not even cigarettes taste the same. It was Dona Alzira who gave him the ashtray, Dona Alzira's husband had been a distributor for the beer factory for over twenty years and got ashtrays for free even though he had never smoked a single cigarette, there were ashtrays in every room of Dona Alzira's house, who knows, maybe she and her husband had taken a suitcase full of ash-trays to the Motherland. Maria de Lurdes, my father says again, annoyed, my sister knows she has to apologise to Mother, I bet she is plotting some revenge in her mind. Girls from the Motherland must also be vengeful. They wouldn't be girls if they weren't.

I'd like to go to Brazil or to South Africa. Even better would be to go to America like Senhor Luís. It must be good to live in America. The flight to America would take many more hours, though, I'm worried about being sick on the aeroplane like

Gegé when he went to the Motherland on holiday. When we were children, Father took us to watch the aeroplanes, we sat in the airport's observation deck sipping fizzy drinks, it was the closest we'd ever been to riding on an aeroplane. We even liked the aeroplanes' noise. In the car, on the way home, my sister asked me to pretend we were in an aeroplane, just imagine the car is flying through the air, only girls could think up such silly games. Gegé vomited on the aeroplane, it is so common that they even had bags for it, Gegé is a liar but I think he was saying the truth about that, if I am airsick I wouldn't even want to catch Father's eye, it would be shameful, a man only vomits when he's drunk or if he's eaten something bad.

The sun appears behind the mango tree's lowest branches and chases away the shadows that covered the deckchairs. We will never again take our siesta in the deckchairs, Father will never sit on the wooden stool while the barber gives him a haircut and a shave, a white barber, because only someone crazy would let a black man put a razor to his neck. My beard doesn't need a barber yet, at my age Father already had the beard he has today, we became men sooner, the barber used to say, I bet all that studying is holding them back, there was a hint of disdain in the barber's voice, studying is the best tool we can leave them, my father replied crossly bringing the conversation to an end. The barber is gone, he must be in the Motherland telling the joke about the midgets, a drunk man sees a group of midgets leaving a bar, hey, hey, the table football figures are running away, Father must have laughed the first time the barber told the joke and the barber told it every time he came here, the barber always laughed at the same joke, just make sure your hand doesn't shake and you slit my throat, Father scolded. The barber must be in the Motherland telling the joke about the midget table football figures, perhaps we'll find him there, Father says the Motherland isn't big, perhaps it will be easy for all of us to find each other, perhaps I will find Paula. On second thoughts, I don't want to find her, Paula is not so pretty and not even that much fun, the only thing in the world she cares about is window-shopping, the hours I spent with her looking at dresses through Sarita's shop window, they're pretty don't you think, do you prefer the blue or the green. I didn't know but Paula insisted, tell me, tell me. The green. And Paula says, but the blue is much prettier, boys are all the same, they have no taste. I need to meet the girls from the Motherland, lovely girls with cherry earrings and dancers' shoes.

Mother doesn't try the rice pudding, it needs some lemon, she says, running her fingers over the tablecloth's embroidered dahlias, I never thought a day would come when I wouldn't be able to find anyone in this neighbourhood to borrow a lemon from. The rice pudding seems overcooked but I keep this thought to myself and swallow it as if it were medicine. Mother begins making the small talk she used to make when we had visitors, this is one of the tablecloths from the suitcase where I keep my linen. Perhaps it is the best kind of talk to have since we are now like visitors. Except that we are sitting around the kitchen table and visitors never entered the kitchen. When I came over to be with your father I brought the yellow suitcase filled with linen I had embroidered myself, I was in such a hurry to come over, I worked in the fields during the day and embroidered in the evenings, I was in such a hurry to come over that I hardly slept, I couldn't believe I would have a house with running water, it seemed impossible, I was in such a hurry that I had to unstitch this dahlia three times, you can still see the damaged fabric here, a house with running water meant I would never have to carry water from the well again, how I hated those blue water jugs, one on my head and one in each hand, from the house to the well and from the well to the house, the path seemed endless carrying all that weight, not a single house in the village had running water, a house with taps from which water ran on demand was only possible far away from that misery, in a place so far away that not even the cold could reach it, I couldn't believe that it would never be cold here, I put two thick woollen blankets in the suitcase with the linen, and at this point Mother always laughed but today she doesn't laugh. The yellow canvas suitcase with the black lozenges in which she brought the linen is next to the sewing machine and will stay there. Today Mother cannot bring herself to laugh at having brought woollen blankets to such a hot place as this. Out of the contents of that suitcase, Mother will only be bringing her linen tablecloth. It is not the one she likes most but it is the one she can sell more easily if necessary.

I won't be able to take my collections of *The Adventures of Kit Carson* or *Captain America* but I can take my poster of Brigitte Bardot and my signed poster of Riquita. I rolled them up carefully so they will arrive in good shape. When I was a boy I used to kiss Brigitte Bardot's poster, I used to seek her mouth and close my eyes, enormous kisses, I never told anyone about that, there are things not even friends can know about. Gegé says that in the Motherland all girls wear shorts and knee-high boots like Riquita, *Riquita, you are so pretty, Riquita, you are our queen and Angola believes in your beauty.* I once asked for her autograph after she paraded down Marginal Avenue, it was difficult, there were so many people I could barely reach her. Riquita has also gone away, I'm sure.

My sister can't decide if she should take her two special-edition photonovels, *The Lady of the Camellias* and *Romeo and Juliet*, or her Percy Sledge and Sylvie Vartan records. I should take my "La Décadanse" record, there is no better music for slow dancing than "La Décadanse", it's like a spell, when "La Décadanse" is playing we can feel up the girls and fumble with their bra hooks. Lee says girls are easy to persuade as long as the right record is playing and that they are as keen to show us their tits as we are to see them, if they weren't they wouldn't wear such tight jumpers or lean forward the way they do. I miss dancing to "La Décadanse" with Paula, and going with Lee and Gegé to spy on the girls in other neighbourhoods, and watching the films shown at the Miramar cinema through binoculars from Ganas' balcony. Gegé says they have no open-air cinemas in the Motherland, I can't understand how it's possible that everything in the Motherland is better than here and yet they have no open-air cinemas.

Father takes the carving knife and uses its sharp tip to rip one of the dahlias that Mother embroidered. Deliberately, as if there were a proper way of ripping the dahlias and Father had learned it just as well as Mother had learned to embroider them. Mother stretches out her hand to stop him but then gives up. We're not leaving anything behind, says Father, thrusting the knife's point towards the centre of the dahlia that Mother embroidered in dark brown, not even the dust on our shoes, they don't deserve anything. By they he means the blacks. All of them. The nameless ones we don't know and the ones we do who have names like people in the Motherland except that they can't pronounce them properly, Málátia instead of Malaquias, Árárberto instead of Adalberto, you have to be a real idiot, a *matumbo*, not even to be able to say your own name properly.

Father used to call them *matumbos* for any old reason but it was always jokingly. Father has tanks filled with petrol in the shed and swore that the last thing he'll do in this place is burn everything down but I don't believe he'll actually do it. We should all go to the airport. We should go now, without waiting for Uncle Zé. Father can't stay behind to burn everything down, it's too dangerous, any property left behind by colonists will automatically belong to the future Angolan nation, no colonist can destroy the property he has amassed, if Father is caught burning down the house and the trucks they will kill him, they will kill us, they will chop us up with machetes and throw the pieces into a ditch, or they will stick us on poles by the roadside, just last week a white man's head was found impaled on the road to Catete. We won't leave anything behind, says Father as he begins ripping into the next dahlia.

Mother looks away, her eyes worried under the blue powder, she must not mind Father ripping her tablecloth, she won't take it anyway, she must be worried about Uncle Zé's delay, it was always difficult to guess what was happening in Mother's mind. Since this all started it has also been difficult to guess what is happening in Father's head, and my sister's, and mine, it's as if we have all become like Mother. Father rips the dahlias and Pirata turns belly up, she must be dreaming because she's moving her legs quickly as if she were in an upturned world and running behind the children in their push karts. We remain silent but don't leave the table. The knife, large and sharp, looks small and blunt in Father's large and furious hand. Father is almost two metres tall and weighs nearly one hundred kilos, wherever Father is everything looks smaller, the seat of Father's chair is sagging, who will sit in Father's chair, who will take our places, how long before they occupy our house, from what side of the street will they arrive, will they enter by the front door or through the garage door, how long before they discover they have to give the electric fan a good whack to make the screeching stop, the electric fan also stays behind, we don't need an electric fan in the Motherland. It's summer there right now but Mother says it won't be warm for long and autumn will be cold.

Mother would know. It was autumn when she came here aboard the *Vera Cruz* with ribbons tied around the tips of her plaits, the way she wears them in the photograph that hangs in the living room. Mother won't ever be able to look at the photograph and tell us what it was like, it was raining when I left my country, my parents took me to the train station in a rented car. Here no-one rides trains, the blacks all hang on to the wagon doors, but that isn't riding a train. I last saw my parents on November 30, 1958, the station clock showed ten past seven, my parents said their goodbyes, they didn't hug me, it wasn't something we normally did, they gave me a bag with Terrincho cheese, some bread and chopped-up chestnuts to eat during the trip, may God bless them. If Father doesn't burn everything down what will happen to the photograph when Mother isn't here to tell the stories about when she left the Motherland, the nine-day journey by boat, the arrival, it was so windy that the dust whirled as if the devil himself were blowing it around, reddened dust, she had never seen anything like it.

We should have gone by boat, Senhor Manuel was more cunning, if we were going by boat Mother could bring the suitcase in which she keeps her linen back to the Motherland. There are no places left on the boats, there is nothing left. Two hours before the *Vera Cruz* moored Father was already waiting on the dock, Mother disembarked wearing a grey skirt and a white blouse instead of a wedding dress. There were two other brides on the boat, proper brides, with veils on their heads. It was so windy that the brides had to clutch the veils, they were worried that the veils would fall into the water. When she disembarked Mother searched the dock for the boy who had fled the village's misery many years ago, the boy in the photograph that hung from her neck on a gold chain. Instead, a man waved discreetly from the dock's furthest corner. The new shoes hurt my feet so much, Mother never forgot to tell visitors about the new shoes and the blisters on her feet that made her take the shoes off even before she reached Father's side. Perhaps Mother already was like she is now, perhaps it is not because of this country, this heat, this humidity, Mother arrived at Father's side with her shoes in her hand and instead of greeting him she said, you don't look like you. Father must still be jealous of the boy in the photograph that Mother carries on a chain around her neck even now. The veiled brides hugged their fiancées so hard that they almost suffocated them, but Father was not like the other men who had scampered onto the stacks of crates in the middle of the dock to wave at the brides and who had put on dark polyester suits and slicked back their glistening hair, your father was wearing a new white shirt, the red dust stuck to him as it would stick to a dog's coat.

Perhaps Father was disappointed that Mother was not

wearing a fake diamond tiara like the other brides, or carrying a little bouquet of orange blossom, Mother greeted Father without embracing him, I didn't even remember your father's voice, I was a girl when your father moved here, I never thought one day he'd write to ask for my hand in marriage. Mother with her back to the sea, not recognising Father, knowing nothing about the land in front of her, the cranes seemed to loom higher than the clouds, the port seemed so large, there must have been one hundred mooring bollards. Mother was scared of the birds that shrieked like the ones in Lisbon, your father told me they were called seagulls. I wasn't scared of black people, there was nothing special about them, they were just black. The port had a sour smell, as if the sea had curdled, in Lisbon the port didn't smell that bad.

Father took Mother to the old house in the green Dodge, the one I learned to drive in before Father gave it to Malaquias, it was falling to pieces, Malaquias was never able to fix up the Dodge, I'd be surprised if anyone can repair it, Father said when Malaquias took it away, but Malaquias seemed happy anyway, he finally owned something, the problem is they don't think straight, by they I mean the blacks, the ones we know and the ones we don't. The blacks. No-one ever bothered trying to explain who these people are, it was always just the blacks, blacks are lazy, they like to lie in the sun like lizards, blacks are arrogant, if they walk with their heads down it's only so they don't have to look us in the eye, blacks are stupid, they don't understand what we say to them, blacks are greedy, give them your hand and they'll want the whole arm, blacks are ungrateful, no matter how much we do for them they are never happy, people could talk about blacks for hours but the whites didn't like to waste their time on that, it was enough to say, he's black and we know what that means. A few months after the military coup back in the Motherland Malaquias' brothers said to Father, go to shit, you white shit, Malaquias' brothers also worked for Father at the shop and that day when Father told them they shouldn't drink during working hours they said, go to shit, you white shit. Malaquias would have apologised to Father but he never came back to work, his brothers were delinquents and must have stopped him. Go to shit, you white shit, they can't even swear properly, if I see you around here again I'll blast a bullet into those horns of yours, niggers, you little pieces of shit, Father knows how to swear. Go to shit, you white shit, it makes you want to laugh.

Father took Mother's hand as they walked to the Dodge parked by the entrance to the port, the sun beating down on them, Mother was amazed that Father owned a truck, I was amazed by everything, the seagulls, the truck, the palm trees, I had never seen trees like that, the red mountains, here they call them hills, Father corrected, people don't use the word like we do back in the Motherland, you don't say a hill of hay, or a hill of laundry to press, they are different things. The heat made Mother's bare feet swell even more, the neighbours had not yet met Mother or else they would have said, only Dona Glória would be a barefoot bride, the neighbours at the old house remember Father arriving with Mother and carrying her in his arms down the road, they remember Mother with her shoes in her hand, the road was unsurfaced, it was a red earth path, as if someone had meant it to be the road to hell.

Pirata goes and sits by the wall in the living room. In the beginning, she was scared of the sound of gunfire but she isn't any longer, she trusts us, she trusts that we won't let anything bad happen to her. Father is already fed up with ripping the dahlias, where is your brother, he should have been here hours ago, Mother gets up without answering. Uncle Zé is late and lateness these days can mean someone's full name being read out in the list of the disappeared on radio before and after "Simply Maria". My sister likes that radio soap opera so much that a few nights ago she dreamed that Alberto from "Simply Maria" was waiting for her as she got off the aeroplane at the Motherland. How could she not be embarrassed to tell us something so childish, my sister coming in all happy and telling us, I dreamed that Alberto from "Simply Maria" was waiting for me at the airport. I never dreamed about the girls with the cherry earrings. I keep their pictures between the mattress and the bed frame but no-one has ever found them, not even Mother who moves the beds around every week to sprinkle cockroach poison.

Father knows, I mean, he doesn't know I keep the pictures of the girls from the Motherland but he knows what I do. He never talked about it with me but I know he knows because on Sunday afternoons, when Mother complained about me staying in my room too long after the siesta and making everyone late for our outing to the Ilha, Father would wink at me and stand up for me, the boy needs to give his brain a rest from all that studying. Father and I are in the same club, whenever I took too long in the bath and Mother needed to use the bathroom to curl her hair or apply blue eyeshadow, Father would say, bathing properly takes time, or if at night I emptied the contents of the fridge because doing it made me so hungry Father would find an excuse for me the following morning, the body grows when it's resting and a growing body needs food. I should stay behind with Father and help him burn everything down but Mother and my sister can't stay alone with Uncle Zé, Uncle Zé is not like us, he doesn't belong to the same club as Father and me, there must be a club for people like Uncle Zé.

But in the Motherland there are beautiful girls. Girls with cherries for earrings, satin ribbons in their hair and skirts up to their knees like in the photographs from the magazines I bought at Senhor Manuel's tobacco shop. Senhor Manuel had the best idea, he embarked with his family on the *Príncipe Perfeito* on December 31 of last year, back then you could hardly hear the gunfire or the clatter of containers being loaded onto ships, I give it less than a year before you're all doing the same, God willing by then there will still be some ships left and enough wood to pack your belongings into crates, God willing.

Now we know that God wasn't willing. But at the end of that afternoon when we sat at the tobacconist's counter God still had time to change his mind, Father laughed at Senhor Manuel, I give it less than a year before you're back, less than a year and you'll be carrying all your luggage back with you, Senhor Manuel insisted, the revolutionaries have sold us out to this black mob, Senhor Manuel was always talking about the black mob and the mulatto mob, this black mob won't rest until they've scalped us, Senhor Manuel hated the revolution and revolutionaries, he often got so agitated while bad-mouthing the revolution that he would choke, Senhor Manuel's pear-shaped head purple from coughing, Father smiled, don't talk nonsense, my friend, things will get better, we'll stop being second-rate Portuguese citizens, the neighbours smiled at Father but kept their arms crossed and their brows furrowed like people with serious problems, have a beer, my friend, you'll see things differently, Senhor Manuel refused, you laugh but the communists from the Motherland want us out of here and they'll succeed, they've already disarmed our soldiers, a white man can't carry a weapon anymore but a black man can carry two, bunch of traitors and sell-outs, and it isn't just the communists, it's everyone, don't even ask what people say about us in the Motherland, what they call us, remember what I say today, there will be a bloodbath here, the violence of 1961 was nothing compared to what will happen here, it will be a free-for-all, God willing it won't be too late by the time you agree with me.

It was.

On the same night that Senhor Manuel and his family boarded the *Príncipe Perfeito*, we went to a New Year's Eve party. My sister wore a maxi-skirt and put on proper make-up for the first time, I had never seen her look so pretty, Father looked at the crowd dancing at the party, his glass filled with Ye Monks, how can all these people leave, Father asked, Mother sipped a fizzy drink in a tall champagne flute, she looked like a film star but less glamorous. All those people cannot have left. The band played out of tune but no-one stopped dancing, *I was minding my own business, when my sweetheart called me, to see the band march past playing love songs, my long-suffering people, forgot their pain, to watch the band march past playing love songs,* people pressing up against each other, the lines of dancers getting longer and the circles in the club's hall getting smaller, nothing had changed, the band marching past playing love songs and the people forgetting their pain, Father began drinking Ye Monks straight from the bottle, Mother never drinks because of her medicine but that night she drank and danced for Father, there were so many people in a circle clapping hands while Mother danced for Father, they can't all have gone away, the midnight bells hadn't rung yet and the slices of eggy bread were already going stale on the tables, the cornbread dry as hay, everyone complained about the damn heat that ruins everything. When the slow dancing started I asked Paula to dance, my hands on Paula's neck, Paula's skin so soft, 1975 was going to be a good year, maybe even the best year of our lives, we were going to stop being second-rate Portuguese citizens, the future was here, Father was right despite the armoured cars on the streets and the gunfire that had already started, despite the blacks pouring into Luanda from all over the country, there are lots of black people in a country fourteen times larger than the Motherland, they seem to crawl out from under every rock, they are worse than a plague, worse than weeds, Father sometimes said things like that when he was drunk, but he also said there was nothing in the Motherland other than hunger and headlice, or that the neighbours were all unhappily married, it's not that Father really believed that, it was because of the Ye Monks, the entire city was celebrating, it could be the last time the city celebrated but it didn't matter, Mother sang along with the out-of-tune band, *and to my disappointment, the sweet moment passed, everything went back to normal, after the band marched past, and we each went back to our corners, and in each corner was an ache, after the band marched past, playing songs of love,* people danced as though there would be no tomorrow, the streamers stuck to the bare backs of the sweaty girls, confetti fell everywhere, it stuck to Dona Magui's eyeglasses, don't go looking at the girls in the miniskirts, she said, Dona Magui's husband laughed showing his gold tooth and twirled Dona Magui in his arms as if they were a young couple, good things are meant to be looked at, he said while Dona Magui danced around blindly with confetti stuck to her glasses, that night no-one was going anywhere. The band was never going to stop marching past playing songs of love, the future would happen as the future should, Paula would agree to go out with me and would let me unfasten her bra, I would get my driving licence and take her to the Miramar cinema, Father would get a loan from the bank to buy the Scania that was on display in that dealership in the city centre, Mother's head would get better and she would no longer have her crises, my sister would finish seventh grade and find a better boyfriend than Roberto who fancied that Indian girl, Lena, who had a crush on Carlos, Pirata would die of old age the way Bardino had died and like Jane had died years before Bardino, the neighbours would continue to begrudge Mother all those things that they couldn't help begrudging her, the only things that would change were the ones that needed to change to make our life more like the life that Father had imagined when he sailed over on the *Pátria*.

During those first hours of 1975 everyone would have agreed that Senhor Manuel had been a prophet of doom, there would be no bloodbath, the violence of 1961 was buried along with its dead. My sister went off to ride pillion on Roberto's motorbike, Father didn't notice, he had knocked back a lot of Ye Monks and Mother danced barefoot non-stop. I took Paula behind the leaves of the palm trees that decorated the walls, we kissed five times, those big kisses with tongues that leave you breathless and with an aching jaw, I had vowed never to ask her to go out with me but kisses always make me forget my vows, Paula said no again, I was so angry at her but I kissed her again, Paula's mouth tasted of apple-flavoured soft drinks and pink fruit. In between kisses Paula talked about Nando, her old boyfriend who was studying in Rhodesia, a good-for-nothing who was into boats and aeroplanes and this made me even angrier with her, but I couldn't stop kissing her. When we got back to where the others were the party was winding down. We went home and Father opened another bottle of Ye Monks, he wanted us to toast 1975 once again, my sister toasted with water, Mother was worried and said that it was bad luck, superstitions, woman, don't believe in superstitions, we raised our glasses to 1975, which was going to be the best year of our lives.

Except that the band never again marched past. Everything went back to normal, and we each retreated to our own corner, and in each corner was an ache, as Chico Buarque said in his song. For a while Father continued to believe that 1975 was going to be the best year of our lives, everything will go well, we'll build a nation, blacks, mulattos, whites, together we'll build the world's wealthiest nation, better even than America, this is a blessed land where anything you sow will bear fruit, there is no other land like this one in the whole world. Father knows nothing about the world and cannot know if there is another land like this one or not, just as he couldn't possibly know what would happen. For some time he would guarantee to whoever wanted to hear him that everything would be fine, he would wager everything he owned on it. But the gunfire and mortar shots did not stop, blacks continued to pile in from everywhere and whites continued to leave, Portuguese soldiers had given up on flying the flag and the communists from the Motherland came over. No matter how much he wanted to believe that everything would go well Father had to shut up, he had to stop placing bets because, among other things, there was no-one left to bet against. Father stopped talking about the future and in his face we could see the shame he felt at having been so mistaken and the worry that it might be too late to do anything about it. The blacks didn't start killing whites indiscriminately straight away but as soon as they got a taste for it they did nothing else and the whites fled even quicker. The city emptied day by day, if Father could have tied up the whites to prevent them from leaving he would have, sometimes he became agitated, they can't just leave like that, at least put up a fight, but the whites only wanted to run to the airport and head for the Motherland, so cowardly, Father didn't know who to despise most, the blacks, ungrateful murderers, or the whites, treacherous cowards.

No-one ever repeated Senhor Manuel's words, there was no need, the violence of 1961 had been child's play, Father became quiet and couldn't even bother condemning Senhor Manuel for what we found out he had done, he had dispatched over to the Motherland a brand new Audi 100S Coupé for which he had paid only the first instalment, Uncle Zé began referring to Senhor Manuel as the imperialist thief. Later it emerged that the imperialist thief had been even more cunning, he had stolen diamonds that his wife hid in the hem of her skirt. Their loathing for Senhor Manuel must have been the only thing Father and Uncle Zé had in common, even if Uncle Zé had more reasons to hate Senhor Manuel, I don't trust people like him, Senhor Manuel used to say of Uncle Zé as he sat at the counter of his tobacco shop, wouldn't be caught dead trusting one of them. To many people Uncle Zé was just one of them but to us at first he was simply Mother's little brother who one day showed up at our house in fatigues, with a tattoo that said Angola 1971.

Mother could not believe that her little brother was now standing in front of her in fatigues, she was so happy she wouldn't let Uncle Zé get through the door, I left you when you were a baby and now you turn up dressed as a soldier, come in, come in, giving him another hug that Uncle Zé accepted before he was even able to put down the presents he had brought from the Motherland, my sister and I watched from the top of the stairs undecided about whether to come down, we had never imagined that one of our relatives from the Motherland could appear on our doorstep. Relatives from the Motherland existed only in those letters that went to and fro with names even stranger than those of the blacks, Ezequiel, Deolinda, Apolinário, except that back in the Motherland they can actually pronounce those names, they aren't *matumbos*, those letters from relatives on very thin paper filled with bad handwriting that strayed off the lines, we lit an oil lamp for Saint Estêvão to make Manelinho sleep better, cousin Zulmira became engaged to Aníbal dos Goivos, the pigs caught fever from passing Gypsies, Zé Mateus will be christened during the feast of Our Lady of Grace, Uncle Zeferino died from the lump on his head, the frost killed our wheat, letters filled with so many spelling mistakes that it seemed to us that people in the Motherland had never been subjected to Miss Maria José's ruler or cane, the first lines in the letters were almost always the same and almost without mistakes, I hope this finds you in as good health as we are in, praise be to God.

Mother taught us about relatives in the Motherland as if it were homework or Sunday school, Mother's side, Father's side, first cousins, uncles and aunts, first cousins once removed, relatives by birth and by affinity, the dead and the living. Every now and then the letters included photographs, babies dressed in thick wool, at a round table covered in a crocheted table-cloth, a newly engaged couple surprised by the flash beside a table covered in the same tablecloth, girls doing their solemn first communion posing like saints with their rosaries and cate-chisms, the same table and the same tablecloth again, there was no other table and no other tablecloth in the Motherland. The photograph that made Mother cry the most was the photograph of our grandparents, two old people dressed in black, Grand-father with a beard and moustache, how my sister and I laughed at Grandfather's beard and moustache, Grandfather standing tall and straight like a prince, a thumb missing on the hand that held his walking stick, he lost it while chopping firewood, firewood often features in Mother's memories, my sister and I pretended that Grandfather had been injured in war and Mother never corrected us in front of other children, Grandfather had been injured during the Second World War and was therefore more important than any other grandfather. Mother bought a frame for my grandparents' photograph and put it on top of the china cabinet, the first and only photograph I ever had of my parents, may God rest their soul. Mother can't bring herself to leave my grandparents' photograph but she has to leave the album with the christened children, the new bride and groom, the saintly girls at communion. If Father does not burn everything down the relatives from the Motherland will end up in the hands of the blacks, the album with the little Chinese girls carrying umbrellas and instruments on the cover, in relief, the bundle of letters at the bottom of a wardrobe drawer tied up in a satin ribbon that Mother bought from Dona Guilhermina the haberdasher, a woman with breasts so large, so large that they must be the biggest breasts in the world, there can be no bigger breasts than hers, even in America where everything is better and bigger there cannot be any woman with breasts bigger than Dona Guilhermina's.

Uncle Zé finally managed to get through the front door carrying the gifts from the Motherland, Mother was still pointing at the roses in the garden and he was already making his way up the stairs, Mother shouting from the garden, careful,

careful with the vases, there were lots of vases on the stairs that Father regularly knocked down, what a bad idea to leave vases on the stairs, who will water Mother's roses now, Mother would never let her roses die, when the days were very hot the neighbours' roses wilted so much you felt sorry for them, but not Mother's, there was nothing that made Mother as proud as her garden. Uncle Zé greeted us, his arms stretched as if he were reaching out from far away, he smelled of sweat, he smelled worse than the blacks whose pong so disgusted Senhor Manuel, our arms open and Mother saying, give your uncle a hug, don't be silly, we hugged him, the smell of sweat on his uniform stuck to us. Uncle Zé said the living room was spacious and nice, he flopped onto the green leatherette visitors' armchair, visitors didn't usually sit like that, they were careful not to knock over the ashtrays that Mother placed over doilies on the armrests, women sat sideways the way they do in magazines and men sat upright even when they crossed their legs and accepted a glass of Ye Monks with ice that Mother would carry in the wine-coloured plastic bucket, her hands unable to fish the ice out with the tongs, the pills always interfering with whatever Mother tried to do.

Hosting visitors was hard work but to be a visitor was even worse, we sat carefully and stayed still like the mannequins in shop windows, we ate with deliberate slowness, we didn't want our hosts to think we were hungry, we never had a second helping of pudding, we didn't want our hosts to think it was the first time we had had a sweet treat. Despite our efforts we were bad visitors, Father dropped ashes everywhere and complained that the whisky was no longer Ye Monks, Mother asked inappropriate questions and interrupted conversations at random like an impatient child, not to mention the laughter, Mother finds things funny that no-one else does, our neighbours were right, there were so many things about Mother that could rub you up the wrong way. My sister didn't open her mouth unless she was asked something, how's school, Milucha, my sister doesn't like studying, I don't like it either, my father says we're as lazy as the blacks and has sworn many times he'll beat the laziness out of us even if he has to whip us with his belt because studying is the best way to get a good start in life. Sometimes Father told us off, you'd better get good grades, we never did, we studied enough to get a pass grade and no more, we were never in the honours group and we never got a school award. Editinha was always in the honours group and Milu was given three awards. But Editinha was ugly as sin and had legs like pocket-knives. Not Milu, though, Milu was pretty and Gegé was always after her.

Uncle Zé, sitting in the armchair in the same relaxed way we sat on the deckchairs, was a visitor who did not behave as visitors should. The news from the Motherland seemed stranger because of the way Uncle Zé spoke, whistling his S's even more strongly than Father or Mother did. His soldier's boots hit the varnished side table and almost knocked over the glass of water in which a lucky bamboo stalk grew vigorously, Mother reprimanded Uncle Zé again, if you'd let us know we would have come to meet you off the boat. We should have been able to see right away that Uncle Zé was not like the other soldiers, he shut his eyes when he sipped fizzy drinks, he batted his eyelashes, he complained of the humidity that made his lungs heavy and gave him bad skin, of the heat that made his eyesight blurry, other soldiers didn't talk like that, and on top of it all Uncle Zé's lips had the shape of a heart like Mother's lips, what a beautiful man you've become, Mother said to him, Father never lets Mother call me beautiful, men should not be beautiful but Uncle Zé smiled gratefully and even blushed the way girls do, men should not blush.

When they finally opened the parcels from the Motherland my sister and I saw cherries for the first time, they had arrived old and shrivelled inside a box lined with straw. My mother ate the cherries with such pleasure that my sister and I were convinced that cherries were the world's most delicious fruit, nothing tastes as good as cherries, my mother repeated, but she was wrong, nothing can taste as deliciously bad as cherries do. Uncle Zé's army boots left marks on the armchair's fabric that Mother wiped off with paraffin the next day. When Father returned from work we went to Baleizão to celebrate Uncle Zé's arrival, Father turned on the car radio, windows open, it was a time before blacks were bold enough to come up to our cars and rob us, the sky was so orange that Uncle Zé said it looked like the largest blaze he'd ever seen, Mother wearing a white turban on her head and Uncle Zé telling her she looked as fancy as the women in Lisbon, it had to be a lie, how could Mother look like the women in Lisbon if even the neighbours made fun of the way she dressed.

When night fell Uncle Zé said that the sky darkened so quickly here that it was as if someone had switched off a light in the sky. We sat at a table and talked, Uncle Zé ordered beer, how do you get rid of this heat, he hardly touched the grilled bread with ham or the Italian cakes Father ordered for everyone. It's late, the children have to go to school tomorrow, Uncle Zé refused Father's offer of a lift, he hailed a taxi, it had been a good day despite the smell from Uncle Zé's uniform and his strange behaviour. Uncle Zé was about to get into the taxi when he turned back and hugged Mother again, they had missed each other, so many years, it was understandable. But then Uncle Zé started crying, a man doesn't cry, especially when he's a soldier, and especially when he sobs like a child, Father tried to separate them but Uncle Zé wouldn't have it, he cried with his face buried in Mother's shoulder and the Angola 1971 tattoo in plain sight until the taxi driver, tired of waiting, started honking the horn.

Then the letters began to arrive from Quitexe. The letters would arrive and Mother would read them to the neighbours while they made sets of placemats and bed-sheet trims. It was not long before Uncle Zé's adventures in the bush turned him into a sort of Tarzan of Quitexe. Afternoons in our neighbourhood were more boring than afternoons anywhere else, including hospitals, prisons and even among the dead in their cemeteries. Our neighbours had the short-sighted eyes of those who cannot see further than their own street and they sought distractions in everything, in rotten drivers who couldn't park at the first attempt, in the street vendors who hawked their fruits too loudly, it all helped to make the neighbours' afternoons go by more quickly but nothing compared to hearing the adventures of the Tarzan from Quitexe, as long as they didn't include beatings or white people getting ripped to shreds.

But one day a letter arrived and Mother lay down in bed, without even turning back the white lace bedcover, and started crying, with the ceiling fan at its highest speed. After that day there were no more adventures of the Tarzan from Quitexe. In any case, by that point Tarzan had already gone out of fashion, even at the movies. My sister was now in love with Trinity, from the cowboy films, and so were the other girls. My friends and I all wanted to be like Trinity but it was difficult to copy a cowboy's style in Luanda. It was the time when I most enjoyed having blue eyes. Not that they were anything like Trinity's but at least they were the same colour. Even married women sighed when they talked about Trinity's eyes being bluer than the lagoon of São João do Sul of which Mother had a photograph with lily pads and flamingos.

After that day when Mother locked herself up in her room

and cried, all letters arriving from Quitexe had the same effect, Mother lying on her bed with the ceiling fan drying her tears. One day Father picked me up at school and on the way home parked the car under a *mulemba* tree and gave me one of Uncle Zé's letters, not a word about this to your sister, girls understand things differently. Night was falling and there were many mosquitoes, you must have realised what's happening, no uniform can cover up what a disgrace your uncle is. The letter was filled with half-spoken words but it was clear that Uncle Zé was like one of the boys caught doing dirty things with others in the school bathrooms. Except that Uncle Zé was no longer a boy and was Mother's little soldier brother. Mosquitoes were biting me and I wanted Father to stop talking so we could go home but Father was agitated and wanted to say many things, I want you to tell me if your uncle starts saying funny things or gets too close to you. The sun must have hardened Father's skin so much that mosquitoes could no longer bite him, Father lit another cigarette, I was desperate to scratch myself but scratching is for girls, men should be prepared for everything and it won't be a mosquito that makes a man behave like a girl so I put up with it and kept still.

Father looked out at the leaves of the *mulemba* tree as if he wanted to find in them a way of correcting Uncle Zé, if I were your grandfather I would have straightened out your uncle even if I'd had to smack him every day, clay can always be shaped while it's still fresh, the bugger won't stop whining to your mother, he takes advantage of her kindness, he's got her in such a state, and your poor mother who, Father became silent, there were never words for Mother's illness, the bugger complains about other soldiers abusing him, of course they're going to abuse him, Father flicked his cigarette butt across the road, its speed betrayed his anger, if there weren't so many black women here your uncle might be in very high demand among the soldiers, yes, because all men have their needs.

I'm not used to having these conversations with Father and it embarrasses me when he talks about those things. It's different with Gegé and Lee, we would spend hours talking about what it would be like to do it with the white girls, we knew it was different with the black girls who don't even use knickers and will do it with anyone and even with two or three of us in a row if we wanted to, Fortunata once did it with seven, one after the other, we even queued like in the school's canteen. Gegé is the only one to have done it with a white girl, Anita. She's not a white girl like the others because she likes to show herself naked and is as keen to do it as we are. I don't think Anita's mother, Dona Natália who worked at Senhor Cristovão's butcher's shop, knew what her daughter was getting up to. Lee says she knew but didn't care because Dona Natália was the only woman in the neighbourhood who was separated and the neighbours said that Dona Natália and Senhor Cristovão were lovers. Perhaps they were. Dona Natália could cut up a piece of meat quicker than Senhor Cristovão and the neighbours were astonished, how could such a small woman have the strength to cut up a whole pig, unless she's thinking about slicing up her husband when she has the meat cleaver in her hand. The husband had shacked up with another woman and hadn't been seen in the neighbourhood since, Lee said Dona Natália had killed the husband and buried him in her back garden.

Because of Anita, Gegé could compare white girls and black girls and he assured us they were different down there, he even drew us a picture but Gegé was never good at drawing. Gegé must have already arrived in South Africa, he left with his family in a convoy over a month ago. I never got a letter from him but I'm sure Gegé wrote and the letter got lost because all the white postmen have left and the black ones can't even read the addresses, you have to be a real *matumbo* not even to be able to read an address. I didn't get a letter from Lee in Brazil, either, we lost touch and if we're lucky we might meet again at the Sears Tower. It was Lee who suggested the Sears Tower, Lee always knew the world records, the world's tallest tower, the fastest car, Lee took the poster of Concorde he had by his headboard, it seems so long ago that we went to see Concorde but it's only been two years, for a few months Lee wanted to be a Concorde pilot but then he changed his mind, better to be a ship's captain and solve the mystery of the Bermuda Triangle, Gegé wanted to be a spy, a spy who could discover who killed President Kennedy and the formula for Coca-Cola, I never knew what I wanted to be, I still don't know, I don't think I want to be anything even though my mother tells me I have to be a dams engineer and Father tells me I have to be a doctor or a lawyer. I miss Lee and Gegé. The last time the three of us were together was at Ganas' house, we had gone there for the umpteenth time to watch the film "Emmanuelle" being shown at Miramar, the best film we ever saw. From Ganas' balcony, each one of us with binoculars, we could see the film as well as if we had been at the cinema and when the actresses were naked we could choose what parts we wanted to magnify to see the differences between white girls and black girls that Gegé used to talk about.

That last day we were so sad that when the film was over we didn't even talk about the difference between doing it with white girls and black girls. Nor did we discuss whether any of the girls we knew did it with each other like they do in the film. But Gegé and Lee still argued because Lee said that simply being able to see Emmanuelle naked had made the coup worthwhile. Lee's father was a supporter of the revolution and taught Lee to see its benefits in everything, according to Lee's father workers would finally be able to walk towards socialism the way that cowboys walk towards the sunset at the end of a film. Lee's father had a flag on his veranda, a flag with the black cockerel, *Savimbi always, Angola always, kwacha Angola, kwacha UNITA*. Gegé's father was sure that the revolution would turn sour, that liberation would lead to debauchery, Gegé's father could not quite explain why it was so dangerous to confuse one with the other but still Gegé was unable to acknowledge that the coup back in the Motherland had brought any benefits, this despite him wanting to watch "Emmanuelle" as much or more than we did, especially the part where Emmanuelle did it with Marie-Ange.

Father never talked about revolution, it's only natural that the book of life says nothing about revolutions because few people are witnesses to a revolution in their lifetimes. Our teacher of Portuguese said we were very lucky to be part of the revolution, the glorious morning in April had been only the beginning, the evil forty-eight-year-long night had come to an end and now it was time to make good on the promises of April and that meant decolonising, democratising and developing. The teacher of Portuguese was young, he had long hair and reeked of *liamba*, he took his guitar to class and sang "Monangambé" as soulfully as if he were black, *in those big fields, there is no rain, it's the sweat on my brow that waters the plantations, in those big fields, the coffee beans ripen, cherry-red like drops of my blood turned into sap*, he didn't sing well but it was better to hear him singing "Monangambé" out of tune, or even *Mon'etu ua Kassule akutumissa ku San Tomé*, than to study the verses from *Os Lusíadas*. The teacher of Portuguese for Class B burned *Os Lusíadas*, the empire should never have existed, and neither should *Os Lusíadas*, which celebrated it.

I saw Lee two or three times after Gegé left but it was never the same, we missed Gegé's tall tales, the table football games at the club, our long school days, the gossiping neighbours on their verandas, the shops we used to go to, all of it was coming to an end and it wouldn't be long before Lee left as well. The two of us were still able to go for a bike ride even though it was dangerous for two white boys to be out cycling. Girls didn't dare leave their homes, the few of them who were still here never came out, if a white boy is a provocation then a white girl is an even bigger provocation. Even the black man who had shone our shoes every Sunday morning for the past five years warned my sister, one of the last times we saw him, be careful, young lady, because someone might do to you the same thing that the whites did to our women. The people who occupied Lee's house ripped up and burned the flag with the black cockerel as they shouted, victory is ours, death to colonisers, the black cockerel is a friend of the white slave-owning colonisers and is supported by imperialist forces, it is a capitalist lackey. Sometimes Gegé and Lee made fun of Uncle Zé. Lee thought it was unfortunate that I had an uncle like that because someone who didn't know me might suspect that his condition ran in the family. I often prayed to God that Uncle Zé would be injured so he would have to go back to the Motherland but apart from the buggering he got from the other soldiers nothing bad ever happened to him. When he finished his tour of duty he had the words Love Sister tattooed beneath Angola 1971 and Mother liked him even more. Instead of returning to the Motherland Uncle Zé found a job in a bar on the Ilha and it was there he met Nhé Nhé, the black friend who blows smoke rings like a girl, with his delicate mouth and his little giggle, look, I did it, look, I did it. After the coup in the Motherland, Uncle Zé began to help the oppressed people to free themselves from the colonial yoke, he carries a party card and everything. He knows the revolutionary songs by heart and learns Kimbundu with Nhé Nhé while they drive around in the Chevrolet Camaro that was confiscated from one of the exploitative colonialists who had fled.

The doorbell rings. We wait for the secret code, two rings in quick succession followed by a pause and a third longer ring. There are no further rings. Mother says Uncle Zé may have got the code wrong but Pirata barks, whoever rang the bell is a stranger. Mother and my sister lock themselves up in the bedroom and turn the key twice and drag a chair up against the door. Father takes the gun from the cabinet's smallest drawer and slips it into his trousers' waistband. Whites can't carry weapons but Father's shirt is loose enough to conceal the gun. When Father opens the door, Pirata runs to the gate. Outside the gate is a black soldier and Pirata won't stop barking. Behind the soldier is a jeep with more black soldiers. The soldier standing by the gate points his gun at Pirata. Father greets them and shouts at Pirata, be quiet, Pirata sits down obediently, wagging her tail. We have to greet each group of soldiers with the right salutation for their movement, blacks from one movement hate blacks from other movements even more than they hate whites, we mustn't confuse the salutations, people have died for lesser crimes. The soldier does not lower his weapon, a white man is a slave driver, a colonialist, an imperialist, an exploiter, a rapist, an executioner, a thief, any white man is all of that at once and cannot avoid being hated. There are children on the jeep, too, some armed and wearing uniforms, they have dry snot between their noses and their mouths and some even on their cheeks, one of the youngest has pus-filled blisters on his head, the rifles look like toy weapons but it's hard to say.

Before the soldier says why they're here, Father turns to me, go find some beers, son, these men are thirsty, bring some cigarettes too. I obey immediately but Father adds, and make it fast, son, these men don't have all day. I think I recognise one of the soldiers, the one sitting on the jeep's bonnet, a square face with eyes half shut, it's not unfamiliar, I've seen him but I can't remember where, perhaps he was doing the rounds some days ago, there are always black soldiers driving around in jeeps. I come back with the crate of beers and a pack of cigarettes that the soldier quickly shares out among the others. Not a glance in our direction. Without the slightest hint of having seen me before, the one with the square face opens a bottle with the tip of his knife and drinks the beer in one gulp, burps, lights a cigarette and opens another bottle. The soldiers' eyes are as muddy as the mountains and their uniforms are soiled with sweat.

Only us, the soldiers and the early afternoon sun on the street. I remember a football game on the clay pitch next to school, the game at which Lee called another player a black fuck because he did a clever feint. My heart beats faster. The black fuck might be the soldier with the square face and the half-shut eyes coming back to take revenge. It was a spat like so many others, black fuck, it was not an insult, we called Lee four-eyes and when he annoyed us we called him four-eyed fuck, we called Gegé lanky but also lanky fuck when we were being rowdy, black fuck was not an insult and only a black could take offence to the point of wanting to hit Lee. Gegé and I held the black lad and Lee gave him a good punch in the stomach. The black lad stumbled out of the field, I hope he learned his lesson, said Lee, and he called Garrincha to play instead. The black lad never played with us again and I can't even remember if he made it to the end of the school year. No, it isn't him. There are lots of blacks with square faces and eyes half shut as if they were difficult to open. It's not this one, it can't be.

Sweat makes the fine fabric of Father's shirt stick to his back. I'm worried that they'll notice the gun, a white man with a gun is asking for trouble big time. I straighten my back and swallow hard, a white man with a gun is a racist unwilling to abdicate his rights, a less evolved being fearful of losing his privileges, an imperialist resentful for no longer living in a world that should never have existed. The soldier standing in front of us throws his beer bottle so that it smashes against our house wall and Pirata starts barking again. We don't want to look at the shards so that it doesn't seem as though we're criticising but the broken glass glints in the sun and it's difficult to look away. The soldier asks, is there a problem, Father and I respond at the same time that there isn't, surely they are aware that we're scared. Father's fear is also obvious in his tightly pursed lips, even when he smiles, but perhaps the soldiers aren't aware of that. The soldier with the square face seems to amuse himself staring at me. It might just be the black lad from the football match. He might have remembered the match. Or perhaps he never forgot and that's why he's here. He's come to settle old scores.

The soldiers talk but we can't understand them. We never learned the black people's language, their languages, in fact, because blacks have many languages and perhaps that's why they don't understand one another, they cannot make sense of what the other is saying. This time we don't need to understand what these blacks are saying, we know what they mean with the weapons they are pointing at us even as we try to ignore them. The shops further down our road are closed and even the houses that have already been occupied have their blinds drawn. Some shops are still covered with the hoardings that their owners put up but most have been looted, the window displays smashed and the doors ripped out. Fear makes us sweat even more than the *cacimbo*'s humidity.

Two shots, one of the soldiers in the jeep shoots twice into the air. Pirata barks again and Father gives her a kick that makes her whimper and curl up beside him. Even if we hit her Pirata never goes away, she likes us, it doesn't matter if we hit her or not. I tell her to go home but Pirata remains in front of us, she is protecting us from the strangers as she always does. Alerted by the shots, the squatters in Dona Gilda's house have come to the windows and onto the veranda and point towards the jeep. People in the houses further away are also at their windows. A group of black children is hanging from Dona Gilda's cast-iron swing. One of Dona Gilda's brown suede armchairs was dragged out into the garden and now it's all wrecked. If Dona Gilda could see what they've done to her house, if she could see the brown suede armchair in that state, she would have a heart attack. Perhaps Dona Gilda is sitting in a better armchair in the Motherland. On the walls of the houses someone has written, *Kwacha* UNITA, and above that in black paint, The Fight Continues, and above that, *Oyé Oyé* Angola *Liberté*, Angola *Populé*. They have also written in bigger and darker letters, Whites on the Street, Whites Out of Here, Whites Back to Their Country and Death to the Whites.

The soldier spits on the ground, the spurt of saliva lands on the hot tarmac and leaves a stain that makes me feel sick but distracts me from my fear. I try to avoid the eyes of the square-faced soldier, he must be here to take revenge and no-one can stop him, not even Father, not even Father's gun. I am so scared I want to disappear, what if I ran off, what if I scampered across the street, what if I hid behind the pharmacy's shutters, a thousand ideas cross my mind but I remain standing, even breathing is difficult. My mouth has never been so dry, the tongue sticks to the roof of my mouth, the bitterness reaches all the way to my throat, my mouth never tasted so bad. Father says, these men need more drinks, go and fetch another crate, the standing soldier stubs out his cigarette with his boot, and more cigarettes, Father shouts, the soldiers in the jeep seem uninterested, the standing soldier says, and make it fast, son, imitating what Father said a moment ago, the other soldiers laugh and so does Father, it looks as if everything is alright, as if they are all men having a good time, but they aren't, if Father had a choice, if he could have chosen to laugh it would be different, Father had to laugh. Before it was Father who chose when to laugh, what's your name, Málátia, boss, what a *matumbo*, you can't even say your name properly, Malaquias also had to laugh when Father laughed, now it's Father's turn to be the last one to laugh, and it isn't true that he who laughs last laughs longest, almost none of the things people used to say are true, Angola is no longer ours, *it was the morning of February fourth when the heroes broke off the shackles to defeat colonialism and create a new Angola.*

I bring more beer and cigarettes. I wanted to drink some water but couldn't swallow a single drop. I try not to run to avoid showing I'm afraid but I know I'm walking quickly and awkwardly and that Father must be ashamed of me. The beers and cigarettes are passed around among the soldiers once again. That is when Father says, gentlemen, and says goodbye with a nod and turns his back on the soldiers. He puts his hand on my shoulder so that I will do the same, I'm afraid of turning our backs to the soldiers' guns, my legs don't keep up with me. Mother and my sister must be watching us through the bedroom blinds, I know I have to turn and start walking, I mustn't be afraid of turning my back to the soldiers' guns, the square-faced lad has come to take revenge, Pirata is already at our front door wagging her tail, I cannot be a coward, all I have to do is go with Pirata, be anything in life except a coward, son, a coward betrays his father and mother, he disappoints his friends, he is serving his enemy, a coward is worse than a murderer, than a thief, a coward has no loyalty except to fear, remember, son, a coward is worth less than a dead person, there are tales of dead people who come back to life but a coward would be scared even to do that, my whole life I heard my father raging against cowards, I cannot be a coward.

Ey you, the smoker, the voice does not belong to the standing soldier, ey you, it was another soldier, perhaps the square-faced one. Before this all began a black man would have been in trouble for calling out to a white man like that, ey you. The soldiers laugh and Father laughs again. Sitting on the jeep the square-faced soldier is more and more amused, the time has come for him to take revenge for the whack that Lee gave him, his eyes are no longer half closed, I pray to God for the soldiers to go away, I promise to say an entire prayer, the ones from that Catholic radio show, I pray to God for Uncle Zé to arrive, Uncle Zé helps the oppressed people, he has a Party card and everything, perhaps they will listen to him and leave us alone, I pray that the soldier does not remember the football match or me, I pray to God for so many things but God, as always, is as deaf as a door, the soldiers are still there taking satisfaction from the fear they are causing us. The square-faced soldier pretends his hand is a gun and points at me with his index finger. He makes the sound of a gun being fired and laughs. He leaves his finger stretched out as if he were going to shoot again. I hate Lee and Gegé, wherever they happen to be, I hate the neighbours who went away and left us here. The standing soldier speaks to Father, we need to ask a few questions, the soldier's eyes look even murkier. Father doesn't move, Father's large body standing straight, his fists clenched, I'm scared of what Father might do, Father hasn't been himself, not long ago he was cutting up the tablecloth dahlias, he puts his left arm over my shoulder, he tells me quietly, go inside and lock yourself away.

I can't abandon Father, we belong in the same club, I'm not a coward even if I can't stop my legs from shaking, go inside, he says between gritted teeth, Pirata barks, go inside. The soldier says, we were told that the Butcher of Grafanil was here. Father creases his brow and throws his weight back, here? he asks surprised. The square-faced soldier points his index finger at Father, he clicks his tongue again, now he's killed us both with his finger-gun, we want to ask you a few questions, Father starts laughing, quietly at first and then louder. Father cannot be the Butcher of Grafanil and knows nothing about the Butcher of Grafanil, Father never went out killing blacks or ambushing anyone. I had never seen Father laugh like that, the guffaws so strong they bend him over, you must be joking, the soldier doesn't know how to react to the guffaws, Father shouldn't have started laughing, the other black soldiers are waiting for their orders, Father and I, side by side, Pirata still there to protect us, I look around, almost all the squatters in the nearby houses have lost interest and gone back inside, the few who remain watch us without paying too much attention, Father walks, he approaches the jeep, look at me, he speaks loudly as if address-ing a crowd, tell me what you see, I'll tell you what you're seeing, you're seeing a man who killed himself working on this land, I unloaded sacks of coffee with you, with you, he points at each of the soldiers, with your father, with your uncle, with your brother, with your son, there is no man who unloaded more sacks of coffee than I did, I worked day and night and now, Father stops speaking and when he begins again he does it more quietly, as if he had difficulty speaking, everything I have is staying here, look at my hands, my hands are completely callused and even so my skin bleeds against the sacks' jute, Father stretches his enormous hands towards the soldiers, all that work to leave everything behind now, Father points at the house, at one of the trucks parked ahead, the soldiers are still quiet, Father seems to be winning, remember my face every time you sit down at my table, every time you pass through the gate to my house, Father raises his voice, the face of a man who was robbed of everything should not be forgotten, remember well, if I weren't so old I could have been the Butcher of Grafanil, if I didn't have a wife and children, if I weren't so tired, Father reaches for the gun, this is the only gun I have and I never used it, the soldiers stir, this is when we will die, the soldiers point their weapons at us, this is when, I have this gun to protect my family, I am not the Butcher of Grafanil, Father almost whispers, the squatters who were at the windows call others, now they're all waiting to see us die, Father raises his voice, I always paid you on time, I drank *cachaça* and ate cassava porridge with you, I never took advantage of your women or your daughters, I gave you money for your children's medicine, do whatever you want.

Father puts his arm around my shoulders again, come on, son, he is not afraid to turn his back on them but I am, I can't turn my back on the soldiers' guns, Pirata jumps excitedly around us, I can't walk, Father nudges me, the soldiers are going to shoot, the white walls of our house make me even dizzier, now I know why birds kill themselves when they crash against the walls on those hot mornings, Father nudges me again, I can't walk, I'm not a coward, I'm dizzy, I'm going to faint like when I had malaria, I must walk, come on, son, I can't look at Father, Mother's rose beds, the soldiers' guns pointed at our backs, I must behave like a man, Pirata is waiting for us by the steps, sorry, Father, the walls of the house are spinning, the house, the street, if we take a step they'll kill us, come on, son, Father tugs at me, let's go inside, I can't walk, Father, the walls of the house are disappearing, come on, son, suddenly everything is dark, my legs buckle and I can't do anything about it, they must have shot, we might not even notice when their bullets hit us, we might have died and not noticed, let's go home, son, let's go home.

The airport today is so different from the airport on Sunday afternoons when Father brought us to watch the aeroplanes, now there are hundreds of people around us, hundreds or thousands, I don't know, I've never seen so many people in the same place, I've never seen such confusion, so many suitcases and wooden crates, so much litter, litter, litter and more litter, on those Sundays, the airport was quiet, the floor so clean it felt wrong to step on it, coming to the airport was good, even hearing the noise made by aeroplanes was good, there weren't all these people, this ceaseless noise, my head feels as though it will explode. The jeep disappearing past Editinha's house.

I'm tired, I've never been so tired, I don't want to sit, I can't sit, I mean, if I wanted to I could, I can sit on the floor, Mother wouldn't mind, not this time, this time Mother wouldn't say, those aren't proper manners, you're no longer a child, she wouldn't say, you'll make your trousers dirty, I'll never get those stains out, Mother wouldn't mind, there are so many people sitting on the floor around us, they're not worried about stains on their trousers, they're not worried about arriving in the Motherland with stained clothes. Father's hands tied behind his back.

Mother doesn't even realise that my sister with her light blue dress, what a bad idea to wear a light blue dress, Mother doesn't even realise that my sister is sitting on the floor, against the wall, her blonde curls crushed against the wall, a girl has to be more careful than a boy, she has to behave differently, if people start bad-mouthing a girl no-one will want her. We gunna killya wid yur gun 'n' yur bullet.

We've been here for almost a whole day, Mother is constantly looking towards the airport entrance but Father hasn't arrived, there is nothing to do but wait, wait for Father and wait for our turn to board an aeroplane for the Motherland. The dust settling slowly.

I wish Uncle Zé would go away but Uncle Zé won't leave, he wants to make sure we'll board, he must be worried that we'll have to go back home, he must be worried that our black neighbours will want to take revenge because they think we know about the Butcher of Grafanil, or that the jeep with the soldiers will come back looking for us, that they'll come back for us, Uncle Zé is right, I want to go back home and wait for Father there. Father's white shirt soaked in blood.

Mother grabs Uncle Zé again, take us back home, and Uncle Zé, we can't, sis, you have to take the plane and fly off with your children, Mother doesn't want to understand what Uncle Zé is saying, she repeats, take us back home, or says, go find Mário, you're a friend to these people, talk to them and bring me Mário. The Ronson Varaflame lighter on the ground by the flower bed.

Uncle Zé tries to reassure us, he tries to reassure Mother, he says that Nhé Nhé has gone to sort it out, the black soldiers will realise they were wrong and will release Father, blacks are fair, sometimes they make mistakes but mistakes can be corrected, Uncle Zé says we can relax. Mother, defeated at the end of the road.

There are also blacks here, blacks from all over, barefoot and dirty, blacks who have escaped from villages and are fearful of war, even the blacks want to go to the Motherland, a soldier calls the passengers who will board the aeroplane that has just landed, it's not our aeroplane yet but Uncle Zé says, when your turn comes you have to go, my heart beats faster and stronger as if Uncle Zé has threatened me, when your turn comes you have to go. Father's blood on the tarmac.

We must wait for Mário, Mother says to Uncle Zé, I can't leave Mário behind, and to us, we can't leave Father behind, Mother doesn't take her eyes off the airport entrance, as soon as Father walks in Mother will spot him, even in the middle of all this madness she will spot him, after all she spotted him immediately when she arrived on the *Vera Cruz* despite the crowds on the dock, despite her saying, you don't look like you. The vases on the staircase knocked over.

Only one suitcase per person is allowed, anyone who has

brought more will have to leave them here, luggage is strewn all over the airport, there are things all over the place, we didn't bring anything extra, we left in a hurry, the suitcases were half empty, so much to bring and in the end we had to pack our cases as fast as we could and leave almost everything behind. Father forced into the jeep.

Father's suitcase stayed behind in the living room, we should have brought Father's suitcase, we have handed over our own, all we have now are the T.A.P. rucksacks that Father gave us, he brought one for each of us, yesterday he came home proudly with the rucksacks, they were difficult to get but I managed. The black soldier's hands on Father's arm.

I never thought it would be like this, I pictured us taking the aeroplane the way we saw those other families doing on the Sundays when Father brought us to the airport, we wouldn't be smiling as much as those people who waved as they walked towards the aeroplanes on the runway but there wouldn't be all these frightened people around us and Father would be with us. My sister unable to come down the stairs.

Father should be here, I don't understand, if Uncle Zé is so sure Nhé Nhé will be able to persuade the black soldiers to let Father go then why did we have to leave home in such a hurry, why did Uncle Zé have to drive at such speed, why are we here instead of being with Father? Pirata whimpering after a kick from the black soldier.

A child starts to cry, the noise of people, the noise of the aeroplanes' engines outside, the child's cries, my sister keeps her head against the wall while Mother shuts her eyes and grimaces, it's not like when we go to séances, it's as if the child's cries hurt her, there are more people here than at the séances but neither Father nor Senhor José are here, I'm afraid but the fear is different from the one I feel at the séances, it's our turn. Father's worried eyes.

It's our turn, Uncle Zé has just said, it's your turn, we look at each other with fright, Uncle Zé doesn't answer when my sister asks, what about Father? The black soldiers laughing when the jeep drives off.

Come on, Uncle Zé puts out his arms to move us along, Mother is glued to the spot with her arms wrapped around herself, Mário hasn't arrived yet, I have to wait for Mário. Father's gun in the black soldier's hands.

Uncle Zé pushes us, Mário will come later, sis, if you miss your turn you'll never get out of here, can't you see all these people waiting for a place, you can't miss your turn, Uncle Zé is not listening to what I say, we can't leave Father alone. Father's own gun pointing at his head.

The guard tells us to move towards the runway, the aeroplane is in front of us, enormous and shiny, more and more people are heading towards the aeroplane that will take us away, the aeroplane's steps are lowered. Mother running through the unsettled dust.

So this is the Motherland, then.

Welcome to the hotel. Please, come in, have a seat in these armchairs. This is my office, please make yourselves at home, here at the hotel we all want to help, you have reached a safe haven. I know how difficult your situation is but regrettably you are not the only ones. Don't worry about the luggage, madam, the receptionist will take care of it. This is just a quick chat, I know you are tired and I don't want to hold you up. You have had a long journey, long and difficult, I imagine. The circumstances are terrible, but it is beyond us to do anything about them. These are troubled times. We will all try our best and I am at your service to help however I can. But before that I want to welcome you as the hotel's manager. You will have noticed that this is a five-star hotel and I assure you that it deserves every one of them. I don't know if you have ever been to Estoril before, I am sure you will like it. Many of the people who have arrived say it reminds them of Luanda, I don't know, I have never been there, perhaps one of these days. This area is very popular with tourists and we are in high season. But I couldn't possibly leave you without a roof, one has to help when necessary. That is why we opened up the hotel, except for the top floor, that is still reserved for paying guests. Not that I don't consider you to be our guests but as you can appreciate you find yourselves in a different situation. As much as I would like to be helpful I cannot close the hotel to our usual customers. Madam, I can assure you that the receptionist will take care of your luggage. You can relax. I understand your concern, it could not have been easy to come over here alone with your two children. A father is always needed and even more so in these circumstances, it's good to hear that he will be here shortly. I know this is no comfort but there are many families here that have been separated like yours, sadly you are not the only ones. We must keep our faith in God, only our faith can save us in these troubled times, God's trials will make us stronger. And you are lucky, your children are almost grown up, a young lady and a young man ready to help. I am certain that they are well educated and respectful, I can tell just by looking at them. But I was saying that I cannot close the hotel off to our usual customers, I have customers who spend a season here every year and of course I couldn't refuse to take them in, there are bookings by foreigners made early in the year. As you will surely understand, those guests must not be inconvenienced, this is a five-star hotel and those guests pay a lot and have to be treated accordingly, there can be no noise, there can be no disorder. No, madam, you misunderstand me. It's not that I think you cannot behave, that is not what I'm saying. No-one is born knowing and what you don't know you must learn and people have different habits in different places. I should be grateful if you did not speak to me like that, madam, you are upset, I understand, but I ask you to calm down. I know perfectly well that you weren't living in the jungle, far be it from me to call anyone a savage, what is happening over here is hardly a good example for anyone. But there are rules to be followed in this hotel, without rules we cannot get along, that is all I mean, whether it's a hotel or a country. Yes, you have told me already that everything you have is in those suitcases but don't worry, nobody will interfere with them, they are safe with our receptionist. You are in a good hotel, very good, in fact, I'd say the best hotel, if you'll forgive the vanity. And you are among the lucky ones, some families are staying on camping sites or in dreary bed and breakfasts, at least you have ended up in a luxury hotel. Not everyone can thank God for the good fortune you've had, you must have seen the masses of people at the airport, I could not believe it when I was there, some of my husband's relatives arrived from Mozambique and we went to meet them. Sadly not everyone is greeted in the same way, there are some people whose families have turned their backs on them, it's true that you only discover who you can rely on in a time of need, there has been so much disappointment. And, of course, there are those who do not have any relatives here, whose parents or grandparents were born in Africa, I don't know if that's your case. Not to mention the coloureds, those poor souls have no-one to turn to, it's a disgrace. People haven't stopped arriving and there are still so many more to come, flights coming in and going out, night and day. If those foreigners had not offered their aeroplanes I cannot imagine the butchery there would have been. I don't mind at all, you can interrupt me whenever you want. Yes, madam, I will keep the forms you were given, let me see. Everything seems to be in order, you don't need anything else as far as the hotel is concerned but you have to go to the I.A.R.N., that's the Institute for the Support of Returnee Nationals, to do the rest of the paperwork, it's warm now but winter is cold and you will need warmer clothes than the ones you were used to over there, and many other things. There are plenty of people who can help you, the churches, the charities. Apologies, madam, I know you are not begging for anything, I wasn't calling anyone a beggar, please do not put words in my mouth. You are hard-working people, I have no doubt about that, but such things can happen to anyone, being in need is no cause for shame. People in need must know how to receive, these are troubled times. But back to the main subject, you have seen that with so many arrivals we must try to take in as many as we can, so I have no choice but to put more people in a single room than would be expected, I am sure you understand, madam, the three of you will have to share a room. We will sort it out later, madam, when your husband arrives we can consider putting you in two rooms but until then you'll have to stay in the same room. I am sure you prefer being a bit cosier in the knowledge that no-one else has been left without a roof, we have to look out for each other, I'm doing the best I can. Keep in mind the great effort that goes into helping you, I am not only talking about myself, we have the same hotel staff but four times as much work. I can't hire more employees. That's another reason why I ask for your co-operation, the more you help us the more we can help you, these are troubled times. So I can offer you a room with two good beds and an extra sofa, you are entitled to breakfast, lunch and dinner served always in the restaurant. It is expressly forbidden to take food into the rooms and cooking in the rooms will lead to eviction. Our rooms are not suitable for cooking. Of course, madam, I know that you will not be cooking in your room. I just want to let you know that, for everyone's sake, I won't allow any serious damage to the hotel. Your room is number 315. The chambermaids clean the rooms once a week and when they do they will refresh your bed sheets and towels. Originally, when only one floor of the hotel was reserved for you, the chambermaids cleaned the rooms daily but no-one seemed happy with this arrangement, people didn't want to be inconvenienced every day, they wanted to relax in their rooms, and it was also difficult for the chambermaids, the rooms are more packed than they are used to and the poor girls could hardly move in there. There was an open meeting and it was decided that the chambermaids would only clean the rooms once per week but that on those days the rooms had to be vacated. So on cleaning days you will have to come down here or go for a wander so that the chambermaids can clean the rooms properly. Of course you'll be notified in advance. If you really need it you can use the vacuum cleaner, just ask for it at reception, as for clothes, you can wash the smaller items in your bathroom but the larger ones have to be taken to the laundry room, we have ordered another wash tub, the washing machines are exclusively for the hotel's use. The most important thing is that you remember that the rules are here for your own protection, disrespecting the rules will make your own lives more difficult. Please do not forget it is forbidden to take food into the rooms and absolutely no cooking in the rooms or anywhere else in the hotel. Of course not, madam, don't get upset. I'm just saying it again because it has happened before and it must not happen again, we cannot allow that in a five-star hotel. I won't take up any more of your time, perhaps you have things to ask. Regarding your question there is no limit, you will be here as long as is necessary, I am sure everyone will manage to find a new arrangement soon. I don't know, madam, that will depend more on you and others than on me, but I can guarantee one thing, no-one will put you out on the streets. Here is the key to your room, there is another copy but it is best if that one stays at reception, many keys have gone missing. I'll ask Senhor Teixeira to show you to the lift and the porter will help you with your luggage, if you need any further information just ring reception, we're here to help. It is free to ring reception, you can call as many times as you want if you have any queries, you only have to pay for external phone calls. Once again welcome, you've arrived safe and sound and that's what matters most. Everything will turn out well. Things will seem better after a good night's sleep, tiredness only makes us say unwise things. It has been a pleasure to meet you, I wish you a very good stay.

It's the first time we've stayed in a hotel, it's the first time we've slept in a hotel room and also the first time the three of us have slept in the same room. In our old house my sister and I shared a room when we were young, we were so young that we were scared of the dark, of slugs and geckos. Mother always slept in the other room with Father. Unless one of us was ill. Then she would move into one of our beds and leave the smell of hairspray on our pillows. But apart from the times when we were ill Mother always slept with Father in the other room. Except that Father is not here. Room 315. The porter who helped us bring up our luggage said we were lucky, the room has a balcony with a sea view. We've never slept so close to the sea.

The three of us in bed, lights out, listening to each other's breathing. Mother and my sister in the good beds that the manager spoke of and me on the sofa we've pushed up against the wall. The neon glow from the photo-lab across the street shines through the drawn curtains and lights up the room. On and off, on and off. The sea is so close that we can hear the waves in the Motherland's night. I don't want to close my eyes. If I close my eyes the black soldiers will take Father again, hands tied behind his back, if I close my eyes I'll pass out again, no, no, I didn't actually pass out, I can't remember what happened but I didn't pass out, Father put his hand on my shoulder, let's go home, son, everything went white, I was blinded the way those birds must be blinded when they crash against the walls and die. I didn't die but once I recovered Father was being forced into the jeep with his own gun pointing at his head, one of the soldiers saying, we'll kill you with your own gun and your own bullet, we won't have to waste anything. No, the bloody bastards wouldn't say that because the bloody bastards can't even speak properly. We gunna killya wid yur gun 'n' yur bullet so we not gotta waste anyting. Uncle Zé and Nhé Nhé will speak to their friends and the bloody bastards will have to release Father, they will even have to apologise to him for having said that he's the Butcher of Grafanil or at least one of his friends. Who knows, they might have already released him and Father might be arranging his plane ticket to come and join us. I'm sure that's it, Father must be on an aeroplane coming to join us.

We didn't even have to agree to keep what happened with Father a secret. It was Mother, despite her feeble mind, who started lying as soon as we got off the aeroplane. We came down the aeroplane's stairway and my sister said, we are in the Motherland. We didn't know what to do. It was strange to be stepping onto the Motherland, it was as if we were entering the map that hung from the classroom wall. The map was torn in places revealing a darkened or dirty fabric behind it, a rough fabric that kept the map stiff and in one piece. We didn't know what to do and it was as if we were entering the torn map, or perhaps the photographs in magazines, or the stories Mother was always telling us, the anthems we sang in the school yard on Saturday mornings. It seemed impossible that we had arrived in the Motherland. More so after what had happened, even more so without Father. I never thought I'd be in the Motherland without Father. Without Father we didn't know what to do but the other families didn't know either, what now, what now, they asked. In almost every answer there was one word we had never heard before, the I.A.R.N., the I.A.R.N., the I.A.R.N. The I.A.R.N. had paid our air fares, the I.A.R.N. would put us up in hotels, the I.A.R.N. would pay for the transport to the hotels, the I.A.R.N. would give us food, the I.A.R.N. would give us money, the I.A.R.N. would help us, the I.A.R.N. would advise us, the I.A.R.N. would give us further information. I had never heard a single word repeated so many times, the I.A.R.N. seemed to be more important and more generous than God. We were told that I.A.R.N. was the name for the Institute for the Support of Returnee Nationals. We are now returnees. We don't know what it really means to be returnees, but that's what we are. Returnees. Us and all the others who are arriving from over there.

It's lucky that Father had gone to change some money for

our journey, the money from over there isn't good for buying anything over here. At the airport Mother wanted to buy a soft drink with money from over there but the vendor said to her, we don't take that kind of money. I don't understand. They are all escudos, Angola is still Portugal, independence won't happen until November. The vendor said that the money from over there had never been any good over here. Father must have known that but we didn't know. Perhaps Mother already knew and forgot. All we have are our suitcases and the twenty contos, or twenty thousand escudos, that Father got in the old city. We were only allowed five contos per person, Uncle Zé suggested to Mother that she should hide Father's five contos in her clothes, Uncle Zé hid them himself, Mother was unable to do anything. Three suitcases and twenty thousand escudos is all we have until we sort our lives out. Sorting our lives out is the phrase most often used by the returnees but without Father we have no idea how to do that. Father knows how to make money, he was seven when he started to help with building roads and he never stopped, roads connecting the mountains in the Motherland's north, roads more difficult to build even than the winding road that goes up Angola's Serra da Leba. The hotel manager does not talk about sorting out our lives, she talks about finding a solution, as if it were a maths problem at school. Rich people speak differently and smell of perfumes that stick to those like us who smell of nothing. The manager's office is large and tidy just as everything must be in the Motherland.

When our money from over there was refused I became worried that Mother would have one of her attacks, you never know what Mother might do, her hands shook and her eyes blinked as if they were damaged but the only thing Mother did was sob quietly. No-one seemed to find it strange, there were lots of women crying and screaming as they held on to their suitcases and their children, Mother's sobbing was like the sobbing of so many others. We went up to one of the queues, all of them led to something connected with the I.A.R.N. The accommodation guides for those who had nowhere to go were also published by the I.A.R.N., but the I.A.R.N. itself was elsewhere. It was the lady who dealt with us at the airport that Mother lied to for the first time, my husband had to stay behind to deal with some business. From then onwards she never stopped lying, she lied to the taxi driver who drove us to the I.A.R.N., to the hotel manager, to the family having dinner at the table next to ours, my husband had to stay behind to deal with some business and he'll come as quickly as he can, she put so much truth into her words that not even the eyes gave her away.

Mother did well to lie, they took Father like they could have taken any other but no-one would believe that. Whenever there's talk of a white man imprisoned or murdered, there is always someone who says, he must have had it coming, they only take revenge on people who mistreated them, they never interfered with me or my family, they know who treated them well. Father knows nothing about the Butcher of Grafanil and always treated black people well. Father is incapable of killing women and children even if they are black, he is incapable of setting native huts on fire or blowing up a lorry full of day labourers. Father wanted to set fire to our house and our trucks but that was different, that was so they wouldn't be laughing at us. Even Uncle Zé, who never got on with Father, thought the charge couldn't be true, Father runs out of breath whenever he has to dash to find shelter from the rain, the Butcher of Grafanil cannot be so old and stocky. Even if he had the will and the courage to be the Butcher of Grafanil, Father has neither the age nor the health, if Uncle Zé could see that everyone else can. That's why it's not a lie to say that Father stayed behind to deal with some business. And they must have released him already, surely they must have released him already.

But we don't talk about what happened to Father even when we are alone. My mother and sister did not see Father being taken away, they did not see my legs buckling underneath me, I thought they were peeping through the blinds but they had hidden under the bed in fear and only came out when they heard my shouts. Uncle Zé and Nhé Nhé arrived shortly after Father was taken away, pack your bags, quick, we've got to go to the airport, you can't be here for a minute longer. Uncle Zé was right, the soldiers could come back to take us away. And the black squatters who had moved into the neighbours' houses would wish to take revenge if they believed we were relatives of the Butcher of Grafanil. We packed our suitcases in a hurry and not really knowing what we were doing, we couldn't think and we obeyed Uncle Zé who wouldn't stop shouting, quick, get ready, there's no time to waste. Pirata barked like I'd never heard her do before, her barks were so upsetting.

We got into the car and Uncle Zé drove off. Pirata ran, ran, ran behind the car as if we were going to stop further ahead to let her in. Sometimes we played that game, and Pirata must have thought we were playing it again because she didn't stop running. She ran as fast as she could but Uncle Zé was driving faster. Pirata fell further and further behind until she was only a white dot on the avenue, a tiny, tiny, tiny white dot. Aboard the aeroplane my sister said, in the end we brought fewer things than we could have, so many things to bring and we didn't even fill up our suitcases. She turned her face towards the small aeroplane window and stared out at the unchanging blue sky.

My sister and Mother must also be finding it difficult to sleep, they're constantly shifting around, the neon turning on and off must be keeping them awake too. I can't stop thinking that if I hadn't passed out they wouldn't have taken Father, let's go home, son, if I had kept on walking, but I didn't and the black soldiers took Father. The jeep disappeared past Editinha's house, the dust took a while to settle, dust in the aftermath, Mother knocked over the vases on the staircase in her hurry to come down, Mother running through the unsettled dust, my sister unable to come down the stairs, unable to believe it, they've taken Father, Mother defeated at the end of the road, the black squatters in Dona Gilda's house talking to one another on the veranda, the leaves of Dona Alda's banana trees swaying gently, perhaps still from the gust of wind made by the passing jeep, Mother standing at the end of the road, not shouting, not saying anything. How do we ever go back home.

I will never tell Mother or my sister about Father's hands tied behind his back, nor about his worried look as he got into the jeep. Nor will I tell them I have Father's lighter with me, I found it on the ground by the flower beds, the Ronson Varaflame lighter we gave him when he turned forty-nine. Father must have dropped it when they took him away, or perhaps he left it behind intentionally so they wouldn't take it and I could keep it. I'm keeping it, I won't use that lighter even once, I want to see Father's face when he arrives and I hand it back to him, he'll be proud of me. Father will enjoy smoking a cigarette on the room's balcony, looking out at the sea, as I was doing a moment ago, after Mother made that call.

I shouldn't have allowed Mother to call, who knows who the black man is that answered the phone over in our house, I shouldn't have allowed her but the phone is on that little bed-side table, how annoying that Uncle Zé doesn't have a phone at home, if he did we'd have news of Father. Nor can we call the neighbours, I know the numbers off by heart, how long before I forget those numbers that are now completely useless. Mother wanted to call home but I shouldn't have allowed it, the phone rang for a long time, no-one answered but Mother called once more, she tried again, and again until a black man's voice answered. Mother hung up in fright but she immediately rang once more, the black man said he knew no-one called Mário and asked who was calling. Mother slammed down the receiver and we remained silent not knowing what to say. It was a mistake, Father would surely not be at home, if they released him he'd be trying to get tickets to come over and join us, why would he be at home? And who was the black man that answered the phone in our house, the phone on the little table by the entrance that Mother dusted every day, the little table with golden legs that stood beneath the white-framed mirror, a pretty mirror but not as pretty as the ones in this hotel. Everything in the Motherland is surely like this hotel, we must have imagined some of the things we saw on the way here.

The Motherland is surely like this hotel that even has a velvet-covered bench in the lift. Portugal is not a small country, that's what was written on the map at school, Portugal is not a small country, it is an empire stretching from the Minho river to Timor. The Motherland cannot be what we saw today from the taxi on the way here, no-one would make us sing anthems on Saturday mornings if the Motherland were so backward and dirty, with streets so narrow that it seemed we would hardly fit through them. Our suitcases and rucksacks didn't fit into the car's boot and the taxi driver had to strap them to the roof.

The taxi driver doesn't think these are troubled times the way the hotel manager does, these are good times, no more soldiers off to the colonies, no more coffins back from the colonies, my comrades. The taxi driver kept addressing us as comrades and Mother got it into her head that he was duping us and was taking us the long way. Mother could not possibly know, she doesn't know Lisbon, she has only been here once before to board the *Vera Cruz*. The roads were full of potholes so big that the suitcases bounced on the car's roof, and Mother was convinced we were going to lose them. The taxi driver tried to reassure her, he said he'd secured them well but it was pointless, another pothole and Mother started again, oh, we're going to lose our suitcases. If they fall we won't lose them, those suitcases don't have legs, the taxi driver joked, but there is no changing Mother's mind when she gets an idea into her head.

No, the Motherland cannot be as we saw it today. Proof that Portugal is not a small country was on the map showing how much of Europe the empire took up, an empire as big as the distance between here and Russia cannot have a capital with streets so narrow that a car can barely fit through them, it cannot be so full of sad and ugly people, or of old toothless men and women sitting at their windows looking so miserable that not even death would wish to carry them away. Back over there old people had very white dentures and went around wearing hats and well-starched suits. When Father saw the old-timers enjoying their seafood at the Restinga restaurant he said, even the elderly escape death here. Father knew what he was talking about, he had gone to Africa to escape poverty, in Africa you could escape everything, death, poverty, cold and even evil, Father used to say to us, here there is enough for everyone, we don't need to gouge each other's eyes out over a sardine. Mother likes listening to Father, your father speaks like a doctor and can do mental arithmetic better than an engineer, even the ones that build dams. The engineers Mother admires the most are the dams engineers, because of the Cambambe dam. There always was a photograph of the Cambambe dam on the calendar that Mother hung up on the kitchen wall and when Father promised that one day we'd visit it Mother would look longingly at the calendar, one day we would have a picnic by the dam. One day we'd see with our own eyes that great work, we'd go down to the turbine hall one hundred and seventy-three metres beneath the ground. One hundred and seventy-three metres, half the height of the Sears Tower but under the ground, which is why the Cambambe dam is a work as impressive as the world's tallest building.

We never visited the Cambambe dam, Father never had a holiday and this is the first night we have ever slept in a hotel. It is not just any hotel, it is a five-star hotel with two lifts and two service lifts, porters in uniforms with golden epaulettes and halls longer than the ones at school back over there. Carpeted halls that no-one seems to walk through and walls covered in wallpaper, wrapped like a gift, the sort of place we never would have dreamed of being in. That must be why I don't like being here. Even if Father arrived and we were able to stay here forever I'm sure I would still not like being here. It may be that you have to fantasise about places the way Mother used to fantasise about the Cambambe dam to really like them. I don't like being in this hotel. I hate the black man who answered the phone, the black man in our house, I hate him so much that if I saw him I could kill him.

The taxi driver told Mother to calm down, so did the lady from the I.A.R.N., no-one is to blame for what happened, we're here to help but if you start shouting we won't get anywhere. Someone must be to blame, Mother said, someone must be. Please calm down, it's no good shouting, we won't solve anything by shouting, madam, you've seen how many people there are here, you are not the only one with problems. The lady from the I.A.R.N. didn't know how to make Mother calm down, the hotel manager did, I had never heard anyone talk like her and had never seen a hotel like that, with such intricately carved furniture and so many cut-glass chandeliers. At the I.A.R.N. the secretaries were old and dirty and the chairs where the return-ees sat when their turn came were wobbly, I was sure they would not hold the weight of a heavy body like Father's. There were returnees from every corner of the empire, the empire was there, in that waiting room, a tired empire, in need of house and food, a defeated and humiliated empire, an empire no-one wanted to know about.

Suddenly my sister says, imitating the manager's voice,

troubled times, these are troubled times. And she laughs as if she has just told a good joke. We have nothing to laugh about but perhaps if we laugh we are less alone. The way the manager speaks is not funny, and if we weren't in this situation we wouldn't have started laughing. Troubled times. We can't stop laughing, the guffaws mixing with each other, we laugh, loud, louder, I can't remember ever having laughed so much and so loudly. These are troubled times, if we laugh we are less alone and perhaps we will be able to sleep.

Mother still has all her food on her plate. She has hardly eaten since we arrived. It's true that the hotel food is bad yet again, the potatoes are half-cooked and the meat is stringy, but Mother could make an effort. When my sister didn't want to eat Father forced her to, we can't live on thin air. I repeat the words Father used to say and ask Mother to eat, we can't live on thin air, the tablets on an empty stomach are worse than acid, Father's words without Father in the hotel restaurant.

I lower my voice because the tables are so close together. They had to add more tables because of the queues at every meal, they start early in the morning at breakfast and everyone complains about how long they have to stand. Lunch is served at twelve thirty but by eleven there are people waiting in line, people with their backs to the wall talking about things over there, my house had this or that, I left this or that behind, gunfire this and mortar-fire that. It's the same with the television, hours before it's turned on the television room fills with people and once again, my house had this or that, I left this or that behind, gunfire this and mortar-fire that. It turns out that the television, the thing that everyone over there used to call the Motherland's home cinema, is black-and-white and small, a rectangle that can hardly be seen and with poor sound, a muted sound like Father's radio when its batteries were starting to die. And there is nothing good on the television, only revolutionaries just saying the same things about the revolution.

There are many people from Mozambique at the hotel but most of the people from Angola don't get on with those from Mozambique. The people from Mozambique keep going on about having lived in the Pearl of the Indian Ocean and they use words in English, they call the black children boys and say they lived in flats, they talk about half-castes and chinks. Dona Suzete in room 310 is Mozambican and is always frying samosas in her room, the whole corridor stinks of fried food, any day now the manager will kick her out. Sometimes the Angolans and the Mozambicans disagree about which was the better colony, the other colonies hardly count. When Father arrives he'll make such a good case for Angola that the Mozambicans won't ever be able to argue. I like to hear the people from Mozambique talking about the Dragons of Death, about their *machambas* or farmlands, about the attack on the administrative post at Chai, about the Polana hotel. I can't understand why they argue so much about which is the better colony if we've lost them both. I mean, Angola is still ours but only until November 11.

Mother plays with her fork, her gaze is fixed on the empty

chair in front of her. The restaurant tables have four places and the empty place reminds us at every meal that Father has not arrived. We feel Father's absence everywhere but it is worse at the table because we know we are thinking about Father and his absence hurts even more. But soon Uncle Zé will have received Mother's letter and will tell Father where we are, soon Father will be here. I can control my thoughts because I don't have Mother's feeble mind and there are no demons bothering me. I can keep my mind busy with whatever I want, how many people are in this hotel, for instance, it's a much more interesting problem to solve than the ones Miss Maria José gave us during arithmetic lessons, tanks filling up at one end and emptying at the other, a real headache that was good for nothing while there are other problems that are actually useful to solve. How many people are in this hotel, the right answer is three hundred and thirty-six people, the hotel is six storeys high, each storey has twenty-eight rooms, each room has two people. This is a more useful problem to solve than the problems about tanks or orange trees that double the number of oranges they produce every year, one day I got confused and the orange trees started producing half oranges instead of whole oranges and our teacher Miss Maria José said, have you ever seen an orange tree growing half oranges, and I tried but couldn't find a way of getting rid of the orange tree in my maths book that refused to grow whole oranges. But this problem is worth thinking about. Three hundred and thirty-six people. If I could always understand the question and if I always had as much time to answer it as I've spent in the queue waiting to be seated I would always get the right answer, I wouldn't even need pencil and paper. I'm certain the answer should be exactly three hundred and thirty-six people but in this hotel the number is approximately three hundred and thirty-six people because the floor for paying guests is almost empty and on other floors there are more than two people in many of the rooms. Three hundred and thirty-six people may not seem like much but it is, especially when they're all together and all want their lunch.

It is easy to control our thoughts but we can't control other people's thoughts and I'm certain that Mother is thinking, some black people are capable of anything, they are not like us, there are many stories of whites captured by blacks, Mother's eyes wide open, and we can almost see Father's big body not quite fitting on a chair, Father's big body never quite fit anywhere. Sometimes it's worse when they don't kill them. Father is sitting down, but not on this chair. Sometimes it's worse when they don't kill them. That must be why Mother doesn't eat, that must be why she looks at my sister and me as if she couldn't understand how we could be so hungry or what Father is doing sitting in a chair that is not the chair in front of her. I'm imagining this, I'm always imagining things, lately I've been doing nothing else. It must be because we are in this hotel with so many rooms and corridors, and a restaurant that was once the venue for an actual princess' wedding reception, with enormous windows looking out onto the sea. A beautiful hotel like only the Motherland could have, the chandelier in the restaurant even more beautiful than the one in the manager's office, a chandelier in the centre of the room with hundreds of drops of cut glass, the first time we came into the restaurant my sister said, it shines so much that it looks like a sun. Mother wanted so badly to have a chandelier for the living room, she spent entire afternoons at the Quintas & Irmão department store choosing chandeliers that Father wouldn't buy, next year, he'd say. Quintas & Irmão did not have cabinets like the ones in the hotel restaurant, nor did they have the sort of plates kept in those cabinets, I had only seen plates like that in history books, plates with illustrations of caravels crossing tumultuous seas. But the nicest thing about the restaurant is the tapestry on the room's far wall, a tapestry with Indians and sailors at the first mass ever held in Brazil, that's what it says at the bottom in letters that look as though they're from back in the days of the old kings, the first mass in Brazil, a tapestry that not even churches back over there would have.

There is no food like my own, Mother says. Mother never liked food that she had not made herself. Even when we went for lunch at Vilela on Sundays Mother said, there is no food like my own, the blue-powdered eyes and the pink lips, there is no food like my own. It wasn't true but Father would never let us say to Mother that her food was bad, so my sister and I didn't contradict her. Father is no longer here but we still won't contradict her, the empty chair is standing in for Father. The chair is empty but Father will arrive soon, if Father were not arriving his cutlery, his plate and his glass would not be on the table. Father will arrive any minute now, he'll say that it's hot, that summer in the Motherland is almost as hot as the one back over there, he'll sit down and order a mug of beer, get me a *canhangulo*. The staff don't want us here and they don't like serving us. They think the blacks kicked us out of there because we exploited them, we lost everything but it was all our fault and we don't deserve to be here in a five-star hotel being waited on the way we were back there. The staff prefer serving the blacks that can't even hold their cutlery properly to serving us, they think the blacks are victims who endured five centuries of oppression and now have had to flee the war. Just let the staff keep feeding those blacks like we did, let them keep serving those blacks and one day they'll see, when the blacks rise up in revolt and they do to them what they did to us, they'll knock on their doors and take them away with hands tied behind their backs, they'll take them away and I'll laugh. People here can say whatever they want but they won't change my mind, blacks are good for nothing. They laughed with us too until they had a machete in their hands, the people here will soon regret it and it will be too late. And I won't feel sorry at all.

But it is the guests, the paying guests, when there are any, that the staff like serving most. The guests who don't mingle with us, guests who sit at reserved tables we can't go anywhere near, the manager's orders, tables close to the window, laid out with many glasses and countless pieces of cutlery. The members of staff seem to glide when called by the guests, they make me sick with their trays and their penguin suits, an exaggerated smile like the ones on talking dolls. There aren't very many paying guests, they must be scared of coming to hotels full of returnees, to a country full of revolutionaries. There is trouble almost every day but the guests are protected, the manager says, access to the floor occupied by guests is forbidden, sitting at the tables reserved for guests is forbidden, inconveniencing guests is forbidden.

Today there is a guest, he must be a foreigner come to witness the revolution. A foreigner like the ones who worked on the ships that docked by the port, the ships from which Father brought back surprises, I have a surprise for you, Father with his hands behind his back but not tied like when the black soldiers took him away. I have a surprise for you, it was so good to run to him then, for my sister Father brought back dolls from Las Palmas, dolls with recordings in their bellies, *Mamá, Papá, yo soy una chica muy guapa*, and for me he brought battery-operated cars. For a few days, in our neighbourhood, we stopped being the children of Dona Glória with all her problems and we became the children who had foreign toys, for a few days we were the most important children in the neighbourhood, at least I was. I think my sister never really took advantage of those talking dolls but I knew how to take advantage of everything

Father brought me, the other children would say, let me play, just a little, I wouldn't let them have their fill, that was the secret, just a little, sometimes the other children would get upset, I'll ask my father to buy me one just like this one, but I always had the magic answer, it's from abroad, it's not for sale anywhere here.

Father would also bring Mother French perfumes and boxes of peaches from South Africa, pink peaches laid on straw that my sister used later to make beds for her dolls, peach-scented beds. There was not a neighbour who did not envy Mother when she got the French perfumes and the peaches from South Africa. The other husbands in the neighbourhood did not bring gifts back from their jobs or else they brought garbage like Dona Alzira's husband, who would want so many ashtrays with the Cuca logo? Or those objects salvaged from farms and brought home by Dona Gilda's husband who worked on Gajajeira Street, they were worth less than dishcloths, it was as good as not bringing anything home. Father brought good things home from the foreign ships, he drove there with his trucks loaded with coffee and brought back such nice things that Mother went from being the disturbed Dona Glória and became Dona Glória who has her problems, which was completely different from being disturbed, we all have our problems, even the neighbours. Mother would show the neighbours her French perfumes and they would say, you must use only a few drops at a time, and Mother would ignore them and slather herself in

French perfume, the smell was so strong that it made us cough and made us dizzy, luckily for us French perfumes always came in small bottles and ran out quickly. The worst part was Mother going back to smelling of Si Frâiche cologne just like the neighbours and then she became the disturbed Dona Glória again.

After the gunfire began Father hardly brought back any gifts from the ships anymore but when he arrives everything will be like it was before, one day soon he'll turn up at the hotel loaded with gifts like the day he brought us a dancing Mickey Mouse and those American walkie-talkies. Gegé and Lee also had walkie-talkies but mine were professional, spies used walkie-talkies like mine. Father always took care of us, any day now he'll turn up here at the hotel and will take care of us again, Father won't let what happened to Hilário happen to me, he won't let Mother end up like Dona Eugénia, Father already knows that Mother's mind is feeble and that she won't let anyone treat her, she's never allowed anyone to treat her head and even less so to treat her other ailments. Boxes of prescription medicine binned, they keep me up at night, they make me feel sick, they make me dizzy, even Senhor Antunes from the pharmacy thought it was a pity, it's a shame to see so much money thrown away, Senhor Antunes from the pharmacy must have also come to the Motherland, one of these days we'll enter a pharmacy and find Senhor Antunes with his white pharmacist's coat and his eyeglasses hanging from a little silver chain saying as he did over there, this is all to do with the nerves, nervous disorders are the most difficult to cure.

Mother puts down her fork announcing the end of the meal. Her medicine bag always used to be on the kitchen counter and before every meal Mother was in the habit of carefully ordering the tablets she was going to take. Now there is none of that, no bag, no counter, not even a kitchen and Mother does as she pleases. As the restaurant tables are very close together I lower my voice and ask Mother about her tablets, I don't need any tablets here, Mother says without lowering her voice, that was a blessed country but not for me because my body always belonged in this one. Mother still belongs to two countries, the Motherland where she was born and where she is safe from everything, even from her crises, and the blessed country to which her body never became accustomed, its weather too intense for bodies not born there. Mother speaks with the tone she used with visitors, a blessed country, the woman on the table to our left nods her head in agreement, you dropped a mango seed on the ground and the next day there was a mango tree growing, and her husband adds, a rich land, coffee, cotton, diamonds, oil. Their children silent like my sister and me. A land of such abundance that there could never be any hunger, says the man at the table on our right, but those people just can't govern themselves, there will be famines that will kill more people than any amount of gunfire, without the whites there those bastards will kill each other, the man at the table on our right adds, whoever refuses a good mother will have to suffer a terrible stepmother. Mother smiles, if only Father were here drinking Ye Monks then we could almost be hosting visitors, even if this is not our home, even if the member of staff comes towards us and with an unfriendly face tells us, you must leave the table now because the queue goes all the way to the lifts. And Mother still in the voice that she used with visitors, I'm sure my husband will arrive soon.

Mourita wants to recover what I've won off him and suggests that we raise the wager to two contos and five hundred escudos. The skin on our hands is all wrinkly from having spent the whole afternoon in the water. I accept his challenge. We take our positions, hands clinging to the swimming pool's edge, Mourita's brother, Paulo, counts us in, one, two, three, I push off, my lungs filled with air, I dive down, further and further down, the blue water, almost warm, I have to hold my breath longer than Mourita, I touch the bottom of the pool, Mourita's body beside mine, I touch the bottom of the pool like Mother used to touch the mantle of Our Lady during the May 13 procession and I pray for Father to come back quickly, I pray for Father to reply to our letters. I'll stay under water, if necessary I'll hold my breath until I pass out so you'll see I'm not joking. Whoever you are, listen to me, I'm not joking, listen to me and do as I ask, if Father doesn't arrive soon or if he doesn't answer our letters you'll have me to deal with. Mourita is still by my side, he doesn't want to lose any more money, he can't possibly imagine that I always beat him because I have wagered much more than he has. Mourita's body floats upwards, it is above mine, I hardly have any air in my lungs, my head is close to bursting, Mourita will lose again, whoever you are you must bring Father back to us, my heart pounding in my chest, if necessary I'll die to prove that I'm not joking.

Rui won again, says Paulo, disappointed, almost protesting, my brother always wins. He used to win, I correct, it's over, now I'm the king of the pool. I put away the two contos and five hundred escudos, I've made enough this afternoon for a pack of unfiltered cigarettes. There are no free sun loungers, we soak up the sun sitting on the ground, we brought towels down from our room, it's not allowed but who cares, the manager can come and tell us off if she wants, these are troubled times. The pool is always packed, no-one in the hotel has anything else to do and the summer days in the Motherland are hot. But it's a different type of heat, it doesn't leave our body dripping with sweat, Uncle Zé was right to complain that over there your skin could go bad from so much humidity, the heat in the Motherland does not leave us drenched in sweat but it claws at our throats and lungs.

From the pool we can see the palm trees in the hotel's garden and we can taste the salt from the seawater across the road. If Gegé and Lee were here with me, instead of Mourita and Paulo, it would be an afternoon almost like the ones we spent at the Alvalade swimming pool. We used to make bets, whoever takes longest to retrieve the locker key from the bottom of the pool pays for the sandwiches at Pólo Norte. The Alvalade swimming pool must be shut down by now. The Nun'Álvares swimming pool, too. It must all be shut down, the Avis cinema, the Restinga restaurant, everything. Mother shouldn't be so worried about not having news from Father or from Uncle Zé, I've told her that there are probably no white postmen left and that black postmen can't read properly and are always getting lost. And besides that there is the war, Father and Uncle Zé can't reply to the letters we've written to them because they have not received them, nothing else has happened. Mother also wrote to relatives in the Motherland who haven't replied either but I have no explanation for that, postmen here aren't black and there is no war, at least for now. Pacaça says we're not far from a civil war, there was a huge demonstration against the commies but the commies are winning, they built barricades at the city's entrance and everything. The television room is always packed when the news is on, everyone wants to complain about what the commies are doing, land reform, nationalisations, the commies are going to ruin everything, they've ruined the colonies and now they'll ruin the Motherland, says Pacaça, but he can go and screw himself because anything that was worth something has already been lost. Pacaça speaks for the returnees with more authority than anyone else at the hotel, he was born in Angola but lived in Mozambique which is why he hates Rosa Coutinho who handed Angola over to the blacks as much as he hates Almeida Santos who did the same thing in Mozambique. Pacaça never utters their names without calling them vile traitors or worse, and if he's outside he'll spit on the ground to show his disgust.

But Mother with her feeble mind is difficult to persuade and she wanted to send Father another letter. My sister pretended to be Miss Goody Two-Shoes, I'm going to the post office with Mother to keep her company, as if I didn't know the real reason, as if I didn't know that she was going to post a letter to Roberto. She thinks she's so clever and she thinks I don't know that Roberto gave her his grandparents' address, she thinks I believe she's writing to Father, hours and hours of writing letters to Father, no-one has that many things to say to their father, least of all my sister who used to complain about him all the time, he doesn't let me go out with my friends, he doesn't give me money for the dress I saw at the boutique on Combatentes Avenue, he won't buy me a new record player. My sister felt ashamed of our record player that came in its own little case as a gift with the English language course. The black man who picked up the phone at our house must have worked out that the little case has a record player, he must have played all our records, even Mother's Roberto Carlos records that no-one was allowed to touch, he must have discovered that the "La Décadanse" record is scratched but he probably doesn't know that all you have to do is lift the needle, all those blacks know is how to accuse inno-cent men like Father. Mother called our house number again but this time it didn't even ring, they must have torn it out, or they haven't paid the phone bill, or telephones are no longer working over there at all. Gegé and Lee's telephones don't work either, nor does Dona Gilda's, the numbers are no longer any good, sometimes I feel like smashing up the telephone on the bedside table or at least tearing off its dial.

My sister must think that when Roberto gets her letter he'll come running to see her, girls are so silly. Roberto liked that Indian girl, Lena, but my sister was always after him, it drove me mad, my sister could have had any other boyfriend she wanted but she got it into her head that Roberto was the only one for her. The boys over there liked her, the boys in the hotel won't stop eyeing her up either, when my sister is by the swimming pool they can't take their eyes off her, it must be the red bikini and the blonde hair. Some people don't believe my sister doesn't dye her hair, luckily my hair is not as fair, luckily only girls can have such blonde hair, it's to do with the Celts. I don't know if Mother even remembers that story she used to tell about the Celts, whenever people found it surprising that we were so fair-haired Mother would say straight away, it's because of the Celts. Before the Romans, the Celts had lived in the village that Mother and Father were from and if someone doubted it, but that was centuries ago, there mustn't be a drop of their blood left, Mother would get upset, our fair hair and our blue eyes came from the Celts and no-one should doubt it. It's been a while since Mother spoke of the Celts but I'm sure she hasn't forgotten about them. Sometimes my sister locks herself up in the bathroom and I hear her sobbing for hours, she comes out with red eyes and a swollen nose, she says that she misses Father, that she wants to go back to our life over there, to our life before the gunfire started. My sister thinks I don't know that she also cries about Roberto.

Let's get out of here, let's go and see the trains, says Paulo, who can never stay still for long. Trains in the Motherland are different from the ones over there, these trains carry people to work every day. Over there we didn't have trains like these, only the freight trains where the blacks hung from the wagon doors. We like to go and watch the trains and to make mischief. The people over here get furious with us but we don't care, and anyway the people over here have never liked us. And it's good to get out of the hotel. Even such a large hotel becomes small when it's filled with so many people with nothing to do apart from going from one side to the other. I already know the hotel inside and out and I know all the people.

Mourita and Paulo are in room 437 with their mother, their father and a grandmother called Dona Cremilde, whose eyes are set so deep that they already seem to be watching us from another world. The rooms on the fourth floor are larger than ours but it's still too many people for a single room, Mourita tells us that his grandmother spends her nights praying for the war to stop, Mourita's father, Senhor Acácio, threatens to put her out on the street but the grandmother keeps on murmuring her Ave Marias all through the night and doesn't let them sleep. Senhor Acácio plays cards with Pacaça and is on sentry duty down by the containers, he is always organising demonstrations, plenary meetings and protests against the revolutionaries and the commies, not to mention against Mário Big Cheeks Soares, who sold us out, our greatest enemy. But what Senhor Acácio likes most is ogling women, there is not a bottom or a cleavage that escapes his attention, I bet he's already ogled my sister and my mother, I'd rather not know, because if I catch him at it there will be trouble. Mourita and Paulo laugh at their father for ogling women like that, they're proud of it, our old man can't see a broomstick with a skirt without wanting to make a pass at it, he hasn't forgotten what's good, he's old but he isn't dead, still they must feel a little embarrassed when Senhor Acácio stares at women's bottoms with his reptile eyes, especially when he's rolling a cigarette and his pasty tongue lingers over the rolling paper, the ring with the Brazilian coat of arms tight around his little finger, because then Senhor Acácio seems truly repulsive. Mourita and Paulo's mother, Dona Ester, is usually in the lounge doing crochet with her swollen legs on a stool, my legs are like this because it was so hot over there, they just won't get better, it's as if they've lost their original shape, Dona Ester complains, as if her swollen legs were her only problem, as if she hadn't lost everything she had over there, as if her husband weren't always ogling women.

Mourita invited Ngola and Rute to come and watch trains with us, it's more fun when there are more of us, we can make more fun of the people here. I put the money I was given and my father's lighter in a secret pocket that my mother asked the seamstress at the La Finesse shop to make, so you won't lose anything. Rute asks her mother to let her come with us, Dona Rosa says, you can only go if another girl goes, it's wrong for a girl to be on her own with so many boys. I make up a lie, my sister is waiting for us, Dona Rosa is satisfied, her turkey neck flapping up and down, that's fine then, and she turns to Pacaça to continue her conversation, our misfortune was other people's good luck, just look at the hotel manager getting filthy rich at our expense. I don't like Rute too much but I've caught her looking at me many times, I think Rute likes me, that must be why she tries so hard to be my sister's friend, it's always hey, Milucha this hey, Milucha that, but my sister doesn't pay any attention, she must find Rute tiresome what with her dreams of becoming Miss Angola. Even if we had stayed there, I doubt if Rute could have been Miss Angola, Rute looks pretty in the picture they took when she won the Miss Samba contest but she's not pretty enough to be a real Miss Angola like Riquita. I left my poster of Riquita over there, I rolled it up so carefully and in the end I didn't bring it, if Uncle Zé hadn't been shouting at us I would never have left behind my Riquita poster. It had an autograph and everything. Rute wouldn't mind becoming Miss Portugal but she can't do that either, the revolutionaries have banned all beauty contests and women have to burn their bras and join the demonstrations so they won't be accused of being reactionaries. Rute would like to live in America, in America women also burn their bras but they still have beauty contests, no-one tells any-one else what to do. If the Motherland copied America instead of the Soviet Union Rute could be Miss Portugal.

I've been spending time with Mourita, Paulo and Ngola but none of them are anything like Gegé or Lee, especially Ngola, who is mulatto and is always boasting, mixed people have the best of both races, he says, just compare mongrel mutts with a pure-breed dog. Pirata was a mongrel but didn't realise that she shouldn't have chased after the car when we left, she didn't real-ise that this time we weren't playing. Who knows, perhaps they let Father go soon after and he found Pirata on the avenue and is keeping her with him. Mourita and Paulo could have been my friends over there, we came to the conclusion that we had done the same things and were even at the same school for a few years, it was only by chance that we hadn't met before. Mourita and Paulo had also watched "Emmanuelle" through binoculars from a friend's house, "Emmanuelle" and other films for grown-ups, they even saw that other film called "Helga" something or other, Gegé and I did not watch it but Lee watched it and told us it was about a girl who has a baby, nothing special. Mourita and Paulo used to have a mini Honda moped, Senhor Acácio had not learned the same things from the book of life as Father had, let the child cry now so the father doesn't cry later, Father would say. I might have had a moped if Father hadn't been so hung up about those things, so there's no harm in saying that I actually had one. I'm just worried that my sister will rat on me, but my sister never talks to my friends, they're idiots, she says, whoever my friends are my sister's opinion is always the same, they're idiots and morons.

I didn't know that days could be as long as they are here, the sun keeps threatening to leave but doesn't. If days had been like that over there then Gegé, Lee and I would have had time to cycle over to the new district and spy on the girls even when school finished at half past six. And Paula would have had fewer excuses, my parents only allow me to be outside while it's light, it always got dark when Paula was just about to let me unfasten her bra, hours of kissing with tongues so Paula would let me unfasten her bra and then nothing. Paula had the same annoying voice as my sister, it's night-time, I have to go home so I won't be grounded, she must have thought she was Cinderella or that other one that dies when night falls, my sister liked those fairy tales but I didn't. The black man who answered the phone must have seen all our books by now, even my sister's special-edition photonovels. Paula also liked photonovels, sometimes she asked me to go to Senhor Manuel's stationery shop to find the latest issues, I never wanted to go, I knew that Senhor Manuel would ask, so you're reading photonovels now. I couldn't explain to Senhor Manuel about how Paula kissed me with her tongue in exchange for the favours, sometimes I think Paula just asked me to do those things so she'd have an excuse to kiss me like that, Paula's tongue twirling around in my mouth, it made me dizzy, sometimes she'd suck on my tongue as if she wanted to yank it out, Paula was no good at snogging, that's what Gegé and Lee said when I explained about Paula's kisses, a girl who twirls her tongue like that or tries to yank your tongue out doesn't know how to snog. Fortunata didn't bother with kissing. She didn't even put her cigarette out. Perhaps Paula is in one of these hotels and any day now I'll see her in the Casino's garden, perhaps here in the Motherland she doesn't have that annoying little voice and she's learned to kiss properly like Anita. Gegé used to say, Anita may be a tramp but her kisses will take you into seventh heaven, one of my regrets is not having kissed Anita, I don't know what I was doing chasing Paula if I don't even miss her now. I miss Fortunata more than I miss Paula. I never thought I'd miss Fortunata who used to do dirty things with the white boys, Fortunata was always a slag, as Lee used to say. But what I want now is to meet girls from the Motherland, the girls with the cherry earrings. I still haven't seen one as pretty as the ones in the photographs but there must be some, they wouldn't have made them up just for the photographs. I could go to the beach, there are pretty girls at the beach, but the water here in the Motherland is so cold I can't even go for a swim, it feels as if my bones are snapping. Not even those who knew this sea before going over there are able to swim in it, our bodies are lazy and get used to the good things and now they only want warm water, Faria said the only time we went to the beach, our lips and the tips of our fingers turning purple, our lazy bodies have forgotten about this chill.

When classes start it will be easy to meet the pretty girls in the Motherland, there must be many at school. Over there, I never wanted classes to start but here I count the days before I go to school. If a civil war breaks out I hope it is after classes have started. I also hope that the strikes and demonstrations that the people here hold every day do not prevent schools from opening. These are troubled times. The hotel manager is always rushing from one side of the hotel to the other, Pacaça says that the manager is running around with a face like a constipated bumhole but that she makes a lot of money at our expense and that she'll make even more now that she has opened the floor reserved for guests to the families crowding into the airport, the manager concluded that there were no guests left and that the empty floor was causing her to lose money, she says it's not due to the loss of money, but to help us, that must be why she has us living four or five to a room and serves us mouldy fruit for dessert. When classes start I'll meet girls from the Motherland. I hope the science classes aren't too difficult, my sister doesn't know if they are, last year we had almost no classes and besides she chose arts subjects, like almost all the girls do. My sister will finish school this year and wants to be a secretary. At least that's what she said over there.

We try to run through as many carriages as we can before the train starts moving, they have to be the second-class carriages because the first-class ones are always almost empty and it's not as much fun, but at the end of the afternoon the second-class carriages are packed tight and to get from one carriage to the next we shout and push so hard that the locals jump with fright, we have to get out, we have to get out. Most fun of all is to jump off the train when it's starting to move. It was a mistake to bring Rute, girls can't run or elbow people out of the way, or jump when the train is moving. On top of it all Rute is always giggling and talking to me, if I'm not careful she'll wear out my name, hey, Rui, look at how pretty the sea is, hey, Rui, would you like to go to the Casino, it almost makes me sick. I like to look out at the sea while we wait for the trains but I like to do it in silence. The sea in the Motherland is as blue as the sea was over there, almost the same sea, perhaps a little smaller. With the sea in front of you the rest of the world is closer, Brazil and America seem to be right there, with the sea in front of you the future can be like Father's on the *Pátria* twenty-four years ago, it can be whatever you want it to be. When I can't look at the sea any longer I turn my back and I watch the Casino's garden filled with returnees, all the nearby hotels are full of returnees and the Casino's garden is a good place to idle the day away. Most of the time you can't find a park bench and sitting on the grass is forbidden, here in the Motherland everything that is good is forbidden, even Coca-Cola, the people who live here have a good reason to be so ill-tempered.

If Tozé Cenoura had not come with us, the bastards from the Motherland would not have felt up Rute. Tozé Cenoura is always around the train station looking for unstamped tickets, he brings boys from the hotel with him and he orders them around in Kimbundu so that people here know he is a returnee. That isn't really necessary because you just have to see the clothes he wears, the people here aren't as stylish as we are and have skin that is white as milk or grey-greenish, skin the colour of something going off. People here are strange and can spot us a mile away. I think Tozé Cenoura speaks Kimbundu just to big himself up, he must think that speaking Kimbundu is like speaking English. Besides his racket with the train tickets, Tozé Cenoura also sells encyclopaedias door to door wearing a coat that he found in the church's charity chest, he looks like the tramp in the Chaplin film but he doesn't care. Tozé Cenoura showed us the tickets he had found, it's easy to falsify the date and then it's just a question of selling them at half-price, we don't normally make much of a profit because we have to rely on the goodwill of the Portuguese and not many seem willing to buy, but on days when there are returnees' demonstrations or when clothes are being handed out then we can make some more money, everyone needs to use the train. As he spoke, Touzé Cenoura did not take his eyes off Rute, he was like a strutting peacock flashing his tail feathers. Ngola asked a few questions about the ticket business and then said, such a terrific idea, making money is not difficult if you have a good idea, a good idea can make you a millionaire, of course, said Tozé Cenoura as if he'd already had one, I was walking around here one afternoon and saw so many unstamped tickets on the ground that I thought, you can falsify the dates easily, all you need is a penknife, sometimes I use the numbers on the ticket, a 3 can easily be turned into an 8, when I got back to the hotel I told my father my idea and we started that very day, now we have all these helpers, he said, pointing at the children. Tozé Cenoura spoke about his ticket racket with more enthusiasm than my father ever showed when talking about his trucks, his chest so puffed up it looked as though he was going to fly away, Rute was impressed, how cool, Tozé, she said in that whiny little voice that only girls know how to make, you've really had a good idea. I'm sure Rute was biting her lips to make them redder, it was Paula who taught me this trick, Paula told me a few secrets about girls and this was one of them, what she didn't tell me was that girls prefer boys who know how to make some money. Tozé Cenoura felt he was a big shot just like Pacaça does when he speaks at assemblies, we sold all the tickets we made and if we'd had more we would have sold them all too, even people in other hotels were asking for tickets, Rute curled a lock of her hair around her index finger and Tozé Cenoura said, if you'd like to one day I can take you into town and I'll pay for your ticket, and Rute went all soppy, and what are we going to do in town.

When the train pulled into the station we hurriedly said goodbye to Tozé Cenoura, let's do four carriages, shouted Ngola, this one's well packed, Tozé Cenoura called Rute, hey, girlie, Rute stopped, her head in profile like the portraits in photographers' display cabinets, Tozé Cenoura asked, what party do

Adam and Eve belong to? We've got to leg it, Ngola shouted again, but Rute stood still, maybe trying to answer Tozé Cenoura's silly riddle, the platform filled with passengers spilling out of the train, people dressed in black and grey, beige and brown, come on, said Ngola annoyed, but Rute did not move, the dumb girl waiting for who knows what instead of coming with us. If she had followed us the bastards from the Motherland would not have felt her up. I ran through three carriages and the inspector was in one of them, the inspector makes everything more difficult because he could pull the alarm and call the police, but everything went smoothly, I jumped off the moving train raising my arms in a V for victory.

Rute was already crying because some bastards from the Motherland had felt her up, we ran after them but the bastards had a head start and got onto the bus. From the window they kept on gesturing and miming that they were groping Rute, you liked it, didn't you, the bus was already moving away and the cowardly bastards were at the open window, all returnee girls are poked by blacks. Rute cried even more, she didn't even stop crying when I asked her, so what party do Adam and Eve belong to?

Bourgeois society has not been destroyed at its deepest root, the fascist beast is still a threat and the struggle for a classless society is far from over, down with salaries that lead to hunger, down with capitalist exploitation, long live the revolution. The hotel workers' committee representative has been speaking for over half an hour. There is such relief when he shuts up that everyone applauds.

I like the plenary meetings. Often they lead to long discussions, they go on until the small hours, some go on through the night, everyone gets overexcited, especially when there is a vote, people threaten to beat each other up, it's like we're in a film. With the furniture rearranged the lounge looks completely different, the chairs for watching television arranged in rows, the card tables placed side by side to make one long rectangular table seating representatives from the workers' committee, the manager, a union representative and three other men I don't know and who are not from the hotel, every time those men talk about the fascists they always use funny words like tormentors and stooges, on our side are Pacaça, João the Communist and the Judge.

The hotel workers' committee representative is from accounting and looks as if he's been shipwrecked on a desert island his entire life, he's a skinny man with a beard down to his stomach and long hair but only at the back because he's bald on top. They say he's a Maoist. Senhor Acácio says Maoists are worse than commies, he's heard that they've been trained for everything, even putting a bullet into the back of an old man's head without showing any pity. The manager doesn't seem to know what a plenary meeting is and is dressed as though she was going to a wedding, her hair all done up, not like our neighbours who were always dolled up, but like the women in the posters at Dona Mercedes' salon where Mother used to go. The manager wears a three-strand pearl necklace, a gold watch and stone-studded rings, almost as if she's asking to be called a reactionary bourgeois and an enemy of the people. She's the only one who doesn't seem out of place in a room with pleated apricot-coloured curtains, the only one who seems to fit in. The hotel workers and the returnees look wrong in a room with a stone fireplace with a golden fireplace guard and paintings on the walls like in museums.

Pacaça wears a khaki-coloured jacket and the white brogues that almost all the old folk have. When I'm old I'll never wear shoes like those. Without his handkerchief and his hunter's hat it's as if Pacaça were suddenly in civvies, he looks like someone else, but I'll bet my Brigitte Bardot poster that the plenary meeting won't come to an end without Pacaça telling the story of how he got his nickname, four hundred and sixty-nine forest buffalo or *pacaças* killed with single shots and two hundred and fifty-seven more that put up a fight, the target was to reach one thousand but someone on high had other plans. When he says this Pacaça points to the sky, someone on high had other plans, and when he says it like that it seems as if that someone on high was forced to choose between a coup d'état leading to decolonisation and the remaining two hundred and seventy-four forest buffalo that Pacaça wanted to kill. I don't know how Pacaça doesn't get tired of telling the same old story, especially the part when he talks about those fraudulent hunters who showed their true colours, the ones that disappeared when the animal charged in their direction, seven hundred kilograms running your way is a lot of animal, three and a half metres in length and one sixty in height, a portent of strength with hooked horns, horns able to cut through a man like a hot knife through butter. At this point, Pacaça offers details of all the buffalo he killed. He also killed boars, deer, leopards and lions, he killed everything except elephants, you can't kill an animal that knows when its time is up and makes its way to a cemetery, an animal that is more intelligent than us. I've killed all sorts of animals but nothing compares to the buffalo whose stuffed heads look so lovely on a wall, I had a wall covered in them, a shame, I left it all behind in Angola because there weren't any in Mozambique, you could only find the buffalo in Angola, they were native to Angola, in Mozambique a *pacaça* is a tree, known to others as an apple leaf or a rain tree, want to see, and he shows the photographs in his wallet, a wallet made from the skin of a crocodile that Pacaça himself killed too. He has photographs of the *pacaça* tree from Mozambique and of the *pacaça* buffalo from Angola and he never fails to say that he is a returnee from Angola as much as he is a returnee from Mozambique, or better yet, I'm not a returnee of any kind, because I had never set foot in this place before, it was my grandfather who left all that time ago and swore that he would never come back.

João the Communist has a flowery shirt and long hair down his back that he flicks away abruptly so he doesn't look like a woman arranging her tresses. I think a serious communist would not wear a flowery shirt but João the Communist is not a communist, they call him that because he's always saying that the empire was shameful, that we should be ashamed at having subjugated innocents for centuries. People have come to blows over this, once Senhor Serpa was about to thump João the Communist, who ran out of the meeting room like a frightened girl, if he hadn't run away I don't know what might have happened, Senhor Serpa just shouted, it's one thing for people born here to say that but you should know better and you should be ashamed of yourself.

The Judge always has his head down as if more interesting things were happening on the table than were happening in the room. Everyone in the hotel knows that the Judge was never a judge, he was never even employed at the courthouse, the people who worked for the state over there are not staying in hotels, their lives are sorted, they were given somewhere to live and pensioned off, some were even given jobs and then pensioned off. They are rewarded as if they'd been in hell while we are treated as if we have to be punished. The returnees who are not in hotels avoid the returnees who are in hotels, they think we're fools, we never took holidays in the Motherland or planned for a life here, we weren't clever like they were, or more precisely, they weren't stupid like us, they didn't sink every cent they ever made into the country we called home. The Judge was certainly not a judge over there but no-one wants to disprove him just as no-one disproves those who claim to have had a house with a swimming pool or two ranches with cotton fields stretching as far as the eye could see. No-one disproves them because no-one is interested, everything is lost, however much or little anyone had. I've even heard Mother say that she used to own a vacuum cleaner, and what a good job it did.

Owning a vacuum cleaner was one of the aspirations that Mother never gave up on, no neighbour owned or even wanted a vacuum cleaner, a broom and a dustpan were enough to clean a house, a broom, a dustpan and a black maid, of course. Except that Mother didn't want to be a housewife like our neighbours, she wanted to be a housewife like the ones in films, like the ones with vacuum cleaners and spotless kitchen aprons, who drank coffee sitting at high counters in immaculate kitchens. Mother also wanted one of those kitchens with windows just by the sink from which you can see lawns that husbands mow on Sunday mornings, she wanted breakfasts with eggs and strips of streaky bacon and those flat doughy discs that Mother didn't have a recipe for. The vacuum cleaner was the key element of this elaborate dream. Father promised every year that the following year would be the year of the vacuum cleaner but it never was. If Mother reminded Father of his promises he would tell her about the payments due for yet another truck he had just bought, or the roof in one of the warehouses that needed repairing, he totted up the domestic expenses, water and electricity, food, school fees for me and my sister, he explained that there wasn't enough money for everything and so Mother postponed one more year her dream of being a housewife like the ones in films. She resigned herself to being a housewife like our neighbours and that's why our living room didn't have lozenge-patterned wallpaper and why there was no Formica bed with integrated bedside tables in Mother and Father's bedroom, no spaceship-style furniture like the furniture in American bedrooms.

Pacaça reminds us that the plenary meeting was convened to solve concrete problems, many of them going back some time, and he reads, overcrowded rooms lacking the most basic conditions necessary for the people living in them, having to queue for as long as two hours for meals, which is not only exhausting for those standing but also causes disturbances that disrupt the calm atmosphere we all value, the terrible quality of the food, a sign of the lack of consideration we are shown. Now he reads out some of the more recent problems, one of the service lifts has been out of order for three days forcing staff to use our lifts and therefore making them even more insufficient, the noticeable slip in standards of cleanliness in common areas as can be easily seen in the very room in which we are meeting, and finally the main reason why the plenary meeting was called, the emptying of the pool with no prior warning, a callous act that deserves our most vehement condemnation. We applaud again, the workers' representatives don't budge. Senhor Acácio is now on his feet shouting, seconded, seconded, but already the Maoist is protesting because the competence and zeal of comrades in charge of cooking and of comrades in charge of cleaning has been called into question. And while he's on the subject, the Maoist talks for close to ten minutes about how peasants, factory workers and salaried employees must resist exploitative landowners, bloodsucking factory owners and capitalists blinded by greed. He adds that the mere existence of service lifts is a threat to the revolution that aimed to abolish such distinctions and reminds us that in other revolutions heads rolled for such affronts to equality. Regarding the emptying of the pool he supports comrade manager's decision, the swimming pool symbolises reactionary bourgeois habits and even when it's empty it is an affront to the legitimate interests of salaried employees, peasants and factory workers.

The manager asks to speak. Whatever she says she will be heckled because we and the workers always heckle her. These are troubled times, the manager no longer lingers over her words, she no longer smells of the expensive perfume that stuck to my hand that first day. She says the same thing at every plenary meeting. She must have learned from Álvaro Cunhal, secretary-general of the Portuguese Communist Party, who makes everyone groan the moment he appears on television, there goes the White Horse again, sounding like a broken record, and people laugh again but there's no harm in them laughing at the same things because the White Horse always says the same things, as though he's swallowed a tape-recording. The television room always fills up because everyone wants to be rude about politicians like Rosa "The Unfortunate" Coutinho, or Otelo "The Meat Cleaver" Saraíva de Carvalho, or Mário "Big Cheeks" Soares, and to all the other traitors and thieves. The manager says she's sorry, she'd like to help but she can't give people what she doesn't have, I have no more available rooms, I have no more cooks, I have no more lifts, I'll help you in any way that I can and you can't ask me for anything more. Moving on to the subject of the swimming pool, the manager sighs and doesn't even try to hide her contempt for these plenary meetings, she fiddles with her three-strand pearl necklace, I had it emptied for safety reasons, there were always more people in it than there should have been, unsupervised children, I was worried that a tragedy might occur. The manager doesn't convince anyone because she doesn't tell the truth, she doesn't mention the hotel towels we inappropriately brought down to the pool, or the enormous grill we set up on the lawn, Senhor Norberto went out to find a gas burner and we had a party, we bought chicken from the butcher, it was as though we were back there, the only things missing were some *jindungo* chillies, some Cuca beer and some merengue, we had a radio but it only played revolutionary songs, the people here are always listening to revolutionary songs, the songs are so bad that you can't even dance to them.

It's always the same thing, it's sickening to hear this shrew who is getting rich at our expense, let's go to the bar and then come back for the voting, says Mourita as he takes a drag from a cigarette so deep that it makes him cough. We don't even have a vote, my friend, we should go and spy on the girls at the other hotels, says Ngola. My feet are killing me from walking over the rocks, Mourita complains, let's go to the bar and have a beer. We never know what to do, but that also happened with Lee and Gegé, we never knew where to go, it was as if we never felt at ease anywhere. I don't know how Mourita does it but he always has cash for a few beers and it isn't Senhor Acácio who gives it to him. I think Mourita is selling *liamba*, Mourita and Paulo whose eyes so often look glazed over, Senhor Acácio must have realised already.

I don't like smoking *liamba*. Back home I smoked once, I had gone over to Helder's house with Lee and Gegé and he offered us some, you've got to try, there's nothing as cool as smoking this. We were scared of getting hooked if we even touched the stuff but Helder told me that his older brother, Vadinho, smoked every day. Vadinho didn't look like a druggie and he went out with Carla, she was so pretty, if Carla had not been twenty years old I would have fallen seriously in love, I think I did for a while. Sometimes I dreamed I was in Mussulo with Carla, that we were both swimming naked, the following morning I had to change the sheets, I was sweating a lot, I'd say, Mother would take the bundled-up sheets from me, she would say nothing or would simply agree, the nights have been hot. I think Mother knew but she preferred to pretend she didn't, Father on the other hand would wink at me because we are members of the same club. Here everything is different. With my mother and my sister nearby I can't even have nice dreams, though I can stay in the bath as long as I want without my mother or sister complaining, they must know that boys have to do their dirty things just like I know what happens with women. My sister thinks I didn't understand when she was talking about the curse with her friends and Mother thinks I don't know what those little towels that they hide in drawers are for but they're wrong. I never talk about it but I know, Fortunata sometimes said, I'm on the rag, but not even that could keep us away, even then she was a slag. After Helder convinced us that we wouldn't become druggies just by trying it, we smoked some *liamba*, Gegé and Lee started giggling like madmen and didn't stop. With me the opposite happened, I started worrying for no reason, I'm going to die, I'm going to die, parts of my body going numb at intervals, I can't feel my leg, I can feel my leg, I can't feel it again, I wanted to shout but I couldn't, I think even the walls in the house started moving. Gegé and Lee were still giggling, I wanted to tell them I was going to die but I couldn't speak or move. When it was over Helder said, you were unlucky, you had a bad trip, sometimes it happens, you have to try it again. Never. I could do without it. From then on every time someone at a party or at school offered me *liamba* I'd say, I have bad trips, as if I'd tried it many times and the results were always the same. Mourita, Paulo and Ngola have asked me to join them, we were by the large wall, I have bad trips, and Ngola said, but you've never tried it, you're making it up, you sissy. I explained about the parts of my body falling asleep and the voices I heard in my head, voices that told me to do things, but Ngola wouldn't stop, what kinds of things, horrible things, what horrible things, they tell me to lie down on the railway tracks or kill whoever is closest to me, Ngola freaked out, if you have bad trips like that it's better if you don't smoke with us and they have never again insisted that I join them for a smoke.

The television brings news of three bombs that the commies set off in Lisbon. Senhor Alcino says, there will be a civil war, as sure as my name is Alcino. We look at each other and start giggling for no reason, Senhor Alcino tries to shoo us away, grow up, delinquents, at your age I had already been through a lifetime of pain, and he chases us down the corridor towards the entrance. Senhor Alcino's bowed legs and curved nose make us laugh even harder, if your parents didn't educate you I'll educate you my way. Queine the night porter smiles, Senhor Alcino gives up and turns his back to us muttering curses, these delinquents don't deserve the food they eat, he almost bumps into Mother and my sister who are coming from the meeting room. They are with Dona Suzete and with her sister-in-law, Gigi, who despite being mute can say a few words that nobody understands, except for Dona Suzete, and that always start with a rrrrrrr coming from her throat as if she were about to spit something out.

Mother's hands fidget inside the pockets of the jacket she used over there during the *cacimbo*. I know what the fidgeting means, Mother is getting worse, her demons are lurking. So it wasn't being over there that made her like this, even over here Mother is not safe from her demons. Father and Uncle Zé have not written yet and I don't know what to think any longer, despite the war, despite the black postmen. I keep telling Mother that nothing has happened to them but it's been such a long time that even I find it difficult to believe what I say. We did, however, get a letter from our relatives in the Motherland, my sister was so happy when Senhor Teixeira said there was mail for us, she even jumped up and down in the hotel's reception, her hands on her head the way girls do when they are happy, oh, my God, we have a letter. She was so disappointed when she saw that the letter was from relatives in the Motherland, but still she tried to convince herself that it might be good news, maybe they were writing to invite us to live with them. My sister was hoping that the same thing would happen to us as had happened to Senhor Flávio from room 211, who went with his wife and daughter to live with relatives who offered them accommodation and food. Senhor Flávio was so excited when he left, the luggage at the hotel entrance and Senhor Flávio saying, whoever has a good family has nothing to fear in this world. Being a hotel returnee is bad because it means there is not a single relative who likes us enough to have us in their home. Our relatives in the Motherland always wrote those lies about how much they missed us, if only we could embrace you, how we miss you, but now that they can embrace us as much as they want they write, we feel terrible for what happened to you. I could have torn up the letter, those fucking weasels, we are sure that everything will work out, God will provide, fucking weasels, I hope that the blacks have also found the family photo album with the little Chinese girls on the cover and ripped it apart.

My sister calls the lift, Mother greets me as if we hadn't been together in the plenary meeting, she introduces me, my son, my son Rui, and asks, have you met Dona Suzete and her sister-in-law. Mother no longer uses blue eye-powder or pink lipstick, she doesn't smell of Si Fraîche. Dona Suzete and the mute girl are in a room close to ours, number 310, how could I not know them if we've been in this hotel for over a month and always see the same people? Mother is getting worse. It doesn't help that Senhor Martins spends his time watching television and saying things like, Big Cheeks Soares will stand up to the commies but he'll lose, we won't escape a civil war. Mother twists the hems of her jacket even more, if there's a civil war here where will we go? There won't be a war, I say it so loud that Dona Suzete is startled. Mother smiles and agrees, there won't be a war. My sister yawns, the lift is here. I'm so worried that my mother will get worse that I constantly think I can spot warning signs in her gestures and expressions. Mother is not getting worse and the demons are not closing in on her. Also there will be no war, if there were where would the people here go, they can't all go to some other country, even if you don't need aeroplanes to leave, they can't all walk over to Spain. We certainly couldn't have walked over here, luckily America lent us some aeroplanes, America and other countries, the newspapers say it is the largest air evacuation ever. Lee always liked records and must be happy, the largest air evacuation ever is something important. If there were a war here I'd like to see all the people here leaving, I'd like to see if they'd leave everything behind the way they made us do. Father was right, that was our country, we should have stayed there, only a coward leaves his country without putting up a fight. Father may not have been as clever as Senhor Manuel but it was Father who was right, they were all cowards, and so was I, I was more of a coward than anyone.

Pacaça is making a speech again, the Judge and the union

representative have left and there are lots of empty chairs in the room, most people are on the balcony, nights in the Motherland can also be very beautiful and full of stars. Pacaça's voice drones on as usual, we have the right to be here, I.A.R.N. stumps up our hotel rates as if we were guests, normal paying guests, but paying guests don't live in overcrowded rooms, paying guests don't get given food that isn't even good for dogs, someone is making money at our expense, says Pacaça with a raised fist, we were robbed once, but we won't be robbed a second time, it's shameful that the hotel is profiting from our disgrace, the manager says that she has stopped reserving the top floor for paying tourists so she can help more families but we all know that there are hardly any tourists, only the odd crazy person or two who didn't want to miss the chance to see a revolution up close, bastards, I hope they enjoy this ridiculous little revolution, the manager wants us to believe that everyone is doing their best to help us but the only thing we're certain of is that they're doing their best to rob us, we want a full pool because paying guests have the right to a full pool and we deserve no less. Pacaça bangs on the table just like the Maoist had done earlier when demanding overtime pay, there is so much applause that it seems as though the hotel is coming down, Senhor Acácio stands up and everyone in the room imitates him, it was Portugal that was the real overseas province, continues Pacaça, he has enough drivel up his sleeve to keep going for over an hour. Pacaça never shuts up, as he says himself, he will only shut up when his mouth is full of dirt, and then not a peep.

We leave the plenary meeting once again and start kicking an empty plastic bottle back and forth between us, that was just like Cubillas says Mourita to impress two chambermaids coming back from the plenary, he does a feint and whistles at them, what a lovely *mataco*, a *mataco* to die for, there goes a bit of *mataco* to make a man dream while awake. When we go to the big wall or to the Casino's garden we say these things to the girls from the Motherland, they don't know what we're saying but they know we're saying dirty things and they get all happy, oh, so cheeky, the returnees are so cheeky. One of the chambermaids is looking our way, there will be trouble, I don't know why Mourita flirted with her, we never flirt with older women, Mourita can't take his drink, if he drinks he starts acting up and no-one can stop him. Father would not like seeing me with Mourita, stay in good company and you'll be a better person, as the book of life teaches. In the end the chambermaid doesn't say anything, Mourita sighs as they disappear, I've had my eye on that little chambermaid for ages, what a lovely round *mataco* she has, it's in things like those that you truly see God's work.

The bar is busier than the lounge. Alongside the people who are fed up with the plenary and waiting for the voting to start are those who come from other hotels. There are always people from other hotels when there is a plenary, we're all in the same boat, what is bad for some is bad for all. They should have thought about that when the gunfire started but instead they all started packing their possessions into crates, whole days of hammering wooden strips around people's goods, they didn't rest until the containers were ready and dispatched to the Motherland, they were like the girls in the girls' school on the eve of their graduation trip, all excited with the move, we're going to the Motherland, we're going to the Motherland. Even I was saying, despite Father's warnings, there are cherries in the Motherland, big and glossy cherries that the girls wear like earrings, pretty girls. Even I was saying those things. The people here should treat us even worse, whoever doesn't fight for his country deserves no respect. And now there's no point in saying, there's strength in numbers, if we stick together nothing bad can happen, it's too late, if we'd stuck together earlier we would never have become returnees, now there's nothing we can do. Some people here call us the removees to wind us up, because we were removed from over there, they must think they're so funny. Returnees can demonstrate with placards all they want and it still won't do any good. Nor will plenary meetings.

Senhor António is on leave and it's only Vítor serving at the bar. Vítor always has frightening outbursts and I wouldn't be surprised if on a busy day like today he picked up a gun and killed us all. They say Vítor doesn't like returnees because his brother went to fight in Guinea and came back crazy. I don't know why we should be blamed for what happened over there to the soldiers who came from here. On top of it all Vítor accuses us of having exploited the blacks but he defends his brother and the other soldiers who went there to kill them. Isn't he a clever one, it's bad to exploit but it's fine to kill. Of course Vítor starts protesting, but soldiers were forced, no-one really wanted to go there, blah, blah, blah. If Vítor had heard Mother's stories, as soon as your father finished second grade the roads were waiting for him, your father always said, if people knew how much sweat goes into making a road they wouldn't lay a foot on them without crossing themselves first, your father's mother had nine children, nine mouths to feed and eighteen arms to help with work, it was the arms that mattered most, the mouths didn't need much, some slices of onion in a few crusts of bread were enough to calm the growling stomachs. If Vítor had heard Mother he'd know that nothing and nobody can force anyone more than hunger and that Father boarded the *Pátria* under more duress than any soldier.

At the bar there are little flags from almost everywhere around the world, they're stuck in a row. I close my eyes and choose one, whichever I touch is the flag from the country to which we'll go when Father arrives. I've played this game many times before and I've picked most countries, even China. Our fate must not have been decided yet, that's why the result is never the same. As soon as Father arrives we'll make a decision but I'm sure Father won't want to stay in this miserable place, he didn't want to be here before he left, much less now. I close my eyes and try to touch the American flag. I got it wrong, but Venezuela isn't so bad either, and I say out loud, when my father arrives he'll take us to Venezuela. Mourita asks for a beer, what's your old man still doing there, it's just blacks over there now, if your old man doesn't come back before independence he'll never get out, they're closing the borders and any whites left will be killed, your old man would only stay if he's too stupid or if he wants to kick the bucket. Mourita makes one of his faces like he's dying, I usually laugh at Mourita's faces, at Mourita pretending to fall over dead, but this time I don't laugh, I grab him by his shirt collar, if you talk about my father like that ever again I'll beat you up so hard you won't walk straight. Everyone is looking but I don't care, Vítor puts Mourita's beer on the counter, I almost knock over the glasses and bottles on the counter, my father had to stay behind to deal with some business and if you ever say that again I'll smash your face in.

Queine the night porter doesn't know that I came to sit outside because I was angry with Mourita. He comes close, what's up, son. Father used to say, so, son. Queine the porter is not like Vítor or the other employees. I've had enough of plenary meetings, I say, they're good for nothing. Queine the porter sits by my side, he's wearing his uniform with the epaulettes of a porter in a five-star hotel with not a single guest to welcome. We're not guests. Queine the porter sits by my side the way Father used to do. I ask him, why do you people not like us, I ask not because I want to know the answer, I ask just for the sake of asking, I'd like to know if they like us or not. Queine the porter shrugs, it's been difficult for everyone, it's also been difficult for us, life was never good here and now everyone's scared that it will get worse, my wife and I once got a letter asking us to go and work in Angola, if we'd gone then we'd also be back now, for sure. If I could tell someone that they took my father perhaps I'd be able to calm down. Our fates are unknown, says Queine the porter, if we'd gone then perhaps we would have met over there, Queine the porter smiles and so do I but, instead of telling him that they took my father or that I'm worried about Mother's attacks starting again, I lie, if we'd met over there I would have taken you for a ride on my mini Honda, it's what I miss the most. Queine the porter has never been in Africa, he avoided being drafted because he had to care for his mother, he can't possibly know that I'm making things up, I talk about the Morro dos Veados, about the Miradouro da Lua, and we get caught up in memories of lives that we never had.

Dear Uncle Zé, I hope this letter finds you in good health. We've gone to the hotel reception every day in the hope of finding a letter from you or from Father but no letter has ever arrived. It's been a long time and I don't know what to think. That's why I'm writing to you. I know that you and my father have never got on well, but I ask you to write and send us some news. I have no good news to give you, Mother is getting worse every day, if Father doesn't join us or write I don't know what will happen to Mother, I don't know what will happen to us. Here in the Motherland I'm not just afraid of the demons closing in on Mother, I'm afraid of everything. The money we brought is going to run out soon, no matter how much we save. I don't know how long they'll let us stay in this hotel and if they put us out on the street I don't know where I'll take Mother and Milucha. I don't know how to take care of Mother and Milucha, I really don't. I want to believe that I do but it's not true. I'm always praying to God that they don't kick us out of the hotel, even though it's horrible to live here. You may not think it's horrible to live in a five-star hotel but it is. It's not just that we're all in the same room, that the hotel is packed, that the food is disgusting, that I don't have a place where I can think about my things, where I can be on my own. I can't really explain. I walk from side to side, sometimes I'm so tired that I can't walk anymore and I just stop. Mother is getting worse because we have no news from Father and because we're living like this. You know that the signs of Mother's crises start appearing some time in advance, as if they were slowly taking over her body. That's how I know she's getting worse. I think Mother sometimes thinks that Father's died, because suddenly she'll go all pale as if she's seen a ghost. And every now and then Milucha will start trembling for no reason. It also scares me to think that Father has died. I try not to think about that. You must write to us. We don't know anyone else here and no-one can help us, even writing letters to the president of the republic does no good. Milucha even wrote to some random general asking for help but she never got an answer. Nobody wants to know about us. Here at the hotel we've never told anyone that Father was taken away. At first we thought Father would join us soon after we arrived and now we don't know how to tell anyone the truth. But also it wouldn't have helped, no-one here could have helped us and on top of everything they would have thought bad things about Father. Newspapers and the television bring news of what's happening over there, they say that they're killing whites who stayed behind and I can't stop thinking about what might be happening. I'm sure not even the blacks believe that Father is the Butcher of Grafanil, or that he knows his identity. Father knew other things, he knew the city like the palm of his hand, he was proud of having helped to muck out the shops when the coastal floods washed everything away, of having seen buildings rising up, and of knowing how difficult it is to spread tarmac, surely you must remember Father talking about how the city was growing, it was as if we were watching it grow ourselves, Father knew all these things but he didn't know anything about the Butcher of Grafanil. I know that you never got on well with Father but this is not the time to settle old scores. Father's advice was always well meant and if I didn't spend more time with you it was because I didn't want to. I could have disobeyed Father. Looking back I realise that you were often saddened because I didn't want to go with you to Baleizão Square or to the tip of the Ilha but over there days passed so quickly that I hardly took any notice of that. Here I have time to think about everything, even about your sadness when I refused one of your invitations. I often get upset with you for not sending us news and when I get upset I call you names, I say things about you and Nhé Nhé. I think Father is right when he says that men shouldn't go with each other and do those things, I won't lie about that. And I don't understand how you can like to go with other men if there is nothing better in the world than kissing a girl. But I'm not writing to talk about that, I get easily sidetracked, I'm writing because I need to have news of Father and because I'm frightened. Milucha must be even more frightened than I am because she seems to be even lonelier than I am and the lonelier people are the more frightened they get. But there's no-one in the hotel who isn't frightened. They all try to disguise it, they disguise it so much that the lounge or the television room can seem like a party. But it's a party of sad people. And now that the summer is over I think the Motherland's sadness is getting into us all as if it were the very air we breathe. And the cold. I never thought the cold would be like this. Last night I dreamed I was in Mussulo and suddenly the sky filled with all sorts of birds, seagulls, terns, cormorants, the sky was so full of birds that there was no air. And yet, despite the unease, I was happy because I thought, at least I'm in Mussulo. I kept repeating it, at least I'm in Mussulo, the birds started to go away and I was left behind floating in the warm seawater with my sight on the coconut palm trees. I haven't seen any coconut palms here, there probably aren't any, there is hardly anything in the Motherland but you must know this better than I do. Nobody here has any hope of going back one day. They all say yes, one day we'll go back, but nobody really believes that. It's hard to know what to believe in. Whether it's good things like going back or bad things like them killing Father. We can't believe in anything but we can't just wait to see what happens either. You must write to me and tell me what happened with Father. I'm ready for anything except for not knowing what happened. I'm scared that Mother will end up like Dona Eugénia who made suits and who never stopped waiting for Senhor Paulino, he disappeared when they lived in the Loje valley. You must remember who they were, when Mother got worse we often went over to them for food, soup, a main dish, dessert, how I loved their mango pudding. I never told Father how much I disliked going on my bicycle to fetch one of his suits because Dona Eugénia always had a place at the table laid out for Senhor Paulino. You too must have heard her saying it, my husband went out to buy some manioc flour and hasn't come back. She repeated manioc flour as if that held the key to the mystery, as if things would have been different if Senhor Paulino had gone out to buy some beans. Dona Eugénia must have known what happened to white people when they disappeared. Even before the gunfire started there was never any mystery about that. I too should know what happens to white people when they disappear. And when they're imprisoned. And yet even Dona Eugénia's children would say, my father went out to buy some manioc flour and never came back. Sometimes Gegé, Lee and I would say to Hilário, who was in our class, the blacks got your father and they killed him. We said it to be cruel, to see him swallow hard, your father won't ever come back. I think I've only just understood this. As you can see it was not only your sadness that I didn't understand. And it wasn't simply because time went by faster over there that I failed to understand so many things. I didn't understand them because I didn't want to. Or perhaps I couldn't even if I had wanted to. I laughed at Hilário and I thought he was a mug because he was always following us. When Dona Eugénia would hear us say to Hilário that Senhor Paulino would never come back, she would threaten us, if I ever hear you messing with my Hilário I'll give you a good thrashing. It was Hilário who followed us, he gave us Captain America playing cards, he did anything we wanted. Now I understand. Our cruelty was nothing by comparison to the wait that Dona Eugénia subjected him to, your father went out to buy some manioc flour and hasn't come back yet. I don't know why I think about these things.

Dear Uncle Zé, I hope this letter finds you in good health.

Sundu ia maié, sundu ia maié, the fucking bitch. I'll kick every door on the way out to the playground, the bitch of a teacher sent me off with a red mark but I'll get my revenge, the cleaners are scolding me, this isn't a jungle, boy, it isn't like back where you came from, there are rules here, *sundu ia maié*, I'm warning you, boy, I take a deep breath and kick another door, they know me now, I stare straight at the old ladies to show them I'm not afraid, I flare my nostrils the way Pacaça says all animals do before attacking, the old ladies with their grey tunics and their varicose veins packed into elastic socks shout at me, you might have been riding lions over there but here you need manners, the old ladies protest but they don't try to stop me, they're scared of me, I walk past the canteen and I hit the tray trolley, all I need to do now is to beat my fists on my chest to show them that I spent more time with the apes than with the lions, the old ladies jump with the clatter that the tray trolley makes, if they want to bad-mouth the returnees I'll give them good reason to do it.

The bitch of a teacher, can one of the returnees answer the question, as if we didn't have names, as if it wasn't enough that they put us all in the same row for returnees only. The bitch tried to justify it, the returnees have lower standards, yes, yes, we must have, we must be as stupid as the blacks, and the people over here must have learned lots after that bummer of a revolution, if the schools are as bad as everything else here they must have had quite some lessons. Even now not a day goes by when there aren't demonstrations, bombs, threats, expropriations, occupations, strikes, there are always people on television reading out communiqués, not only the Armed Forces Movement, or the Revolutionary Council, or the Continental Command, now it's people in the commissions, too, in the committees, in the co-operatives, there are more and more of them every time, I don't know where they find so many revolutionaries. This morning there was no bread in the hotel and the manager tried to justify it, bakers are on strike because they don't want to work at night. Fuck the bakers and the manager, I kick the door to the playground, the hinges squeal more than the old ladies, it's fucking cold out here, I do up my coat, I light a cigarette, I huddle in my corner, if the cleaners don't want trouble they'd better not come near me.

If there are no bread rolls at least give us some baps, says a mischievous Senhor Acácio with his eyes on Dona Juvita's breasts. They say that Senhor Acácio and Dona Juvita are having an affair and that they meet in the boiler room by the swimming pool, Mourita laughs, my old man still knows how to wet his wick. They also say that Dona Ester asked a black priestess, Preta Zuzu, to put a spell on Senhor Acácio so he'd stop ogling women. Preta Zuzu is famous for her *uangas*, or spells, and for casting *xicululos* or evil eyes so powerful that some people cross their fingers when they go past her house. Dona Ester also asked Preta Zuzu for a spell to make Mourita develop the skills of an engineer and another to make Paulo develop the skills of a doctor, that's what they say. If it's true, Preta Zuzu is no great priestess, Senhor Acácio is still chasing women and Mourita and Paulo are always bunking off, though this is understandable because there are teachers like the maths bitch who just sent me out with a red mark. The nice teachers can't do anything about the ones that mistreat us.

The maths bitch made all the returnees sit in the row furthest from the windows, in the worst-lit seats, she must think we're like Mother's roses, that we'll wilt without sunlight, that must be it. Can one of the returnees answer the question, the bitch never says our names, can one of the returnees answer the question, just what we needed, I never open my mouth, can the returnee at the back answer the question, the bitch insisted, as though she was taunting us. Is it so hard to say my name, if I were called Kijibanganga she might have an excuse but Rui, for fuck's sake, such an easy name and even if I were called Kijibanganga it's the bitch's duty to learn it. But no, can the returnee at the back answer the question, I wouldn't speak even if she had pulled out my fingernails and my teeth, not even if someone called the thugs from the secret police, the P.I.D.E., who took away Helder's father, Senhor Moreira, who was never the same after prison, poor Senhor Moreira who was left all disoriented, sometimes he didn't even know what he was saying. Helder said his father was left like that because of the sleep deprivation and because they beat him with steel cables that stripped off his skin, poor Senhor Helder, I hope he's better.

The bitch thinks I care about the red mark but I shit on it, I'd rather be out here, I'm tired of hearing all that crap. The only thing bothering me is the cold, the cold in the Motherland gets into your bones, so when the wind blows down the aisles that we have to cross to get from one classroom block to another it feels as though it's freezing your blood. And it's not even winter. They say it will get worse, I can't imagine how that might be, it's already so bad, my hands never warm up, no matter how much I rub them against each other, and often I have itchy fingers and horrible skin blotches that hurt as if they are burns. Mother says they're chilblains, I didn't know that word, nor did I know the word chapped, which is when our lips crack and even start bleeding when we laugh. That must be why the people from over here don't smile, who would want to smile when you know your lips will start bleeding. And the people from here who went over there would complain about jigger fleas and roundworms, as if the Motherland's chilblains and the chapped lips weren't worse. In photographs winter looked pretty, with snow on the tiled rooftops, families huddled around fireplaces, cats playing with balls of yarn and children in parks wearing colourful hats and gloves. But the cold is nothing like that, it is people hunched over and rubbing their hands, it is people stamping their feet on the ground to warm them up, it is sad people with lint-balled sweatshirts. Lint-ball is another new word we use often, the sweatshirts we get at the clothes depots always have lint-balls. We have no choice, either we wear the sweatshirts with lint-balls or we wear our pyjamas underneath our old clothes, our clothes from over there. Whatever. This morning, when we went for breakfast, I noticed Mother wearing her flannel night-gown underneath her dress. When the cold began we were embarrassed to wear our pyjamas underneath our clothes but we're used to it now.

Sometimes my sister looks at herself in the mirror and tears come to her eyes, over there I used to make fun of her when I saw her sobbing but now it's different. To be in the Motherland is even worse for girls, the boys here don't want to go out with returnee girls. Maybe if it's just to have some fun but never to date them properly, the boys here say that the returnee girls used to go out with blacks. And the girls here don't want to be friends with the returnee girls to avoid being talked about, returnee girls have a bad reputation, they wear short skirts and smoke in cafés. My sister shouldn't mind that the girls from over here don't want her as a friend, we won't stay in the Mother-land for long, we'll leave as soon as Father comes. Father will come. I mustn't worry about Father not coming. Uncle Zé still hasn't replied to the letters I wrote to him, fucking queer, he hasn't replied to me or to Mother. The fucking queer hasn't said a word but Father must be well, he must be well and about to come and be with us, the airlifts will stop on the day of Angola's independence. There's less than a month to go. Father has to come to us before then, he has to come, he has to come, he has to come. Whoever you are, you know what our agreement is. Sometimes, when we're in the restaurant, Mother speaks as if Father were there in front of her, I think even the people sitting at neighbouring tables notice it. We can't keep on waiting, any day now Mother will start sounding like Dona Eugénia, Father has to come quick, there's not much time before independence. And I'm so frightened. I don't want to be frightened but I am. If Father doesn't come before independence it's because he won't come at all, it's because he is dead. You heard me. Whoever you are this time I mean it, it's not like the games I used to play before. If Father doesn't come before independence day you killed Father, if Father doesn't come before independence it's because you wanted those black bastards to kill Father. Whoever you are, listen to me, I'm not joking. You cannot make me wait forever. You cannot do to me what you did to Hilário.

It's cold. Very cold. But what makes me tremble is fear, I grind my teeth hard and try not to think of Father, I have to think of other things, even if it's the maths bitch who's been on my case since the very first day of class. On that very first day she said, oh, look, such a blonde returnee with such blue eyes, what did the bitch mean by that, returnees come in all colours, there may well be green returnees with yellow spots. But today the bitch wouldn't stop, answer the question, I'm talking to you, what's the square root of nine? It's a shame Mourita and I aren't in the same year, Rute is the only one in my year but we're in different classes, probably a good thing, I'm sick of hearing about the Miss Samba beauty pageant. Square root of nine, the returnees in my class are so spineless, they never challenge teachers, they're scared of being expelled from the classroom after too many red marks. After everything that's happened to us we shouldn't be afraid of anything, much less of being expelled from a classroom, bunch of spineless bastards. The bitch at my side trying to intimidate me, answer, her mouth stinking of coffee, they're always drinking coffee, the people here are always asking for some, a tiny coffee, a small cup, and they're all so happy with the crap they get that tastes as bad as everything else. And the soft drinks, how bad are the soft drinks in the Motherland, everything is bad. Square root of nine, and me, *sundu*, silence, *ia*, silence, *maié*, the other returnees start laughing, the bitch doesn't understand, what does that mean, it's the answer in Kimbundu, would you be kind enough to speak in Portuguese, we speak Portuguese here, square root of nine, *sundu ia maié*, that's what they taught us over there, they all laugh, out of the classroom this instant with a disciplinary notice, Teresa Bartolomeu is keeping her head down so she won't be caught laughing. Teresa Bartolomeu likes it when I'm lippy with the teachers. It will be break time soon and Teresa Bartolomeu will come and find me, hey, Didja, I like it so much when Teresa Bartolomeu calls me Didja, that's the only reason I don't mind wearing this silly white coat I was given at the clothes depot.

Teresa is the coolest girl in the school and when she wears the light pink jacket her parents brought from Paris she could be Miss World. Mourita doesn't like girls from the Motherland, those skanks are silly, they don't want to be seen with returnees but they do like to go behind the fence with us and they are the ones who put their hands up our sweatshirts and down our trousers, the skanks from the Motherland are hypocrites, they are always bad-mouthing us but then they want us to cop a feel. Mourita is right but Teresa Bartolomeu is different, Teresa Bartolomeu spends her breaks with us and never says stupid things. The girls from the Motherland are almost always stupid, if we ask them for a favour they'll say, do I look like a black girl, they play hard to get until they want to go behind the fence. Behind the fence they don't seem like themselves, they don't even mind being like the black girls, they go and fetch us cigarettes, snacks, everything we ask them for, they even carry our books, and if we pat their bottoms and call them *quitatas* they're all giggles. Gaby, one girl I kissed with tongues right at the beginning of the school year, said that she liked being with me, that when she was with me it was like being abroad. And how is it to be abroad,

I asked, Gaby didn't know, she had never left the Motherland but she didn't think that was an odd thing to say, it was like being abroad, that's the kind of thing that girls from the Motherland say.

But Teresa is different, soon it will be break time and Teresa will come to be with me, hey, Didja, Teresa is the only person who calls me Didja, I don't let anyone else call me that. When I was given my coat I asked what it meant but nobody at the clothes depot knew. It must be something important, nobody would have written Didja in fat black letters on the back of a coat if it wasn't important. Soon it will be break time and we'll go behind classroom block C. Mourita says that Teresa Bartolomeu is a druggie, the skank only hangs out with us to smoke *liamba* for free, your problem is you're jealous, Teresa is a very cool girl, Mourita doesn't give up, I wouldn't get too excited, you've seen her mother, she has an arse like a wardrobe, a few years from now Teresa will look the same, what does Mourita know about what Teresa will look like a few years from now. Teresa must be waiting for me to ask her out, I'll invite her to go onto the rocks, if she says yes then it's certain she wants me to kiss her, every girl knows what it means to be invited onto the rocks. To get to the sea you have to climb down some rocks covered in green, they're very slippery, girls always need help, or they pretend to need help, immediately we're holding hands, and it takes only a moment to go from holding hands to kissing. And then there's the Giant's Grotto, which is a cavity in the rocks, it's not scary at all but the girls get frightened and we have to put our arms around them, and once you've got your arms around them you have to kiss them, even if the girl is ugly, if we don't try to kiss them people will think we're sissies. That's why I never go near the Giant's Grotto with an ugly girl, Rosarinho has been trying hard to take me there but I always sneak off, I don't want to end up kissing a girl with a metre-long nose, she'd gouge an eye out.

I think Mourita is jealous of Teresa and I can understand why, Teresa lives in a nice apartment close to school, we went there once when we were bunking off, it has a living room with round sofas like the ones Mother was always asking Father for and a stereo record player, how my sister would love that record player. My sister never hangs out with the returnees, she is always running after a group of morons who gather outside the staffroom, morons who think they're so clever, my sister is like a puppy chasing after them, I don't chase after anyone, not even Teresa, who is pretty like no-one else and has a maid in uniform who brings her a snack during the long break and parents who buy her presents all over the world. But I do like Teresa. I like her because she's pretty, almost as pretty as the girls with the cherry earrings. The truth is that there aren't very many pretty girls in the Motherland, generally they're ugly, much uglier than the ones from over there, they have greasy hair that tumbles horribly down their backs and crooked teeth crusty with plaque, it's like they don't brush them, and they smell like lunch boxes left out in the sun back there, a vinegary smell that sticks in your nose and makes it itchy. But Teresa is different. And I also like her because she doesn't mind always having her fingertips stained with ink from ballpoint pens, little plump fingers with bitten fingernails. And because she eats cake without picking the sugar from the corners of her mouth the way other girls do, pressing their mouths into an oval and using their fingers like tweezers. And because she doesn't let out little shrieks when she gets hit while playing dodge-ball. Mourita may think I'm foolish for liking Teresa but I think he's even more foolish for chasing after Rute, who bunks off to go with older local boys who drive her around in their cars and give her presents. My sister is always eyeing up Rute's nice clothes. One day I'll buy a whole shop full of dresses for my sister and then my sister will be the coolest girl at school.

It's good that my coat is warm, Mourita was unlucky, he only managed to get a cold trench coat, the colour of shit, when he wears it he looks like a detective in the old films, Ngola has an Elvis-style striped coat and Paulo has one that belonged to a fireman, we look like clowns. It's even worse when we wear woollen jumpers that are four or five sizes too large. Almost everything they give us at the clothes depot is too large, they say that warm clothes come from America, from Canada, from Germany and that the people over there are large, but we know that the people here rob us of the best clothes, there can't be only giants living abroad, there must also be people our own size. Next time they are giving away clothes I will be there the night before and they'll have to give me good clothes, otherwise there will be trouble. My sister needs warm clothes so that the teachers will stop sending notes home, the pupil is very cold, the pupil is always shivering during class, the pupil must come to school dressed more warmly. We never show Mother the notes our teachers send home and we forge her signature, Mother is so easily distressed, she hardly eats or sleeps, I never imagined I'd send my children to school with no books and shivering with cold, I never imagined this would happen to us, after all your father's hard work, years and years of work without a single day off and now we don't have a ten-cent coin to our name. The last thing Mother needs now is for us to show her the teachers' notes.

My sister is ashamed of being a returnee, she pretends to be from over here and hides the I.D. card with the red stamp on it, the one that says returnee student, the one that entitles her to a daily snack at the canteen. My sister who goes hungry but is ashamed of going to the canteen where the local students might see her card, returnee student. My sister who thinks she might pass herself off as a non-returnee despite the oversized clothes, despite the skin still darkened by the sun from over there, despite laughing without fear of her lips chapping, a nice smile, my sister who pretends she is not a returnee, who says morning meal, icebox, omnibus, playing truant, instead of breakfast, fridge, bus, bunking off, my sister who does not want to be a returnee but wakes up saying, last night I dreamed I was eating *pitangas*, my sister who is so sad that she doesn't even argue with me or call me an idiot anymore. When we leave this place my sister will be like she used to be, she'll get annoyed with me about everything and nothing, you idiot, you hurt me, you idiot, you ruined my book. When we're in Brazil my sister will once again enjoy straightening her hair and making herself pretty for parties, reading photonovels, Brazil is not cold and there are fruits like the ones back there, my sister can eat as many *pitangas* as she wants. I wonder if there are still any *pitangas* on our *pitanga* tree, Mother says she's certain that the rosebushes have died of sadness, that the flowers lost their petals one at a time until they were left with their hearts exposed. She never let us touch the roses, you shouldn't touch things that die, Mother always said odd things. One day we went for a daytrip to Barra do Cuanza, by the river's mouth, Mother couldn't take her eyes off the vegetation growing by the sides of the road and she said, I'd like to get to the heart of this country, to the place where the birds cry out, where vegetation is so dense that not even the sun's light gets in, I'd like to feel this country's dark shadow. I don't know where Mother gets these ideas from, sometimes I'm scared that it's her demons making her say those things and my heart starts beating faster. But that day she was calm and talked slowly, I don't think it was the demons speaking through her about a place where shadows are so dark and so thick that trees can live with their roots out in the open, this country will never belong to us as long as we don't know its heart, as long as we don't know its heart this country will not preserve our traces and will not recognise our footsteps.

Any minute now it will be time for break, Teresa Bartolomeu will come and join me and the playground will fill with people. It won't be quite as cold and the fear will also go away. Or at least it won't make me tremble.

Father died.

The television room is full, people are sitting on the ground, on chairs, standing by the door, leaning against the wall, perched on the windowsills, so many people that the room looks smaller and darker. The crystal chandelier is switched off, there are only the opaque wall lamps and the glare from the television lighting up the faces of those who are closest, Goretti's hair looks blue, Francisco's face looks washed out, Senhor Campos' ears seem to be glowing. Today is the day. Today is the day of Angola's independence. Angola is finished. Our Angola is finished. I don't know why I'm watching television, I don't know why I'm here.

The men have pinned black ribbons to their jackets, it was Pacaça's idea, today I'm in mourning, he said, today my country died for me, today I became uprooted, we live with the certainty that our country is forever, we live with the certainty that the country where we buried our dead will always be ours and that our children will never be without the country where we gave birth to them, we live with that certainty because we never imagine that our country can die for us, but today my country died for me, today I have lost my dead and my children have lost the country where we gave birth to them, my children are uprooted like I am. Pacaça shuts up and Senhor Belchior starts talking, I'm in mourning for the country where I became a person, before going there I was nothing more than a belly filled with hunger and a head covered in lice.

Not all men are wearing black ribbons. João the Communist isn't, those lands did not belong to us, it's only fair that they are handed back to the people we stole them from, and on television some revolutionary is saying, the empire is coming to an end, our shame is coming to an end, today we can say we are proud of Portugal, long live Portugal.

I'm not wearing a black ribbon, I don't know what's fair, I feel no pride, I feel no shame, and I don't even know what they're talking about. The only thing I know is that they killed Father. But nobody knows, Mother sitting in a third-row chair doesn't know, my sister sitting on the floor doesn't know. I can't live hoping that Father will arrive. No-one can ever live always hoping for something like that. Whoever you are, you must exist so that I can stop hoping. Whoever you are, I know you exist and I will stop hoping. Whoever you are, you chose to kill my father.

Father died.

I know the words, I'm sure I know the words, I never say them, I'm afraid of them, I don't even say them in my head but I'm sure I know them.

I knew that road. The car's headlights shone only on the grass covering the verges. Beyond the verges and the tall grass nothing could be seen. Perhaps that was where the heart of the country was that Mother sometimes talked about. It was a hard road to follow but Father was a good driver, you don't own eleven trucks if you're not a good driver. And if Father was able to drive the car all the way to heaven, he could easily drive it to hell. We were on the way to hell. Mother was by Father's side, upright, her neck rigid and her body stiff, hard like a plastic doll's. This was not the same Mother from our trips to the tip of the Ilha, the Mother who on Sundays wore a new dress and put on more blue eye-powder, the Mother who made us cough with her French perfumes.

The Mother sitting next to Father in the car was the same Mother who is now leaning against the wall of the corridor in the dinner queue, me on one side, my sister on the other, and all these people around us, it was the Mother with the illness doctors couldn't treat, the illness we never talked about. Mother could take pills and more pills but it did her no good, the illness couldn't be cured with pills, the doctors couldn't cure her illness, it wasn't a normal illness, it wasn't even an illness. It was demons. It was demons taking over my mother's body, and they had to be expelled at séances. Father learned how to expel the demons from Mother's body, he knew how to say the words that had to be said when they take her over. But Father isn't here, nor is Senhor José, there is nobody here to rescue Mother from that darkness that the demons are now dragging her towards.

My sister also knows what is going to happen and she's frightened. Growing up together may not have made us very close to each other but we know each other's fears and what makes the other suffer. We know what is going to happen and we're frightened. For the time being Mother is quiet but we can see her chest rising and falling beneath her dress, rising and falling, her breathing shallow, the tormented eyes of someone seeing horrible things. After her attacks Mother never remembers what happened, we don't know what happens to Mother while she's having her attacks but Senhor José used to say that Mother is seeing the demons that want to get into her body. Mother's body is like the bodies of the dolls from Las Palmas that Father used to get for my sister on the ships, except that, instead of saying *Mamá* and *Papá* Mother says terrible things in a voice that isn't hers, sometimes we couldn't even understand what Mother was saying and Senhor José explained that Mother was speaking in another language, that demons come in all sorts of shapes and speak in all languages. Mother always said that the attacks were caused by that country, that the demons hadn't entered her body before she went there, that in the Motherland her body was closed like other people's. It may be that this is true and that now the demons are lurking around Mother but can't get into her.

Mother never wanted to go to the séances or to Senhor José's house but Father took her, Father never stopped trying to rescue her from the demons that made her kick and scream, that made her pick up knives and threaten to kill us. Doctors said she was having nervous crises because of her feeble mind, your wife's illness is not something that doctors can do anything about, said one of the hospital porters one day as Mother left, leaning on Father, I know a place where you can take her. And Father started taking her to healers too. First the white healers and then the black healers.

The corridor is full of people all the way to the lifts, a huge queue for dinner, I don't want anyone to see what is going to happen but I can't stop it. There were lots of people at the séances too, except that many were like Mother, here there is only Mother for the demons to get into and neither Senhor José nor Father are here. I'm sure I know the words, but I don't know how to say them, and I'm frightened of what might happen if

I don't say them correctly. Senhor José used to explain that someone had put a spell on Mother, or perhaps someone envied her, which is even worse, the evil eye, there are people who give you the evil eye without anyone noticing. Father did not believe any of it, he did not believe in healers or in doctors but he took Mother to all the healers and all the doctors he could. I don't know how many places Father took Mother and her demons to, how many boxes of medicine and home-made remedies he bought. Mother's demons always won, the proof of that is in the faces Mother is making now as she leans against the wall. Dona Rosa has realised that something is not right and says, this hotel would drive anyone crazy, Senhor Daniel agrees, instead of treating us well after we've lost everything they do this to us. For now Mother is only acting strange, nobody can know that the demons will take hold of her and that I don't know how to cast them out. It was Father who did that, Father or Senhor José who was black and who could talk to white demons and to black demons. He was the best healer but even he could not cure Mother.

We never talked about Mother's illness but we knew that everyone in the neighbourhood talked about it, Mother was Dona Glória who has her problems or, when the neighbours were feeling bolder, Dona Glória who summons the demons. The neighbours crossed themselves every time they talked about the demons that attacked Mother, they were frightened that their words would summon them, let them rest in peace, the neighbours would say, but Senhor José would banish the demons to the depths of hell. I remember him from when we went to the séances, there could be over a hundred people gathered near a baobab tree. Séances were banned and the meeting place was always changing so the police wouldn't catch people, they think they're demonstrations against Salazar, Senhor José would say, but they were just gatherings to expel demons from people whose bodies were open like Mother's. No matter how often the meeting place changed, Father never got lost on the roads. We could never go in the daytime, I don't know whether it was to do with the police or with the demons. All those cars parked at dawn in the middle of nowhere, near some baobab.

Sometimes we also went to Senhor José's house past the Cuca brewery, I don't know if it was where Senhor José lived, it was an almost empty shack. Everyone took their own folding chairs as if it were a picnic, the chairs had to be arranged in rows in a semicircle, like in cinemas, Senhor José at the front grappling with Mother's and other people's demons. Mother was among those who shouted the most, her body shaking, her face unrecognisable, Mother shouted until Senhor José raised his hand, in the name of God almighty I expel you. These are the words, in the name of God almighty I expel you.

We couldn't tell anyone about the séances. I think Gegé and Lee may have suspected something but didn't say anything, it was impossible that people in the neighbourhood didn't know, the neighbours often saw Father bundling Mother into the car or raising his hand and saying, in the name of God almighty I expel you. My sister and I hoped that it would all be down to nerves, the nerves that overwhelmed Mother's feeble mind and not the demons entering her open body. We never went to the séances willingly but Senhor José would say to Father, the whole family has to be blessed, and Father was frightened that the demons would jump out of Mother's body and into ours. Mother never wanted to go either, Senhor José said it was the demons making her refuse. Even when they weren't inside her the demons controlled Mother, the demons knew almost as much as God, and were almost as powerful. God won in the end but it was necessary to be very vigilant, because the demons took advantage of any weakness. Mother never shouted at Father except to refuse to go to the séances or when the demons were inside her, she implored, please, my love, don't take me again, Senhor José would also say that it was the demons making her implore and call Father my love, the demons were devious, Senhor José knew everything about demons and said he could see the future, he said he could see the future as though he was watching a film. He should have told us about the gunfire and about Father being imprisoned.

It's happening. Mother is wrong, it wasn't that country's fault. The demons have taken hold of Mother. The queue breaks up and everyone stands around Mother's body as it shudders on the blue carpet in the hotel corridor, Mother's screams so loud that even the people in the restaurant come to see, no-one says anything, at first they seemed surprised, then scared, Mother's features distorted, her legs splayed without worrying about showing her knickers, Mother who always gets worked up when my sister crosses her legs too carelessly, but Mother on the floor is not Mother, it is the demons. People start talking at the same time, what's her problem, it must be her nerves, she might be epileptic, I never saw anything like that, it must be exhaustion, Dona Rosa crosses herself and says a prayer, it doesn't help, Mother is kicking Faria who is trying to hold her down, more people are crossing themselves and saying prayers, someone calls Preta Zuzu and without taking the cigarette from her mouth Preta Zuzu says, it's the spirits that have taken over her, but she doesn't do anything, she just watches like the others.

Father knew how to say the words that would reclaim Mother's body from the demons and he knew how not to be frightened of the threats that the demons made through Mother, I'm going to kill you, or on the way to the séances, I'll make you drive the car into the bay. Father could confront the demons that wanted to take Mother away, he would raise his hand, in the name of God almighty, you cannot hesitate otherwise the demons will attack, you cannot be a sinner and I am a sinner, I'm frightened, the demons take advantage of any weaknesses. Senhor José used to show us the scars he had all over his body from the hundreds of battles he'd waged against the demons, I am a sinner, I do that dirty thing boys do almost every day, I get into fights all the time, I insult teachers and a few other idiots from over here, I'm often bad, I use God's name in vain. Mother on the floor and so many people around her, Pacaça, Senhor Acácio, Preta Zuzu, João the Communist, my sister at my side crying, I breathe deeply, I will raise my hand and say the words, I mustn't be frightened, I will raise my hand, I won't be frightened, there is no-one else here to save Mother, it has to be me, I raise my hand, and what if my voice won't come, what if I tremble, my arm is stretched out towards Mother, my hand is open, Mother screams even louder, everyone has seen my raised hand, I won't be able to do it, I know the words, I won't be able to do it, I know the words, I have to say the words, I have to say, in the name of God almighty I expel you, in the name of God almighty I expel you. In the name of God almighty I expel you. My hand is raised and I hear my own voice. Mother calms down. Now we just have to wait for her to come round, to ask what happened, dazed, to rearrange her dress and take my hand so I can get her out of here.

A room can be a home and this room with this balcony from where you can look out at the sea is our home. Mother and my sister don't agree with this so when we're out on the street they never say, let's go home. They always say, let's go back to the hotel. Sometimes, Mother fixes her gaze on the sea and sighs, there's no place like our home. The same thing she used to say when we came back on the ferry after spending a day at the beach. Except now we can't ever go back and there's no point in gazing across the ocean. But whenever I disagree with Mother and I say, we can never go back, our home no longer exists, Mother gets worked up, you're just trying to upset me, and I say, our life over there is over and it's best to forget our home and stop pining after it, it's best to forget everything, Mother gets even more worked up, I insist, we have to forget, Mother tells me to be quiet, how we need your father here, you've become disrespectful, how necessary a father is. I say nothing about Father. In time my mother and my sister will find out what happened. And in time the longing I have for Father will stop making me cry when I'm alone.

For now I need to find a way for us to go to America. Our fate is a sealed letter, as Queine the porter says, but I'm certain everything will be easier in America. I've asked for an English-language dictionary at the library and I'll learn it all by heart, I'll start with the letter A and then carry on until the end, by the time I've learned it all I'll be able to speak English and find work in America and support Mother and my sister. This was my backup plan in case Father died. The book that came with the walkie-talkies my father brought back from a foreign ship said that any good spy must have at least one backup plan. I have several, and if the America plan doesn't work out I have others.

In the meantime, we have to accept this room and this balcony from which you can look out at the sea as our home. It's the only way to carry on. Father used to say, the sun might be blinding you but if you turn your back to it your own shadow might hide what you're looking for. Or perhaps I imagined that Father used to say that during one of my afternoons on the hotel's rooftop terrace. I like going up onto the terrace, spending my afternoons there. I found a way to force open the door at the top of the service staircase and I go there often but I haven't told anyone so I won't lose the only place where I can be on my own. Things will be different now that Queine the porter has found me a bicycle. I was so happy when he told me about the bicycle that some neighbour was going to throw out. He's very cool, Queine the porter. And so is his wife. I had seen her before here at the hotel, Mourita tried to hit on her. I didn't even know Queine the porter was married.

With the bicycle I can go far away. Here at the hotel there are always people around. It's difficult to think with so many people around. Even when I'm quiet it's as if I were talking to others and as if others were guarding my thoughts. When I'm on my own I think differently. This is a good thing although sometimes it scares me. And also I can't stay out on the street too long because of the cold. I can't stand the cold for too long. I can't stand the cold or the thoughts that I think.

I don't like the cold in the Motherland but I really like the seasons, over there we only had the *cacimbo* and the rainy season and even then they were very much the same. Here it's different, everything is always changing. The autumn sea is more frightening than the tidal waves from over there, here the waves fold up on themselves dark and heavy, they drag seaweed, broken shells, pieces of wood, the dirty foam runs over the sand, it crashes against the sea wall and reaches the road. The sea getting out of place is frightening. The autumn sun is more golden here. I like riding my bicycle even more beneath this sun, I only need to fix the seat, it's been hard work but it's almost as good as new.

A room can be a home and this room with this balcony from where you can look out at the sea is our home. The proof is that Mother is inside making placemats and my sister is studying for a test she'll have on Wednesday. The sound of the radio in the Judge's room reaches us through the open balcony door, there's nothing good on but it keeps us entertained, I don't know how the people over here aren't fed up with all those revolutionary songs. Mother must have realised by now that there's no point in wasting her energy doing crochet, she can never sell her placemats to families from the Motherland. Mother and my sister show the placemat sets to the people strolling along the seafront but nothing happens, they try to sell them on sunny Sundays when people might be better disposed but the families from the Motherland say, if you were offering some ivory tusks or carvings we might be interested, we have enough crochet here. My sister tells me that Mother replies, we had those things and many more besides but we had to leave it all behind. Mother shouldn't say things like that, we never had carvings or ivory tusks and anyway people from the Motherland seem to think that we are being rightly punished for oppressing blacks. Mother used to make crochet placemats with the neighbours on long afternoons back over there, just as she now does during long afternoons at the hotel, not much difference.

My sister also told me that Mother wanted to sell her linen tablecloth to the rich people in the green house next to the hotel. Dona Rosário had sold them a china tea set, those people understand the difficulties we're going through, I didn't want to get rid of the tea set but better to lose the rings and keep the fingers. Mother and my sister knocked on the door of the rich people's

169

green house but they weren't as lucky as Dona Rosário who must have gone on about her illnesses, they had to take out a piece of my stomach, it was the size of a walnut, not to mention my bad spine. Other people's illnesses are not like Mother's. Nobody talks about Mother's illness and neither do we, nobody says a word about what happened the other day when we were queuing for dinner but I'm sure they must be talking about it behind our backs the way the neighbours did over there, just one look at her and you can see she has problems, I feel sorry for the children, with a mother having attacks like that they have to be very good. Mother hasn't had any more attacks. She seems calmer. But I don't like to think about what happened, I'm scared of summoning the demons.

Dona Rosário's illnesses are the sort of illnesses everyone likes to hear about, they are illnesses for doctors to treat and they can affect anyone's body, you today and me tomorrow. That's why Dona Rosário benefits from them, because of the piece of her stomach she had taken out Dona Rosário is entitled to special food, her bad spine entitles her to free laundry service and she can also have coffee for free at the bar so she won't faint from her dizzy spells, I'll just collapse, she complains, nobody can say whether her dizzy spells are connected to the piece of her stomach she had taken out or to her bad spine or to some other problem. Dona Rosário has had so many problems that the doctors at the university hospital once said to her, we're giving you an injection that will either save you or kill you, the doctor gave me the injection and I felt the heat inside me, it was like my blood was boiling and I thought my life would end there and then, but I didn't die and I'm still here, God bless the injection. Dona Rosário must have told that story and many others at the rich people's green house, they might have even bought her china tea set just to make her shut up. But Mother's illness is not the kind you can talk about and the rich lady in the green house didn't want to know about Mother's tablecloth, we have lots of those, and she shut the door, Mother and my sister could still hear her say, returnees again, these ones wanted to sell me some tablecloths of the kind we already have so many here, and badly made at that.

A room can be a home and this room with this balcony from where you can look out at the sea is our home. Queine the porter's house is different from other people's too. Queine the porter could be one of us, if he were like the people over here he would never have thought about me when he found out that a neighbour was getting rid of the bicycle, it's old and rusty but maybe it'll work for you, it's no mini Honda but it will let you get around. It will be good to go for long rides and to cycle to school. Teresa Bartolomeu will like me even more when she sees me doing a wheelie or when I give her a ride the way I used to do with Paula, Paula sitting on the handlebars and me pedalling down the road with her hair in my face.

Queine the porter's house is far away. Queine the porter took me there on his day off and even by car it felt like we were never going to get there, we went on and on and on, Queine the porter's car was so slow that it would have been faster to go on foot. The car is small and old, even the dashboard is battered. Queine the porter apologised, we had to buy a plot of land all the way up here, the closer you are to the sea the more expensive land is. Queine the porter's plot couldn't have cost more than a ten-cent coin because there can hardly be a piece of land that is more desolate and further from the sea than his, that must be the Motherland Father and Mother always talked about, the Motherland with unpaved roads. The road got narrower and more potholed, until Queine the porter stopped the car and said, this is it. A house of bare breezeblocks, greyish metal door and window frames and a garden with dark earth, not a single flower, on one side a washing line full of clothes flapping in the wind. It was so windy that Queine the porter had to shout and even then it was difficult to hear him, I left the bicycle in the shed, I'll go and find it. Queine the porter walked away and disappeared behind the house. There were no other houses nearby and the ones in the distance seemed even smaller and poorer, the narrow road cut through fields of tall grass that the wind blew this way and that, further down the road stood two tall and slender trees that Queine the porter called cypresses, not even the most shrivelled-up baobabs seem as lonely as those two dark trees standing in the wind.

I heard the car, said Silvana opening the door, and then when she saw me there, so you must be Queine's friend. She said something else about me and about the hotel that I couldn't catch, besides blowing around our coats the wind blew away the words. I didn't know what to say but Silvana didn't seem to mind, she was wearing a flower-print apron and rubber boots, the boots looked too large for her legs even though she was wearing thick woollen tights and the wind ceaselessly blew her ponytail from one side of her neck to the other as though it was a whip. At the clothes depot my sister was given boots just like those, they're called galoshes, it's another new word from the Motherland, over there not even jiggers made us wear shoes, we splashed around in puddles with bare feet and when we saw rainbows we'd shout out, it's raining and there's sun so the witches will bake us a bun.

I must have been unable to hide my disappointment when Queine the porter emerged from behind the house with an old and rusty bicycle, luckily Silvana said, let's go inside or we'll get blown away. Inside, the house is also made of breezeblocks, the only difference is that the breezeblocks are not clammy and stained green by the rain and the cold like they are on the outside. We were in the kitchen, me and Queine the porter sitting at a table covered by an oilcloth with pictures of fruit while Silvana stood by the sink rinsing some dishes and carefully placing them on a blue plastic dish rack. Silvana's face seemed familiar but I would never have remembered that she was the chambermaid that Mourita was flirting with on one of those plenary meeting days. Silvana finished rinsing the dishes, do you know why everyone calls him Queine, she asked, gesturing comically as she pretended to be a wrestler, they call him Queine because of that T.V. series, do you remember it? I didn't remember it because over there we had no television and over here I hardly watch it. Artur got it into his head that he could learn wrestling just by watching that man Kane, or Queine, on T.V., Silvana explained as she covered the dripping dishes on the blue plastic dish rack with a tea towel.

I only realised that Silvana was the chambermaid from that night of the plenary meeting when she asked, so tell me then, what is a lovely *mataco*? I must have flushed red with shame. I was worried that Queine the porter would be angry with me, I was furious with Mourita for being so stupid. I kept quiet but Silvana didn't give up, you don't have to tell me what it means because I know what it means, I just don't know if you agree with your friend. I could have died right there, if someone had pricked me not a single drop of blood would have trickled out. When Silvana and Queine the porter started laughing it occurred to me that this was all an elaborate trick, that Queine the porter had taken me there to settle scores with me. But Queine the porter grabbed Silvana and gave her a pat on the buttocks, what a lovely *mataco*, now leave the boy alone. They laughed again and so did I. Queine the porter and Silvana are so friendly that they hardly seem to be from the Motherland. Do you want anything to drink, Silvana asked. People offer out of politeness, Mother taught me that I should always accept a glass of water because it's rude not to have anything, it may look as though we're snooty. Silvana brought me a glass full of dark water, it's water from our borehole, we have a well here. I didn't know what Silvana was talking about but I didn't ask, the water tasted of earth but I drank it anyway. Even though Queine the porter's house has taps it mustn't be very different from the house Mother lived in before going over there. No, it must be different, the house where Mother lived had no gas-burning stove or fridge or dishwasher and this one does. Mother often said, our kitchen had nothing but a fireplace and a stool, two cupboards and a tub. We sat at the table, Queine the porter talking about his house, maybe by the end of the year we'll have enough money to paint it, but who knows what will happen, they said nobody would be able to own anything, that the land reform and nationalisation were only the beginning, that the revolution would press ahead and that there would soon be no property but now it looks as though it might not be like that, it looks as though everything is going backwards, who knows what they're doing.

I like to see the ships passing in the distance. We won't be able to stay forever in this room with this balcony from which you can look out at the sea which is why Mother and my sister are right, this room with this balcony from which you can look out at the sea is not a home. Much less our home. If it were, it would feel good to smoke a cigarette here. Like when I used to smoke behind Senhor Manuel's tobacco shop. But here it's different, here it's smoking a cigarette in a place I don't belong and where I will never belong. Queine the porter says, the closer you are to the sea the more expensive land is, and we don't even have the ten-cent coin that it must have cost Queine the porter to buy his plot of land at the world's end. Any day now they'll kick us out of here and who knows where we'll end up. That's why smoking a cigarette here is more than just smoking a cigarette with a view of the sea. I don't know when things started feeling like more than just themselves. Smoking a cigarette should be just smoking a cigarette. Lighting a cigarette with Father's Ronson Varaflame lighter should also be just that. I shouldn't be thinking that it's the lighter that Father wanted to use to set all our things on fire over there. I shouldn't be imagining our things on fire. I long for the time when smoking a cigarette was just smoking a cigarette. Nothing else. I must go back to thinking and feeling only one thing at a time. A room can be a home and this room with this balcony from which you can look out at the sea is our home until we go to America.

The pawnbroker's waiting room is small, there are chairs against the walls, a table with old newspapers in the centre, the windows are covered with dark velvet curtains and the wooden floor is chequered like a draughts board. In one corner there is a plastic Christmas tree with a golden star at the top and beneath it a hut with a baby Jesus lying on a clay cot, Mary and Joseph. Our nativity over there had the three wise men with their gifts, shepherds, lambs, donkeys and cows and a river that my sister would roll out, a wrinkled and colourful river made from chocolate wrappers. I made the mountains with green cardboard, cut out triangles with cotton wool at the top to resemble snow, and I stuck sand from the beach onto the floor made out of brown cardboard. We knew the baby Jesus could not have been born over there because there was no snow over there, only heat, a lot of heat. It was as if Christmas were a lie over there, nobody could believe in a Christmas happening on a beach. Here Christmas is for real. The girl who had asked us to wait apologises, my grandfather is running a little bit late, about ten minutes, please wait here, make yourselves comfortable, she smiles calmly as if she hadn't seen Mother's troubled eyes, as if she didn't know what we were there for.

We've been waiting for over half an hour and Mother hasn't stopped talking, Zé Viola was wrong to do what he did but the manager and the workers' committee reacted even worse, no-one likes to be accused unfairly, the manager should not have accused Zé Viola of destroying that tapestry with the scene of the first mass in Brazil without proof, to accuse someone without proof is a very serious matter, Zé Viola is not a boy anymore, he has a wife and two children, and not even a boy likes to be accused unfairly, I don't know why the man from the workers' committee swore that he saw Zé Viola with a pen-knife in his hand slashing the tapestry from top to bottom, if he hadn't been able to prove that on that day he was out of the hotel Zé Viola would have found himself in a nice mess, the manager could have kicked him out and where would Zé Viola go with a wife and two children, what would become of those people without food and a roof over their heads, the manager is also right to say that smashing chairs and tables is not the way to solve things, in that she and the workers' committee are right, no matter how upset he was Zé Viola should not have smashed up the card table or the chairs, luckily nobody got hurt, what I'd like to know is who cut up the tapestry with the penknife, it must have been a man because a woman would not have the strength to do that, such a thick tapestry slashed from top to bottom, I don't understand how anyone would be able to do that, especially because the restaurant remains closed except at mealtimes, the tapestry didn't do anyone any harm, it was so pretty, it's the manager's fault, if she treated us better these things would not happen, what I wouldn't give to leave that hotel, even if I have to spend the whole day scrubbing floors, I was never afraid of working and I've scrubbed many floors, my mother taught me how to do it when I was a girl, though a child only works a tad, not to take advantage of it would be mad is what she used to say, it seems as though there are no more floors to scrub in this country, or there are but they just won't let us, it's like we're lepers, what awful people.

Mother folded the red scarf she had been wearing on her head and put it on her lap. She took the silver bracelet out of the handbag, your father gave me this bracelet when I turned thirty, you must remember it, it was such a lovely day, we went to get a cake at Riviera, I had said to your father that I wanted a bracelet with my name engraved on it, like the one Dona Amália had, you must remember Dona Amália, she lived in the blue house by the butcher's, the one with the pond and the little water fountain in the garden, your father didn't give me the moon because he couldn't, how I miss him, I'm sure the first thing your father will do when he arrives is to get us out of that hotel, not even animals could live like that, and still the manager complains that everything is ruined, what was she expecting, she took in three times as many people as could fit into the hotel, sometimes it seems as though the hotel is so full it's going to burst at the seams, even a child could see it wouldn't work, it's true that people don't need to be quite so mean, those armchairs in the lounge all full of cigarette burns, such expensive armchairs, it's heartbreaking, the carpets all full of chewing gum, they will never get that out, I can only imagine what happens in the rooms, the chambermaids refuse to go into certain rooms, I don't even want to think what Dona Suzete's room is like with all her frying of samosas, how disgusting to have the smell of fried food all day long, our clothes always smell of fried food, the manager must have been sorry for what she did, that must have been why she proposed the idea of a New Year's Eve party, we don't need parties, what we need is to be treated better and for her to stop calling us vandals, poor Zé Viola, he wasn't even in the hotel when someone was slashing the tapestry, one of these days there will be a tragedy, one of these days someone will lose his head and then who knows what will happen, I don't know why they haven't called us, we've been here so long.

This house is not like Queine the porter's. It's a house close to the sea with a wood-panelled door, a chocolate-coloured door with a metal knocker in the shape of a lion. Before we rang the bell Mother arranged her hair underneath the red scarf that she wore on windy days, she smoothed the pleats of her blue *cacimbo* dress, she made sure the silver bracelet was still in the handbag and she rehearsed a smile, we've got everything. Now that the girl tells us her grandfather will see us, Mother smooths the pleats of her blue *cacimbo* dress again, she retouches the hair bun that the red scarf was concealing, but she forgets to rehearse her smile. The girl is younger than I am, her hair is tied with a lilac-coloured ribbon, her eyes are still sleepy and she is wearing flip-flops. The hall is dark and long with doors on both sides, the girl guides us without hesitation, a cat joins us, it must have come out of one of the doors we walked past, a white cat with long hair that drags on the floor. Neither the girl's flip-flops nor the cat make any noise, only my footsteps and Mother's. The girl opens one of the doors at the far end of the corridor, please come in, and she leaves us with her grandfather, an old man sitting at a desk in a small room.

The old man remains seated and we don't know whether to shake hands with him. He gestures for us to sit, there are two chairs in front of the desk, Mother sits in one and I in the other, upright, as if the way in which we are sitting might determine what will happen next. Senhor Teixeira suggested that we come to see you, we're at the hotel, says Mother, showing the old man a piece of paper. He looks at the piece of paper in which Senhor Teixeira recommends us to him but he seems uninterested. Behind him are cabinets filled with glasses, silver trays like the ones used in churches, Christs in many sizes but all nailed to their crosses, binoculars, cuckoo clocks going tick-tock. At first I don't hear the clocks' noise. Tick-tock. The half-open blinds let in beams of light like the ones that shone onto our kitchen tiles at lunchtime, I wonder who is sitting in the cool of our kitchen now. Dust specks glow in the air as they are caught by the beams of light, outside the clouds must be covering and uncovering the sun because the beams of light appear and disappear.

Mother is nervous, her forehead is beaded with sweat even though the room is cold. She has taken the bracelet out of the handbag and holds it in her tightly shut hand. Mother suddenly looks so tired, her hair tied up in a bun the way the old ladies do here, Mother not noticing the beams of light landing on her body. Finally the old man says, how can I help you, the old man sunk in his black leather chair, a surprisingly confident voice in such a frail body. Mother puts out her hand and opens it, her gesture almost child-like, I want to sell this bracelet. The old man takes the bracelet, the end with the plaque engraved with Mother's name hangs out of the old man's hand, Glória, Mother's name swings back and forth, tiny letters that can only be read close up but I know they're there, Glória. The old man puts the bracelet onto a weighing scale, the bracelet clinks as it falls into the dish, a weighing scale with copper dishes, small, unlike any other I'd seen before, the old man adjusts the weights, he pauses for a moment but the clocks continue their tick-tock, tick-tock, Mother's forehead beaded with sweat, two hundred and seventy-five escudos, says the old man looking at Mother and instead of her rehearsed smile Mother has a grimace of desperation. The white cat jumps onto the desk, it sits solemnly by the weighing scale and distracts the old man.

Mother swallows hard but even then her voice is hard to hear, it was a gift from my husband. Dear lady, the old man says patiently, I pay by weight, I don't pay for an item's craftsmanship or sentimental value. Mother wrings her hands, we lost everything, I have two children, this one and a girl who is finishing school this year, you must know how painful it is not to be able to take care of one's own, we were only allowed to bring five contos per person, we've been here for many months, the money is running out, you know that nobody can live without money and I can't find a job, either there aren't any or they won't give me one, my husband worked his entire life, we can't be blamed for anything. The old man interrupts Mother, dear lady, I am only a man with weighing scales, I only know what the scales tell me, please pardon me.

Mother sits back, her spine pressed hard against the chair, as if that will help her to understand. Dear lady, you don't have to decide now, the old man's voice filled with patience, if you wish you can step outside and give it some thought, you can come back another day, I am always here. Mother says, my husband stayed behind and I still haven't had any news from him, I don't know when he'll be able to join us, the cat seems more interested than the old man in what Mother is saying, dear lady, there isn't a day when someone doesn't come here to sell gold and silver, everyone has a story, some people share it and others don't, I have never refused to listen to anyone and I never refuse to buy whatever they bring me at its legal price,

I cannot do more than that. Mother raises her hands very slowly, Mother's feeble mind will betray her in front of the old man, Mother will start to shout or say strange things. But no. Slowly Mother takes her hands to her neck and the old man who seems to understand what Mother is doing takes the bracelet off the weighing scale, Mother unfastens her gold chain, the locket with the photograph of the young man Mother married slides down the blue *cacimbo* dress. Not the young man she married, the boy who lived before the young man that Mother married, the boy who no longer existed on the docks when Mother disembarked from the *Vera Cruz*, Mother's gestures so slow, I could try to stop her, Mother seems to sense what I'm thinking, she looks at me and says, it's not important, and the clocks carry on, tick-tock, tick-tock, the cat is busy licking a leg until the chain falls into the weighing scale's dish. The old man rearranges the weights, the clouds cover and uncover the sun, they make and unmake the beams of glowing dust that fall on the desk, they counter the precise timing of the clocks, tick-tock, the cat stands with one leg raised, waiting, three thousand nine hundred, and Mother says quietly, it cost more than twenty thousand, and the old man, I don't doubt it, madam, but as I said I am only a man with a weighing scale who buys silver and gold at its legal price.

Tears cannot be running down Mother's face because I can't hear even a single sob. Tears cannot be running down Mother's face with this old man and this cat staring at her. I could kill this cat with its glazed eyes fixed on Mother, I could put my hands around its neck and squeeze until I hear the bones crack the way the boys over here do to pigeons outside the school, they twist their heads around to watch them walk in circles, the pigeons walk in circles for so long before dying that the boys get tired of watching them and leave. That's not the way to kill a cat. I never killed one but I often saw Dona Arminda put them into barrels full of water, sometimes it was rainwater. When they were newborn the barrel didn't move but if they were older Dona Arminda had to call one of us to sit on top of the lid because the cats put up a fight, a racket so unlike the clocks' tick-tock and Dona Arminda said, they say cats have seven lives but they seem to have twenty. They were the same barrels that her husband, Senhor Delfim, filled with diesel when he travelled through the bush to his farm. I liked helping Senhor Delfim to prepare the barrels, Gegé and Lee too, the barrels had to be emptied, cleaned and left to dry before Senhor Delfim could fill them with diesel again. We also liked climbing into the empty barrels and rolling inside them, we had to be careful not to roll downhill, despite the lack of air, the darkness and the bumps on the rocks it was cool to go rolling inside the barrels, Senhor Delfim told us off when he caught us, one day you'll get killed when you run into a car, we laughed, we weren't afraid at all, before the gunfire started we weren't afraid of anything.

The cat must have read my mind because it jumps onto the floor, Mother picks the gold chain off the dish, she isn't able to sell it, the chain is a part of her, when she is anxious she holds the locket with Father's photograph and calms down, Mother will put the gold chain around her neck again and will say to me, let's go. Mother opens the locket, takes out the photograph of the boy who was not waiting on the docks, she puts the chain back on the desk, I want to sell both, she says with no hesitation.

I never thought that Pacaça would invite me to join the group that guards the containers on the docks. Mourita got tired of saying to Senhor Acácio and even to Pacaça himself that he wanted to do a few shifts but they never took him, it's a man's job, you have to spend the night out in the open and be prepared for whatever happens, any thieves we catch have to be punished. Last week Dona Celina's and Senhor Marques' containers were burgled, the thieves couldn't steal much but they broke the fridge, the stove, the furniture legs, not even the image of the Sacred Heart of Jesus that once belonged to Dona Celina's mother was spared, the thieves must have been communists, only communists hate churches and saints' images, look at what they did in Russia, normal thieves would never have broken an image of a saint, says Pacaça.

Mourita was furious when Pacaça invited me, especially because he made his invitation in front of everyone who was watching the *sueca* card game. Pacaça had switched the suit to clubs and the room had gone silent because Senhor Belchior was going to lose once again. Senhor Belchior is as bald as Chris from *The Magnificent Seven*, he is always scratching his shiny head and betting whiskies on how he will beat Pacaça but he never wins. Pacaça had switched the suit to clubs in order to trump Senhor Melchior's diamond knave, he turned to me and out of the blue said, you seem like a straight sort of kid, I've seen how you take care of your mother and your sister, if you want to you can come with us tonight, we have many kilometres of containers to guard and we need more men for sentry duty, if we don't defend what is ours nobody will. Pacaça trumped Senhor Belchior's diamond knave, with such good luck in gambling you must have been very unhappy in love, Senhor Belchior said in a huff. Playing cards requires some skill but love is the only game in which you rely entirely on luck, replied Pacaça, shrugging.

I was so happy I didn't know what to say, count me in, when do I have to be ready, should I bring anything? Steady on, we're not talking about a picnic for ladies or for boy scouts, said Senhor Belchior, lighting a cigarette despite the lungs that wheezed like Father's, we'll meet downstairs around ten, two words of warning, if you suffer from cold you'd better not come, down by the river it can be so cold it makes us cry, and if you are squeamish like a girl it's also better if you stay, things can get ugly, if I get hold of a thief I'll beat him to a pulp. I'm not afraid of the cold or of thieves, I answered. That's good, kid, says Faria, shuffling the cards, you don't have your father here and it'll do you good to listen to some man talk, talking to women isn't the same, talking to women is about shutting up and listening because they won't accept any other type of conversation. Faria put the cards on the table, Senhor Acácio cut the deck, Pacaça said, my friend Faria has never uttered such true words, it's been years since my wife passed away and I can still hear her nagging me, may God rest her soul but she was worse than the diseases you catch from the whores. Pacaça took one more drag and snuffed out his cigarette in an ashtray piled high with stubs. Despite being so large the lounge smells so much of cigarette smoke that it seems as though Father is always nearby. Senhor Belchior looked at the cards he was dealt, this is it, my friend Pacaça, this is it, Pacaça kept his calm, if you'd like to bet another whisky I'm in, and Faria, I just hope we get the scoundrels tonight, I'll chop the hand off the first one we get, it's what Israelis do to thieves. I don't think it's Israelis, said Senhor Acácio as he rolled a cigarette while looking at Dona Juvita, who had just come into the lounge with a décolletage that made her breasts leap out. Happy are the eyes that see you, Dona Juvita, said Pacaça pretending that Dona Juvita's breasts weren't the centre of attention. I've been congested, said Dona Juvita, this hotel makes me ill, as if things weren't bad enough. It's this cold, replied Senhor Belchior, you need to cover up. The men play so often that the cards are dog-eared and worn, Faria held his cards in a fan, if it's not in Israel that they chop thieves' hands off it's in India, it's one of those countries, it doesn't matter what country it is, what matters is that it's a good idea, losing a hand should give a thief pause for thought.

We always go in Pacaça's car, the one with the steering wheel on the right-hand side because it was bought in Mozambique. We park where the docks begin and the containers are lined up along the river as far as the eye can see. Senhor Belchior says that the containers are the dregs of empire, it is ironic that they are rotting away in the exact place where the Portuguese empire started, this must mean something, this should teach us something, everything in life has its reasons. Senhor Belchior always talks in riddles and it can be tiresome to listen to him for a long time. Although the car is Pacaça's it is always Senhor Belchior who drives because Pacaça doesn't see well at night, it's because of those lands at the ends of the earth, I don't know what ruined my eyesight more, whether it was the light or whether it was all the coal-tar pitch. Pacaça says this because there is nothing the old-timers like more than repeating themselves. The old men in the hotel can't stop talking about the empire for which they still wear black ribbons as a sign of mourning. Those in João the Communist's faction call them reactionary imperialists and there's often trouble. Enough with your commie propaganda, my friend João, even the people over here have put the commies in their place, says Pacaça and João the Communist replies, and they'll regret it, they'll regret it.

The men in the hotel wouldn't argue so much if they had jobs or if the loans from the I.A.R.N. weren't so late. Almost all of them think the way Father did, my politics is to work, he used to say, except that the only work they have is looking for work they can never find. They have enough spare time to play cards, to discuss politics and to stare at Dona Juvita's and other women's breasts and bottoms. And to frighten themselves with the daily rumours, that foreigners are no longer sending aid money, that the communists are encouraging the hotel workers' committee to take over the hotel and that the first thing they'll do is kick us out, there's been enough scrounging. But what they do most of all is waste away the hours remembering everything they've lost, if I start to think about the things I left behind I'll shoot myself in the head, I must have heard every one of them saying such things at least once.

The men also want to find work to prove to the layabouts from the Motherland what stern stuff the returnees are made of, if we can build nations in the lands we were forced to abandon we'll certainly be able to improve the backward life of the Motherland. The people from over here like us less with every day that passes, they say we went over there to exploit the blacks and now we're here to steal their jobs alongside destroying their hotels, destroying the lovely Motherland that will never be the same. Pacaça says that the tragedy we suffered is nothing compared to the tragedy that never stopped happening to the people over here and even João the Communist who always disagrees with Pacaça seems to concur, there is no worse tragedy than never to have left this place, amid such misery the only thing that can grow is envy.

Mother does not like me joining the group that guards the containers, the last thing we need is you staying up all night looking after other people's things, and with this cold. Persuading her is always a challenge, the coat and the boots I got from the clothes depot are warm, we take blankets from the hotel to wrap around ourselves and we always light a bonfire, but Mother insists, it's dangerous to do that, this country is on its head, I don't know what I'd do if something happened to you, what would your father say, I won't let you go, I don't want my son spending sleepless nights and catching colds to look after other people's things. I could turn my back on Mother the way Mourita does with Dona Ester, Mother would be furious for a few hours and would then forget about it just as other mothers do. But I'm scared that her demons might start lurking so I try to reassure her as best I can, you mustn't worry because there won't be any trouble, it's just one night spent by a bonfire. Mother doesn't like Pacaça, I can see it when she talks about him, she has no time for his stories about how many buffalo he killed, I tell her that Pacaça's stories are a lie, he's just showing off, it's harmless, there is no-one in this hotel who isn't lying. Mother looks down as if I've told her off, it's easy for someone to delude himself when he remembers things that happened so far away, and she always ends by saying the same thing, you can go as long as you stay warm and you don't miss school tomorrow, I don't care if you're sleepy, you have to go to school to be someone in life, if I had studied we wouldn't be in this hotel but my parents needed me to thresh the rye and to harvest the olives and now with no schooling I can't even get a floor to scrub.

I don't know what Mother would do if she found out I'm bunking off. I sneak behind classroom block C to smoke with the other returnees, I climb down the rocks to look at the sea or else I cycle around lost in my own thoughts, thinking about Father's death and our departure for America. I haven't spoken to Mother and my sister about it, first I have to break into the containers that used to belong to the dead of Sanza Pombo. It's the only way to get some money for plane tickets. When I get tired of thinking about bad things, I think about what it would be like to kiss Teresa Bartolomeu or about meeting Gegé and Lee at the top of the Sears Tower. Gegé wanted to organise a meeting on the day of his eighteenth birthday but Lee wouldn't agree to it, why your eighteenth birthday and not mine or Ruï's, because I'm the last one to turn eighteen, how they argued about it, they often argued over nothing. I suggested New Year's Eve, it must be good to watch the fireworks from the top of the Sears Tower, we swore we'd meet at the top of the Sears Tower on December 31, 1978, I have so many things to tell them. Gegé and Lee must have even more, there must be more things happening in South Africa and in Brazil than in the Motherland, in the Motherland nothing happens apart from the revolution.

I don't know what I'd do without the bicycle, sometimes I

get tired and so cold but even then it's better than being in the classroom, everything is better than classes. It's not just because of the maths bitch, can one of the returnees answer the question, I don't pay her any attention anymore, I want her and everyone who doesn't want us here to go and fuck themselves, I don't like being in class because I can't pay attention, I'm not interested in what they're teaching, the only thing I'm interested in is how I'm going to take Mother and my sister to America, and to get to America one year of school more or one year of school less makes no difference. I have to keep on memorising words from the dictionary, memorising words is easier than I thought, there are many whose meaning I don't even know in Portuguese, what does apostate mean? But if I have never needed those words in Portuguese until now, I surely won't need them in English. My sister knows I've been bunking off but she hasn't told Mother. My sister seems different, besides not ratting on me to Mother, which she did all the time over there, now she wants to be a good pupil and is always studying. I don't know how the Motherland can change people so much. They taught us so many things about the Motherland, its rivers, its railways, and they failed to teach us the most important thing, that the Motherland changes people.

It fell to me to do the first round of the containers with Faria. We had lit the bonfire and Pacaça had put some water on for coffee. Bonfires remind me of hunting expeditions, he said, come to think of it this is also a hunting expedition, if we catch someone getting his dirty hands on the containers I'll beat him to a pulp, they've already robbed me of what they had to rob me, word of honour and word of Pacaça. Faria has a small machete and a lantern that won't be necessary today, there's a full moon and even the water in the river is glowing. This river has no crocodiles and no hippopotami like there are in the river Cuanza, it's not true that all rivers are the same, two riverbanks and water in between. The containers have been here for months but their owners can't get them without having somewhere else to put them, they have to sort out their lives first. It's strange to see so many crates stacked along the docks, crates of all sizes built out of wooden planks of all colours. I still remember the wooden planks in Senhor Manuel's back garden, and in Dona Gilda's back garden. We never had wooden planks in our back garden because Father kept saying, I give them a year before they're back again with all their belongings, this is our land. Father was wrong, the crates are still stacked up along the river and will never go back over there. Faria stopped to investigate non-existent noises, there wasn't even a rat and much less a thief, Faria must be keen to apply the punishment used by the Israelis or Indians, I'll chop the hand off the first one we get.

Do you know when your father is coming, Faria asked as he ran his hand over one of the plywood slats used to secure a crate. I had never told anyone that Father had died, not even Mother or my sister, I wouldn't know how to explain. Not yet, I answered. The river so close, if this is the place from where the old ships once set sail for Africa it is also the place from where I'll be able to leave for America. Shush, said Faria as if he wanted me to stop thinking about going to America, and looking alert again added, I think I saw something move over there. It was nothing but Faria pressed his back against a container as he peered down the lane between two rows of crates, like in police films. Keep your eyes and ears open, kid, because these thieves are clever. The only things moving are us and our shadows. Trust me, your father'd better hotfoot it out of there, the proper war hasn't even started, the F.N.L.A. and U.N.I.T.A. have Luanda under siege, Americans and South Africans will push back against the Russian and Cuban commies from the M.P.L.A., your father'd better come before it's too late.

I pretended to examine one of the crates to change the subject but Faria continued, what was it your father did over there, he was a trucking entrepreneur, I replied, when I say it like that it sounds more important than being a doctor, he had trucks, he carried coffee, cotton and sisal, I explained. Faria shook his head, coffee, cotton, sisal, you see the difference, here there is only potatoes and cabbages, how can you make money with potatoes and cabbages, but if your father is waiting for the war to end he's wasting his time, things over there will never improve, Angola is finished, kaput, coffee, cotton, sisal, palm oil, diamonds, crude oil, kaput, everything is finished, all that remains are these crates, and most of them are filled with old junk because whoever sent over good things has probably picked them up already, what's left are the crates of those who have no money to take their things away or no house to dump their junk in, every time I see this I am infuriated, what a miserable life, if I could only get hold of that Rosa Coutinho I would put my hands around his gullet and squeeze until he couldn't even squeak, he was the son of a bitch who incited the blacks to kill our women and our children, if I could only get hold of him, him and all the others who betrayed us, Big Cheeks and his friends, if I could get hold of them not one would remain alive, I wouldn't care if I rotted in prison.

On the banks of this river Mother would not be able to talk about the heart of the country, like she did when we went to the Barra do Cuanza. Here the vegetation is never so thick that even the light of the moon cannot get through. The Motherland is old and there isn't a single patch of overgrown earth in which Mother can try to find a heart.

The damn cold, is your coat warm enough, asked Faria. It is, I replied. It's a shame the coat is white, Faria continued, well, at least it's your size, I wasn't given anything that fit me, I threw it all out when I got back to the hotel, one of the sweatshirts was even eaten by moths. I got this sweatshirt and it's very warm, I open my coat to show the sweatshirt with the red reindeer. Oh, so now you're wearing little animals, Faria joked. And I also got these boots, I raised them to show Faria the bootlaces and the rubber soles, proper winter boots. You were lucky, Faria grumbled, and what's that written on the back of your coat, Didja,

Faria read, what does that mean? I don't know either, and then Teresa Bartolomeu's voice between the containers, hey, Didja, Teresa Bartolomeu's voice is enough to make the night warmer, hey, Didja. Who knows what Didja means, Faria said, intrigued, mark my words, if we all spoke the same language we'd understand each other so much better, even the blacks would have understood us.

These ones really mess me up, said Faria, standing beside the containers that belonged to the dead of Sanza Pombo, every time I see these containers I feel a knot in my throat that hardly lets me breathe, when you think about them you realise how lucky we are in spite of everything to still be alive, these poor bastards couldn't escape, two entire families, a massacre, they found the heads near the entrance to Sanza Pombo and the other parts spread out who knows where, the sons of bitches killed people and then dispersed the body parts to stop them from resuscitating, they think that a body has only truly died when its parts can't be put together again.

The names of the dead of Sanza Pombo were often read out among the lists of the disappeared that were broadcast before and after *Simply Maria*. I remember my sister waiting impatiently for the reading of the list to be over, she wanted to know what was going to happen to Maria and Alberto, my sister fed up with having to wait, they're always repeating the same names, everyone knows they've disappeared. Perhaps Uncle Zé called the radio station to give them Father's name, perhaps

Father's name was read in the list of the disappeared, but nobody cared, apart from us and Uncle Zé, nobody knows that Father has disappeared. My sister didn't mean ill, she wanted to listen to her soap opera on the radio and the list of the disappeared delayed everything, when you didn't know someone who had disappeared and you liked the soap opera as my sister did, it was easy to lose patience with a list that grew and took longer to read every day.

I can't tell anyone about my plan to break into the containers that belonged to the dead of Sanza Pombo. Not even Mourita. He's jealous because he hasn't been asked to join the group that guards the containers and so Mourita might snitch on me to his father and then it wouldn't be long before Senhor Acácio told Pacaça. I can almost hear Pacaça, a man capable of stealing from the dead of Sanza Pombo is not a man, he's a rat. For Pacaça there are only two types of men, proper men and rats, and there's not a chance that a man can be a little bit of a rat. Pacaça always offers the same explanation, the soul rots quicker than the flesh, if a rotting finger that isn't cut off can kill a man, if this happens with flesh that is in plain sight, imagine what happens with a soul that nobody can see and from which you can't cut off the rotten part.

At first I was unsure about the idea of stealing from the containers, there were nights when I dreamed that the dead of Sanza Pombo were angry with me, they asked me, how dare you steal from us after everything we've been through, but then I thought, the containers will all rot away, all the things inside will fall into disrepair on the docks or else be stolen by someone else. If Father were with us and we stole from the containers it would be different, Father knows how to earn a living and would only steal from the containers to make some money not out of idleness. But Father is not with us and never will be, now I'm the head of the family and I have to take Mother and my sister to America. Surely nobody will come to claim the containers, the dead of Sanza Pombo don't have any relatives here, if they did they would have given an address for them and not just written PORTUGAL in big black letters. I'm not stealing from anyone since you can't steal anything from the dead, despite what Pacaça says about men and rats. And I bet that Faria, Pacaça, Senhor Acácio and some of the others who are guarding the containers have thought about stealing from the dead of Sanza Pombo. Even João the Communist who claims he has never done anything wrong in his life must have thought about it at least once. The difficult part is to concentrate on the stealing, even if you don't want to you start thinking about bodies cut into pieces, and what those people went through, and you lose the desire to touch their things, let them rot on the docks if they have to. That's what usually happens and it would keep on happening to me if I didn't have to take Mother and my sister to America. But I do and that's more important than stopping to think about what's right or wrong, what's good or bad, we've spent the twenty contos we brought and we have no more gold chains to sell.

These containers must be full of good things, says Faria, running his hand over one of them as he might run it over the bonnet of a car he didn't want to scratch, they were rich farmers, it was their own employees that killed them, who knows what happened in those farms, in the countryside things were murkier, there were whites abusing blacks, I can't deny it, but however bad the things those poor bastards did were, they were leaving. Faria stamps his feet, my feet are so cold I can hardly feel them, if a man thinks too much about everything that's happened he'll end up shooting himself in the head.

I'd like Faria to stop talking for a moment, I don't understand why people who get older can't stop talking. They must be scared like Pacaça, who will only shut up when his mouth is full of dirt, and then not a peep. When I'm an old man I'll always be quiet. Faria continues, he's like a radio that's always switched on, decolonisation wasn't bad for everyone, no matter how big the tragedy there are always people who profit from it and many did profit and now they live better here than they did over there, and I'm not talking about the blacks that lived in the shantytowns over there and now live in hotels, I'm talking about the whites who stole what they could, watch it kid, don't get so close to the edge when you piss, if you slip you'll end up down there and there's no way I'll be going to find you, right, I'll have a piss as well, it's true what they say that when one Portuguese man is having a wee you'll always find another two or three, hey kid, what a long face, I'd swear you're suffering a romantic disappointment or something like that, the year just started and you have that face already, what's bugging you, new year new life, what's up? Nothing, I replied, nothing's up. I won't tell Faria that I'm trying to find the best way to steal from the containers that belonged to the dead of Sanza Pombo, I won't tell him that while he rants about opportunist thieves I am trying to find a way to break into the containers to take the smallest and most valuable things. Something's up with you, kid, nothing, I reply again. It's all Faria needed to hear before launching into his favourite monlogue, there are always people who profit from others' tragedy, when the *Titanic* was sinking there were people stealing jewels from safes, you've heard of the *Titanic*, yes, it was a ship that crashed into an iceberg, well, kid, when you put it like that it sounds as though the *Titanic* was a boat like any other, the *Titanic* was the most luxurious and the safest boat in the world, but it still sank on its first voyage, if we're scared of standing by the edge of the docks for fear of falling into the water imagine falling into a sea full of ice, the survivors said the orchestra never stopped playing until the end, I get goose-bumps just thinking about it. Faria zipped up his trousers, well, kid, I think we've checked everything here, we can go back to the fire, in a while Pacaça and Belchior will do another round.

When we got back to the fire Pacaça was winding up Senhor Acácio, tell us what's happening with Dona Juvita. Senhor Acácio took a drag from his cigarette, it's all rumours, too many people confined to the same place, Dona Juvita is a proper lady, she just has that little problem of wanting to show off her flesh. Faria took a swig from the bottle of spirits, the thieves must be asleep or else they're cold, give the kid a drink of coffee, then you can have some firewater to warm up, at your age I was already polishing off a whole bottle. Drinking spirits always makes me cough but I held it in so they wouldn't make fun of me.

Since I saw you wearing that white coat a few months ago, I've been trying to think who you remind me of and I've only just worked it out, said Pacaça, you remind me of the pimp in the Bairro Operário. He turned to the others, look at him and tell me if he doesn't look like Jacques Franciú from the Bairro Operário. Senhor Belchior laughed, leave the kid alone, he spent the whole day queuing at the clothes depot to get that coat, you mustn't look a gift horse in the mouth. But don't they look alike, Jacques Franciú was also blonde with blue eyes, he just wasn't so tall and so thin. They all agreed that the white coat made me look like the pimp in the Bairro Operário whom I had never heard of before. I didn't want them to know that I was the only one who didn't know who Jacques Franciú was and so I didn't answer any questions. How I miss the *munhungu* in Bairro Operário, said Pacaça, poking the fire with a stick, how I miss it. When I was in Luanda I went there every week, how I missed those floozies when I was in Lourenço Marques, how I miss them here. Faria shook his head and smiled longingly, none were better, he said. I even miss Jacques Franciú, Pacaça continued, always wearing those strange coats, I don't know how he could stand to wear those coats in that heat, but if we said anything he'd reply, you're just jealous, with that sissy voice of his, and we laughed at him, one thing's for sure, I never met women more beautiful and more fragrant than Jacques Franciú's. All the men seemed to agree, Faria started talking about Bairro Prenda but Pacaça shook his head, no comparison, Jacques Franciú's women were four times more expensive than the ones in Prenda but worth every penny, some were so pretty they looked like film stars, and all so well educated, not one of them could be outdone by some girl from a rich family sent to a convent school.

The icy fog blowing in from the river made us tremble even though we were wrapped in blankets, no matter how tightly we're wrapped in blankets the Motherland's cold always finds a way to get into our bodies. Pacaça threw a stick into the fire sending up a yellow flame that immediately died out before we could warm our hands. Jacques Franciú's floozies, Pacaça continued as he exhaled a cloud of white water vapour, looked like convent schoolgirls but in the bedroom it was as if they were reading our minds, and they were always cheerful, black and white, there was no sadness there, the white women cost three times as much as the black ones but boy, could they stop traffic, some married men with children were prepared to leave everything and run away with them, not to mention the unattached men who fell madly in love and then loitered in the neighbourhood like stray dogs. And the soldiers, there wasn't a soldier who didn't go there. Once a sergeant spent an entire month's wages buying rounds for everyone, the poor man kept saying, I'm in heaven, this can only be heaven, I didn't know heaven was like this, if I'd known I would have let the blacks kill me earlier, one of them must have killed me and I didn't even realise it.

Pacaça put more coffee on the fire, the first time I went to the *munhungu* in Bairro Operário it was still the old Jacques who was in charge, it was just before I turned twelve, my father chose a black woman and said to her, I'll give you twice your price if you turn this boy into a man. I knew what I was there for and for the last few days I hadn't thought about anything else but when I found myself in the room with that black woman I didn't know where to hide. After fifteen minutes my father knocked on the door, how are you getting on in there. I was worried that the black woman would tell my father that I was a limp wimp, but the black woman answered as if she were out of breath, he's more of a man than many men with full beards, it runs in the family, my father said with pride on the other side of the door, today the drinks are on me, I finally have someone to carry on the family name. The black woman suggested that I wait a while so my father wouldn't suspect about me being a limp wimp. We stayed in the room, me lying on the bed staring at a cockatoo cage hanging on the porch and the black woman painting her fingernails and telling me stories of the village she lived in before old Jacques discovered her and brought her to the city. It was the first time I saw a woman with long fingernails, my mother had short fingernails to avoid hurting her children when she blew our noses. I woke up with my father knocking on the door. Despite my sleepy face he suspected nothing, even a real man gets tired, he said. On the way home he gave me the advice any father has to give to his son, the same advice I passed on to my son, the other black women aren't as clean as the ones from the *munhungu*, careful with diseases, if a black girl ever comes up to you and tells you you've made her pregnant send her over to me, they rarely say that because for them having children is a whole different thing, but if they see you so young they may want to take advantage of your innocence, if you want to go with a black woman who has a husband you have to speak to him first, you'll see he puffs up with pride, it's an honour for a black man when a white man wants his wife, you may have to pay a fee, a bottle of *quimbombo* or a shaving blade, they're small things that help to keep everyone sweet, if we have to live with one another it's better to do so in peace, if she's a *quilumba* it's different, then you'll need to speak to her father, fees for *quilumbas* are higher but at least you're guaranteed that they won't have any diseases, at least not the sort that they can get from other men, but even then you have to be careful, many say they're *quilumbas* but they've already been with who knows how many men, it's in their blood. After he gave me this advice my father never again talked about the subject and if we came across each other at the *munhungu* he pretended not to see me. He was a good man, a respectful man, said Pacaça, choking up with emotion, a man who taught me to respect everyone, no matter whether white or black. They don't make men like him anymore. The second time I went to the *munhungu* in the Bairro Operário I went on my own and with money I had saved. I told my mother I was sleeping over at a friend's house and in the early evening I scrubbed up and paid a visit to old Jacques. The soldiers there made fun of me, look at that runt, they don't sell lollies of the kind you want here. I didn't let that bother me. I asked old Jacques about the black woman, I knew her name was Nívea and that she came from near Nova Lisboa. As soon as she saw me she showed me her fingernails, I've already painted them today, she said, poking fun at me. I showed her the money I had, we went to her room and I didn't leave until next morning. That was a while ago. Jacques Franciú wasn't even born. He must have been born some five years later, he must be around fifty-five by now. Jacques Franciú's mother was one of the most beautiful white women that old Jacques ever had there. When old Jacques found out he'd made her pregnant he set up a house for her near Corimba and got her out of the business. He was also an honest man. Jacques Franciú was brought up with the best of everything, he was so coddled that he turned out the way he did, I never met a queerer queer than him, so many beautiful women within hand's reach and that faggot was only thinking about cocks, it's true that you can have too much of a good thing. All the things I remembered because of that white coat. Hey, kid, stand up and give us a twirl, Pacaça said, you all tell me if he doesn't look like Jacques Franciú.

If I refused to do a twirl it would be even worse, I didn't want them to notice I was furious. I humoured him and I even pretended to be having fun, but when I got up to do the twirl I already hated Pacaça. We begin hating someone from one moment to the next, it's not only our thoughts that we can't control, it's also our feelings. I used to like Pacaça, but he went on, they could be relatives, I swear. Maybe Pacaça found out about Uncle Zé, it can only be that, he was saying that me and Jacques Franciú could be relatives to hint that he knows about Uncle Zé. Gegé and Lee were right, everybody thinks it's a family thing, I should have found a girlfriend at the hotel, I've got to have a girlfriend so others will know that we're not a family of faggots, I could have a girlfriend at the hotel and not say anything to Teresa Bartolomeu.

Give us one more twirl, says Pacaça and I do it. I laugh too, I laugh more than everyone else. And what does the writing on your coat mean, Pacaça asks. I just asked him that, says Faria. Pacaça gets up, puts his hand on my shoulder, you should have asked the person who gave you the coat, you shouldn't be wearing clothes with writing that you don't understand, maybe it says queer in Russian or some other language like that, at least take the fur off the coat's collar, that fur is certainly for queers.

It's not only Pacaça I hate. I also hate Senhor Belchior who won't stop laughing while he says, fuck me, the things you remember, and Senhor Acácio and Faria, I hate them all and I'm still twirling the way Pacaça asked me to, Didja, one more twirl, Didja, so different from Teresa Bartolomeu calling me, hey, Didja.

I twirl once more, I'm not like Jacques Franciú or like Uncle Zé, Pacaça and the others are mistaken, when I get home I'll rip up this coat, better to die of cold than to be walking about with a queer's coat, they'll see, I just hope that the people over here steal from their containers, fingers crossed, they deserve to have their containers burgled, they deserve to have been expelled from over there, they deserve everything that happened to them, they even deserve the gunfire, they must think they can make fun of me the way they made fun of the blacks, or they must think I'm black, I twirl once more, I'll keep on twirling until I fall over.

You know the way to my house, I can't get the question out of my head. You know the way to my house, Silvana's voice inside my head. I'll never get well. If Silvana hadn't kissed me and if she hadn't crawled into my bed, I wouldn't mind being poorly for a week or two. It's good not having to wake up early to go to school and I always liked having a fever, you see things differently, I like the hallucinations that a fever causes, I even like that dull pain that takes over the body. But when she said goodbye Silvana asked me, you know the way to my house, and that's why I have to get well soon. I'm sure that's what Silvana asked, it wasn't a hallucination from the fever. It wasn't. I had never even thought of Silvana that way. Even though she is pretty. I'm sure it happened, Silvana standing by the door, her face still flushed and her hair loose, I loosened her hair, you know the way to my house. I have to get well as soon as possible so I can go to the house with the bare breezeblocks and the garden with dark soil and no flowers. I haven't forgotten the way, go down the big avenue, turn left, then left again, then right, even if I forgot one part, I'll find my way to the unpaved road, and from there onwards it's straight ahead, for a long time, always straight ahead, further and further from the sea, fields of grass on either side, yes, I know the way to her house. The house that is not only her house, it is Queine the porter's house. But for now I won't think about Queine the porter, I can't think about everything at the same time.

The dawn light is already brightening the room but here in the Motherland the sky takes a while to reach its full morning blue. I can see the contours of Mother's and my sister's sleeping bodies, I can even see my sister's face and her blonde curls spilling over the pillow. I know their sleep patterns so well that I only need to hear them breathing to know if they are having good dreams or bad. If Mother and my sister were awake I wouldn't be able to think about what happened with Silvana. I must still be feverish, I feel my body burning and my head is spinning as if I were on a carrousel. You know the way to my house. Perhaps Mother's episodes also start with a single thought that takes over everything.

I think Silvana came over to see me and not to clean the room, perhaps she had even planned everything that happened, if I don't understand girls I can understand Silvana even less because she's married and at the New Year's Eve party she asked Tobias to show her how to dance the merengue. Tobias is the son of Celeste, who is Preta Zuzu's sister, but he's a mulatto because his father was a white man. Celeste's dream is that

Tobias will marry a white girl, that's what she says, and he's always flirting with my sister, my Tobias likes blonde girls, Celeste says to my sister, my Tobias might ask you to go for a stroll with him one of these days. Everyone talked about the way Silvana danced with Tobias. Even if Silvana were not married she should never have allowed Tobias to grab her so tight, she should never have allowed his hands to slip down to where they shouldn't be, Tobias' mulatto hands on Silvana as she threw her head back. It wouldn't have been right for Silvana to let a white man do that but to behave like that with Tobias was even worse. It's lucky that the husband is as drunk as a lord, is what Senhor Acácio said about Queine the porter, who watched everything and laughed, his reptile eyes glued to Silvana's bottom and Tobias' hands, I know what that woman is after, he licked the cigarette paper, his tongue white with saliva, I know what that woman is after and I'd give it to her right now, if her husband wasn't so drunk there would be a big ruckus here.

The two paper angels that Mother bought at the tobacconist on the corner and stuck onto our bedroom window made our Christmas seem even sadder but the New Year's Eve party felt as though we were back over there, the women with short backless dresses and the men drinking beer as if it were hot. Senhor Bento took out the records he had brought from over there and even the hotel workers who were on leave came back to see what a returnees' party was like. Mother did not wear blue eye-powder or pink lipstick but she danced barefoot the way she used to dance for Father. My sister straightened her hair just as she used to do back in the days when she didn't like her curls and she danced holding Tozé Cenoura tight, her face against his chest and hardly moving. I don't understand what my sister sees in Tozé Cenoura who wore a suit from the church's charity chest even to the New Year's Eve party. I danced the whole night too even though Teresa Bartolomeu did not show up. Mourita was right, Teresa Bartolomeu would never come to a returnees' party, I don't know why she said she'd come when I invited her, girls are truly hard to understand. I danced with Rute and with other girls, pretending that it was Teresa I was dancing with, I didn't even have to close my eyes. But that was before Silvana kissed me, when I was still a master of my own thoughts and I could choose to think about Teresa Bartolomeu or any other girl.

You know the way to my house. I do, but it's also Queine the porter's house and he is my friend, he got me a bicycle, he lends me comic books and sometimes gives me cigarettes, I shouldn't want to go there. I shouldn't want Silvana and Silvana shouldn't want me to want her. You know the way to my house, a man must not betray a friend, even if his wife does what Silvana did to me. I'm sure that Silvana came here on purpose, that it didn't happen by chance. Mother let the receptionist know that I was in bed and that the cleaning would have to wait until another day. Even so Silvana opened the door and didn't seem surprised when she saw me lying on the sofa bed. I told her that Mother had let reception know I was sick but Silvana just said, I'll take care of you. I remember putting my arms under the bed sheet because I didn't want her to see that my pyjama sleeves were too short. I must have grown since I arrived in the Motherland, because over there the pyjama sleeves weren't short.

She put her hand on my forehead, you're burning, she said. Her hand was cool and it felt good. I'll wet a towel in the bathroom to put on your forehead, Silvana's voice seemed different but it must have been the fever because her face also seemed out of focus, it was very close to mine but if I hadn't been feverish I should have been able to focus on it. My mother and my sister went out for lunch but they'll be back soon, I said, and she, they'll be a while because the queue is very long, and me, I'm fine, I don't need anything. Silvana put her finger on my lips, shush, sick boys don't talk. She locked the door from inside and drew the curtains, the Christmas angels Mother bought at the tobacconist were left outside stuck to the window, bright light will hurt your eyes. The room was in twilight, I could smell Silvana's green-apple smell, I could hear the tap running in the bathroom, Silvana sat on the side of the sofa bed and put the wet towel on my forehead, it feels so good, and Silvana said, I know it feels good, her voice was different, as if she were hoarse, I know it feels good.

Perhaps this lasted no more than a few minutes but fever changes our perception of time, to me it seemed like a long time, I opened my eyes and I felt more rested, my body and my head lighter. She put cool water on my lips, they're bursting

214

with fever, she said. Everything Silvana did felt good, her fingers moving slowly over my lips, I closed my eyes and begged that when I opened them again Silvana would still be by my side. I think my eyes were closed when Silvana moved onto me, I only remember feeling her breathing very close to my face, I opened my eyes and her lips were close to mine, so close to mine, Silvana's mouth was cool too and also tasted of green apples. Perhaps it was a feverish hallucination, you know the way to my house. No, it was not a hallucination. Silvana kissed me like no girl had kissed me before, not even Teresa Bartolomeu when I asked her out and I played "La Décadense", I'm getting mixed up, "La Décadanse" was not Teresa Bartolomeu's favourite song, that was Paula's favourite, Teresa's was another one, I can't remember which. You know the way to my house, it's because of that question that I can't remember anything else.

It sounds like one of Gegé's lies but it isn't, Silvana didn't give me just one kiss, she gave me many. My mouth was hot with fever and Silvana's cool mouth felt so good, I know it feels good. Silvana said, so young, I'd forgotten the smell of a young skin, and she uncovered me, I was embarrassed, about the short pyjama sleeves or about something else within me, who knows, embarrassment or fear, perhaps fear that Mother or my sister would open the door despite it being locked. Or perhaps I only realised later that this might have happened, the taste of green apples in my mouth and Silvana's cool hands on my chest didn't allow me to think of anything else at the time. Silvana said, you have to sweat to get rid of the fever, I don't know if Silvana said that, perhaps it was Dona Gilda when her husband had malarial attacks, you have to let the fever out through your pores. Silvana unbuttoned her uniform and put my hands on her body, my hot hands on Silvana's white skin as she unfastened her bra, Paula would hardly let me touch her bra hooks and now Silvana unfastened her bra, it's what Gegé said that Anita would do, we don't even have to ask Anita to show us her tits. Silvana's pink nipples so close to my mouth, Silvana's smooth belly, Anita showed us everything without us having to ask her, Silvana must be like Anita because she took off her knickers without me asking her, the tuft of black hair, her hand guiding mine down there, like that, slowly, whispering, my hand, and Silvana whispering, don't be afraid. I wasn't. And I'm not afraid now. You know the way to my house, I do know it, I only have to get better soon, I'll get my bicycle and nothing will stop me.

I think I loosened her hair, I think my hands were trembling but I managed to loosen her hair. If I had been with another girl before it would have been different but Paula behaved like she was some kind of saint and Fortunata was black, black girls aren't like white girls, their cooches are showing and they have their babies standing up, it's what the neighbours used to say. If I had been with a girl I would have known what to do, I wouldn't have kept still when Silvana lay down on top of me, Silvana almost nude on top of me, so pretty, her thighs and her breasts so white and soft, her smooth belly and that tuft of black hair, have you been with a woman before, she asked, you can tell me the truth, you don't have to be ashamed. Not with a white woman, I replied, but I've been with many black girls before, I wasn't going to tell her that I'd only been with Fortunata and that almost doesn't count, there wasn't a boy in the neighbourhood who hadn't been with Fortunata, she did it as easily as if she were ironing clothes, she didn't even put out her cigarette.

I couldn't verify if Gegé was right and if there's any difference between white girls and black girls, there must be. It was good to do it with Fortunata but not as good as doing it with Silvana. Perhaps it was the fever. Silvana seemed to lose herself in a way I cannot describe, it was like she was being taken far away and she had to claw her fingernails into my chest to stop herself from going. The more I felt her body holding on to mine the more it seemed like Silvana was drifting away, and I was drifting away too but in another direction, Silvana on top of me and me not afraid of anything, not thinking about my father's death, about going to America, about my plan of breaking into the containers belonging to the dead of Sanza Pombo, about war, about the hotel, about the Butcher of Grafanil, about Mother's demons, about my sister's sadness, about the Motherland, Silvana on top of me more beautiful than the girls with the cherry earrings, Silvana with her eyes almost shut, breathing as though she was frightened, her hardened legs pressing against my legs, my body ever deeper inside hers and her body, ever hungrier, asking for mine.

Someone knocked on the door of our room in the middle of the night, using the secret code we invented over there when the curfew was imposed, two quick knocks and then a pause followed by a third louder knock. I got out of bed thinking that the Judge was feeling poorly again or that one of Dona Suzete's grandsons was drunk again and knocking on every door. Despite the daily arguments amongst ourselves it was also true that we looked out for one another, we have to stick together, the people over here like us even less than the blacks did over there. I also thought it might be Pernalta, the crazy man who is always loitering about the hotel and who, when he manages to slip past the porters and the receptionists, sits in one of the armchairs in the living room like a king or else runs around the corridors. Pernalta never manages to stay long in the hotel, there is always someone who will throw him out, sometimes even Senhor Teixeira in reception who takes him by the shoulders and puts him out on the street. Senhor Teixeira doesn't like having to throw Pernalta out because he worries about his three-piece suit with a pocket watch and a gold chain getting dirty. Pernalta stinks, he must not have had a single bath in his entire life, Dona Juvita says she saw some fleas jumping on his head, no-one wants to touch him and that makes it even more difficult to throw him out. When he is about to be thrown out Pernalta sometimes shouts that he was black in an earlier life and so has a right to be in the hotel, or he swears at the manager, fascist slut, communist slut, whatever takes his fancy. Almost everyone has fun watching Pernalta being thrown out and when they see him in the garden some people encourage him to go in, come on in and go to the bar and ask for a whisky, whoever was black in another life deserves to have a whisky in this one. And Pernalta does as he's told.

Nobody comes back from the dead but Father is standing outside the door to our room. A black rucksack in his hand, a grey beret and a checked jacket. I cannot believe it is Father, Father who was taken away by the blacks with his hands tied behind his back, Father who did not arrive before independence day, Father whom I had to convince myself was dead. Nobody comes back from the dead and knocks on the family door in the early hours, nobody comes back from the dead wearing a beret and a checked jacket and carrying a black rucksack, Father is dead and he will be gone when I wake up. No matter how wide I open my eyes and how much I rub them, Father is still in front of me, almost the same as Father from over there, he is thinner but Father's large body still makes the corridor look small just as over there it made the kitchen look small, the face is more wrinkled but it is the same face with the yellow teeth in the same smile. Father is smoking, Father was always smoking. I have no voice, like in those dreams when you want to shout and can't because your tongue seems to be numb. Don't you recognise your father anymore, Father's voice is the same, have you forgotten about your father, son? Father is standing in front of me and I don't know what to do.

I call Mother and my sister, it's Father, Father's here, Father's come to be with us, I say the same thing in many different ways and even so I can't believe it's true. My sister tripped as she got out of bed, Mother stumbled, she embraced Father, my love, you're here, my love, I can't believe you're here, how I dreamed of this day, my sister, her blonde curls tousled by sleep, crying with happiness the way only girls do. The four of us embraced in the hotel corridor, Mother took two steps back and said, it's you, it's you, my love. Mother no longer has the smiling boy in the photograph hanging from her neck like the day she arrived on the *Vera Cruz*, it's you, my love, it's you, Mother holds her hands together in prayer after looking up at some imaginary sky in the hotel corridor's ceiling, thank you God, and as if this weren't enough she kneels, almost next to the black rucksack that Father dropped on the floor, thank you, God, for granting me such a blessing. My sister and Mother are so happy that they can't stop crying, I don't cry, men don't cry not even when a father comes back from the dead.

People in other rooms wake up with our cries, even Dona Fernanda and her husband who are at the far end of the corridor open their door to see what's happening. People are saying, Milucha's father's arrived, Dona Glória's husband's arrived, they are repeating it to one another and everyone is joining in our happiness, Rui's father's arrived. Father doesn't seem surprised to see so many strangers standing in the corridor in their pyjamas nor does he seem surprised to see us treat those strangers in pyjamas as though we're all one big family. They all greet Father who hasn't taken the beret off his head nor has he taken off his checked jacket. The Judge goes back to his room to fetch an almost empty bottle of whisky and offers Father a sip, welcome, friend. Father takes a sip even though it isn't Ye Monks, there's a party in the hotel corridor, Dona Fernanda's husband says he regrets the bar isn't open, I'd buy you a drink, friend, you must need one, let's go to the lounge, suggests Sandro, Dona Suzete's youngest grandson, one of the boys who helps Tozé Cenoura collect train tickets, let's have a party, everyone laughs because Sandro is yawning while he insists on celebrating. Dona Fernanda says to Father, how your poor family suffered while you were gone, they talked about you all the time. It's a lie, I haven't talked to anyone about Father since independence day. Senhor Tadeu says, you have a truly mighty woman, a lioness, Mother in her flowery flannel nightdress with her tangled hair grinning like a girl, we're all so happy, Gigi the mute makes those sounds nobody can understand, rrrrrrrrrr, and

Dona Suzete tells her off, you're not letting anyone talk.

I'm so happy I pick Sandro up in my arms, Father is here and I'm no longer the head of the family. Sandro kicks his legs, put me down, I'm seven years old, Dona Suzete laughs, we all laugh, even Father. I no longer have to take care of Mother and my sister, I don't have to steal from the containers that belonged to the dead of Sanza Pombo to take Mother and my sister to America, I throw Sandro up into the air, put me down, I'm so happy I throw him up into the air once again. Father's skin is dry and dark, it looks as though he's brought the dryness of the baobabs into the carpeted and wallpapered hotel corridor, everybody asks him questions, so how are things there, Father replies in short sentences, and Mother repeating, my love, I'm so happy, I touch Father's arm tentatively, despite having Father in front of me I still can't believe it's true. But it is.

Father gives thanks for the welcome and apologises, it's been a long day, if you don't mind I'd like to have a bath. I pick up Father's rucksack, it feels light, Father tries to stop me but changes his mind, it's all I'm carrying, he looks at Mother and says again as if he were apologising, it's all I could carry. Everyone looks at the black rucksack in my hand and everyone wants to say something but cannot find the words, the Judge opens and closes his mouth like Editinha's mother's fish, a red fish in a glass bowl on top of the fridge that opened and closed its mouth all day long, it was the only thing the fish did apart from dying, every time one died it was replaced by another identical one that came in a plastic bag filled with water, the glass bowl on top of the fridge was never empty so that Editinha's mother's kitchen would always look nice, the kitchen cupboards had fruit-shaped stickers on them, how my sister pestered my mother to buy fruit-shaped stickers for our kitchen cupboards, but Mother never allowed it, the blacks kept a much-loved house. Perhaps Father managed to burn everything. Or perhaps they were laughing at us. But now that Father is here none of that matters.

The welcome party ends as quickly as it started, people go back to their rooms and close their doors. Once inside Mother says, this is our room, and she hugs Father, the scar on Father's right hand is more visible now, it must have been them that did it. This is where you've lived, Father asks, a room can be a home and this room with this balcony from where you can look out at the sea is our home. Mother says, the manager promised to give us another room when you arrived, when I shut my sofa bed the room looks bigger, I add. What happened, Mother asks looking at Father's hand, Father looks away, it's nothing, it'll go away in time. It's a different kind of scar from the one the motorcycle left on his shin, Father liked talking about that one. Mother runs her hand over the new scar, what did they do to you.

We are all in the room and so happy, Father has come to be with us, we are all together again. And Pirata, I ask, as if I had just returned home and Pirata had not come to greet me. Mother and my sister look worried and signal me to shut up, Father doesn't reply, as if he is checking whether Pirata is in the back garden or making sure she isn't ruining Mother's flowers, I never saw her again, he replies at last. Mother starts talking, tomorrow we have to ask the manager to put us on the waiting list for the rooms that become available, then me again, and Uncle Zé, once again Father takes some time to reply, I never saw him again either.

Mother won't stop talking, perhaps she is afraid of what I'll ask next, she explains the hotel rules as if that were an important topic, Father has come back from the dead and Mother is explaining about the schedule for meals and the mandatory cleaning day for rooms, like the manager on the day we arrived, Father listens without interrupting, Mother doesn't say these are troubled times. I am so happy to have Father with us that I could talk until the morning but Father says, I have to take a bath and rest, tomorrow we'll talk about other things, my sister hugs Father once again, her blonde curls against Father's large body, a thinner body but still Father's large body. I pull two bedcovers off the beds, I keep one and give the other to my sister, I say to her, let's go downstairs, Father needs to settle in. My sister hesitates, she looks at Mother and Father, I think she's waiting for someone to say, nonsense, stay here, but Mother and Father stay quiet, I insist, let's go, and my sister follows me carrying the blanket.

The manager doesn't like us sleeping in the lounge but

once doesn't count, my sister and I are in the large sofa, the one closest to the stone chimney, my sister's head is on one of the armrests and mine is on the other, our legs crossing in the middle, each of us covered with our own blanket. Mother and Father needed to be alone, I say, trying to make my sister less angry with me, fine, I get it, you've said it a hundred times, girls like my sister don't want to know about the things that parents need to do. There is nobody else in the lounge and it's almost completely dark, only the night lights are on. There is nobody in reception either and even Queine the porter is asleep on one of the chairs in the hall. If only Queine the porter knew what Silvana and I are doing, I wonder what he thinks when he sees me come back so late. Once he said to me, on cold nights like these it's good to go for a ride, and he winked at me, he offered me a cigarette and we sat together smoking on the steps. As we sat side by side I worried that Queine the porter would notice something, that he'd detect something about Silvana on me. He didn't seem to suspect anything, when he said goodbye he even gave me a pat on the head, get some rest, kid.

My sister and I don't want to sleep, Father came to be with us, we're not going to waste such a happy night sleeping, we've told each other many times, we mustn't sleep. It seems impossible, I know, I still can't believe it, I feel as though I'm dreaming, me too. The last time my sister and I slept in the same bed we weren't even in school and now we're on the same sofa foot-wrestling, be still, you idiot, my sister is even calling me idiot again. We could have each stayed in our own armchair but Father has returned and so we wanted to stay together like in the big bed in our old house, so long ago, before school and everything else, we'd stay awake looking out for fireflies, there's one, there's another, bubbles of green light moving silently, and if one of the fireflies landed on a wall we'd say, stay there, firefly, don't turn off, stay with us because we like you. But the firefly would stop glowing, the firefly died, my sister would say, keeping my sister from crying was easy, it's sleeping, I would reassure her, my sister would ask, how do fireflies sleep, they close their eyes just like us, tell the firefly to stay awake, I would make up an excuse, the firefly has small babies and has to wake up early to go to work, and my sister, where are the babies, I didn't know what to answer and so would say, you're one year older than I am, you're the one who should know, my sister would be quiet for a while and then say, the firefly died and it has no babies, girls are more melodramatic and don't like games that are too hard to play. Mother would tell us to be quiet from the room where she slept with Father, you have to sleep, if you don't sleep you'll be small forever like Vicente the Midget. Vicente the Midget helped at Senhor Santos' shop and would not have been amused by the table football story that the barber used to tell. My sister and I were scared of staying small like Vicente the Midget and we were even more scared of being taken away by the Caterpillar as Mother said we would be if we didn't eat our soup. Do you still remember the Caterpillar, I ask my sister, my sister does an impression of Mother's voice, I'll tell the Caterpillar to take you away in its bucket. The Caterpillar was an excavator digging up the foundations for the building in a nearby neighbourhood. That monster terrified us but we couldn't help going to watch it do its work. And so the neighbours would say, poor children growing up so wretchedly, and in danger of falling into the foundations of the new building, and my sister and I laugh about the Caterpillar in the lounge, by the stone chimney that we never saw lit. When we stop talking the only noise is Queine the porter's snoring.

Queine the porter always does the night shifts and Silvana is alone at home, you know the way to my house. I did know. I do know. Getting to Queine the porter's house is easy, it's easy to lie down on Queine the porter's bed with his wife. I must be one of those rats Pacaça talked about, a man would not do that to a friend and Queine the porter is my friend, he gave me the bicycle, he offers me cigarettes every now and then, he lends me Spider-Man comic books and I'm sure he'll be happy when I tell him that Father has arrived. It's a shame he's sleeping, otherwise I'd tell him now. But Queine the porter being my friend does not stop me from being with Silvana. I must be a rat, one of the biggest. If the neighbours over there had known Silvana they would have said she's an unhappily married woman like Anita's mother, unhappily married women get involved with other men and have wild mood swings. Since the revolution anyone can get a divorce but Silvana never talked about that and still wants to paint the house that she and Queine the porter have been building for over five years. When Silvana tells me this or shares their other plans for the future, I'm happy to see Queine the porter all bent as he sleeps in a chair when I get back to the hotel. I think I'm jealous of him, I'm glad nobody knows, anyway I'm only a little bit jealous. But it's true that Silvana has her mood swings. With the flowers, for instance. There are days she accepts the flowers I pick up on the way, you're so sweet, she says, almost with tears in her eyes. I think being sweet is not very manly but the sweeter Silvana finds me the longer the kisses she gives me. Other days she says, flowers again, flowers are not an everyday thing, and she doesn't put them in a vase nor does she stop whatever she's doing to kiss me, eating, washing the dishes, sleeping, those are everyday things, flowers aren't. I don't like it when Silvana talks to me as if she hasn't missed me, as if she didn't want to take me into her room and lie down with me.

When will you tell Father that you failed for skiving, my sister asks. I should have imagined that my sister would already know, Mourita is a little snitch, I'm glad I never told him about Silvana or about my plan to steal from the containers that belonged to the dead of Sanza Pombo. Father will be so angry, studying is the hoe you'll need for the field of life, whenever he got angry he clenched his fists and pursed his lips and if I tried to get away he'd give me a good hiding, Father will be angry because I failed for bunking off. Maybe not as angry as when I stole his car to take it for a spin with Gegé and Lee, that time he whipped me with his belt until he got tired. But I can't ruin this night thinking about the hiding Father will give me, my sister brought it up on purpose to annoy me, she's upset because I brought her down to the lounge, they say girls grow up quicker but they're wrong, girls grow up so slowly it's annoying.

Did Roberto ever reply to your letters, I ask. My sister doesn't want to answer but in the end she says, I think he found a girlfriend over here. He's an idiot, the girls here are no good, I say. But I always see you at school with a girl from over here. Oh, that one, as if Teresa were one among many, her name is Teresa but she's not my girlfriend anymore, girls become boring after a while, they always want to do the same things. My sister says, it's the same with boys, but that's not the reason they're boring, it's because they're always boasting, like you. I feel as though I'm dreaming that Father is back, pinch me to know I'm awake, you idiot, not so hard, tomorrow I'll have a big bruise on my arm, you really are an idiot. My sister is calling me an idiot again, everything will be well.

I was sure Father had died, I mean, I thought they had killed him. My sister sits up in the sofa, she folds the blanket, I was also afraid that they'd killed him but Mother assured me he was alive and I believed Mother, Mother knows things that we don't know. I had everything worked out to take you to America, I even knew how to get money for the plane tickets but now Father will take us to America, Father won't want to stay here.

When we stop talking the lounge seems larger and more run down, do you think Father has become like Helder's father, my sister asks. Senhor Moreira became a little crazy because he was in prison for many years, I reply, they tortured him for many years. My sister says, you couldn't tell at first that Senhor Moreira was crazy, you had to talk a lot with him. I know, but Father isn't crazy. I still remember when they took Senhor Moreira away, it was in the middle of a May 13 procession, we were very young, we must have been in primary school. Father was doing a late shift at the docks so Mother took us to the procession. It was unusual for us to be out so late. We liked seeing so many people with their lit candles, it was like daytime in the middle of the road and night-time beyond the pavement. Helder told me that Senhor Moreira knew Salazar wanted to lock him away and he had everything ready to escape to Belgium, that he had gone to the procession because he thought they would never arrest him there. I remember him two rows ahead of us with his family. Not all of them were there, only Helder's two sisters and one of his grandfathers. Helder had caught the jigger flea and couldn't use shoes so he was wearing flip-flops. You were wearing those shoes that Mother had bought you for Paulinho's baptism. Sometimes the bearers disappeared in the fog, the image of Our Lady entered that fine mist and disappeared, all you could see were the candles burning. Helder lost one of his flip-flops when he tried to stop them from beating his father, after the chaos I saw the flip-flop and I picked it up to give it back to him but I ended up throwing it away. Why? It was stupid to go to Helder's house to give him a flip-flop. Why was it stupid? You're a girl, you just don't get it, a boy doesn't go to another boy's house, here, I got your flip-flop. Boys do things that are even stupider than that. Helder had a large family, his mother, Dona Elsa, the four sisters and the older brother, Vadinho, who went out with Carla. And the grandmothers, one older grandmother and one younger grandmother. I can't remember the name of the grandfather. Senhor Justino. That's it, Senhor Justino. He was always belching. I know, disgusting. Senhor Moreira had a Chevy Bel Air. Light yellow. And they had a house with an enormous piece of land, the mother wanted such a large piece of land to plant roses. But it was so far away, Mother would have been scared of living outside our neighbourhood, even there she was always afraid of burglars and troublemakers. The real troublemakers didn't usually burgle houses, the real troublemakers stayed in the bush. For Mother all blacks were troublemakers, even the ones who worked for Father. Do you remember the banana trees that grew around Helder's family's property. They were scary at night-time, Helder said he had seen ghosts coming out of them. Helder was always making things up. And the pond in Helder's back garden, the water was so green that it looked as though you could cut it with a knife. And the two papaya trees by the entrance. They were so tall they seemed almost to touch the sky. They must have been the tallest papaya trees I've ever seen. Zezé Preto had to climb up them to get the papayas, no white person could climb so high. Zezé Preto liked us even if we were white. Belmira the washerwoman did too. People here are wrong when they say that the blacks didn't like us, the blacks liked us and wanted us to stay, it was the people here who told them to throw us out of there. Why would they do something like that? Envy, people over here are very spiteful. How do you know if you hardly know anyone here? It isn't necessary, you just need to look at their faces, they all have the faces of spiteful weasels. I was so scared of taking a dip in that green pond, the water weeds stuck to our legs and arms and didn't let us swim, one day I went underwater to get to the bottom of the pond and I couldn't get back to the surface. That water was disgusting, I don't know why you liked swimming there. Gegé pulled me out, if Gegé hadn't pulled me out I would have died. Now you're making that up. No, I'm not. If Gegé had saved your life you would have mentioned it before, you're making things up, you're like Mother. I swear it's true, it was during the March holidays before the procession. You're such a liar. In the end Helder was always smoking *liamba*, he didn't even go to school. If they were all going to Belgium, Helder didn't need to go to school. You also need to go to school in Belgium. But the schools are different. Maybe they're all in Belgium. Or in a nearby hotel. If they were we would have seen them. There are so many hotels and so many people in the hotels that we can't see everybody. Helder was so happy when he heard there had been a coup in the Motherland. When they released

Senhor Moreira, Gegé and I cycled over to Helder's house just to have a look. Uncle Zé used to say that Senhor Moreira had gone crazy because the P.I.D.E. had subjected him to sleep deprivation. Uncle Zé always called them P.I.D.E.'s tormentors. Tormentors or executioners. I wonder where Uncle Zé is. Father said he didn't see him again. He must be with Nhé Nhé, you don't know what Uncle Zé did with Nhé Nhé, it's like they were a couple. I know, it's dirty. Queers. Don't forget you mustn't smoke in front of Father, I can't believe Father is back, I was so worried that they wouldn't let him go, they never release the whites that they lock up. But Father didn't know anything about the Butcher of Grafanil, even Uncle Zé could see that. Tozé told me he once saw the Butcher of Grafanil in Cazenga and that he was short and stronger than a bull. Tozé Cenoura is always telling stories, I don't know how you don't get fed up with him, he never shuts up, he's even worse than Pacaça and those others who like appearing on television, there's nothing special about television, everything they said about the Motherland is a lie, but Father will get us out of here, Father will find a way to get us out of here, did you hear what I said, you're falling asleep, Milucha, don't fall asleep, Milucha, Milucha.

I shut my eyes tighter. The cold wind gets into my coat and whips my hair about as if it were going to pull it out. Gegé and Lee will be arriving soon. I open my eyes as wide as I can, I'm at the top of the world, the wind blows in my face. Lee will make fun of me because of my beard, it's a proper beard now, it's no longer just a few blonde bristles sticking out that can only be seen when they catch the sun. They arrive and we punch one another the way we did every time we stopped seeing each other for a while. Gegé and Lee won't believe me when I tell them what the Motherland is really like, they know it from the maps in our classrooms, and Gegé has been here on holidays but neither of them know what it's like to live in the Motherland. When I tell them I bet they'll say, you're pulling our legs. The three of us finally at the top of the Sears Tower, saying over and over again, how long has it been, how long have we waited to be here together. With my eyes shut tight and the wind blowing in my face it's easy to believe that Gegé and Lee are arriving soon. But there are still seven hundred and eighty-four days to go. In seven hundred and eighty-four days the three of us will be on top of the Sears Tower. We'll have to pinch ourselves so many times to believe it. Me, Gegé and Lee at the top of the world telling one another our stories, all at the same time, proud of having kept our promise, the three of us in America on the last day of 1978, me and Gegé and Lee interrupting one another, let me finish, dammit, Lee always struggled the most to make himself heard, Gegé would say, let the little lady talk, and Lee would say, your mother was a little lady until she met your old man, Lee and Gegé arguing about everything and nothing. None of us will get sentimental, we won't even say we missed one another, that's a girl's thing.

What you see from up here on the hotel's rooftop terrace mustn't be too different from what you see from the top of the Sears Tower. There, the cars below must look even smaller, buildings must be just like the ones in Spider-Man books, very tall and regular buildings, with windows that look the same, and people so small they almost disappear. Though it must be a bit different from here because everything in America is different. Seven hundred and eighty-four days. Seven hundred and eighty-four days and I'll be at the top of the Sears Tower with Gegé and Lee. I have to remember everything I see to tell them, I can almost hear them, how tall was the hotel, how far away was the sea, how big was the terrace, and the pool, Gegé and Lee were always asking questions about everything, sometimes it was almost annoying, we could spend a whole afternoon discussing why papaya trees were so tall, hours and hours talking without reaching any conclusion. Now it feels as though our afternoons there were so long, and our holiday afternoons even more so, the afternoons were long even when we went to spy on the girls in another neighbourhood.

There is no autumn in Brazil or in South Africa. Gegé and Lee must have never seen this golden sun and must not know that the parks fill up with the yellow leaves that fall from trees and muffle the sound of footsteps. They may have trouble imagining a swimming pool filled with leaves like the one in our hotel, leaves and rubbish, since the manager ordered it to be emptied last year she never had it cleaned again, she must have forgotten that this is a five-star hotel, that the hotel has rules and that rules have to be followed for our own good. And if we complain the manager fiddles with her three-strand pearl necklace without even trying to hide her annoyance at our complaints and she doesn't even answer. It's been so long since Pacaça first complained about the pool's closure, now there aren't even any more plenary meetings, this summer nobody even mentioned the empty pool. Senhor Marques did complain about the air conditioning not working inside the rooms but the manager said, if you're hot go to the beach, few people are lucky enough to be so close to the beach. The manager doesn't even use the excuse of these being troubled times, in fact she doesn't even say troubled times anymore, she now says these are terrible times. This summer I went to the beach and the water didn't seem so cold, maybe next summer I'll find it even less cold. Despite what Faria says, our lazy bodies do get used to anything.

Only seven hundred and eighty-four days to go before I'm with Gegé and Lee at the Sears Tower. It sounds like a lot but it isn't, from now on the days will go by faster, time goes by slowly when you're only waiting and in the hotel we're always waiting, not only waiting for a place in the dining room or the television room, but waiting for the big day, the day we leave, and that wait makes the days blend into each other, the big day is so long anticipated that all other days are filled with little more than waiting. But the wait is over for us. Tomorrow we leave the hotel. Tomorrow we'll sleep in a new house.

I will never be here again. This is the last time I see the world from up here, the small cars on the Marginal, the houses with the red-tiled roofs side by side like in that game of Monopoly that my sister liked playing so much with her friends, they locked themselves up in her room and they bought Rossio Station and Ouro Street, Santa Catarina Street and Aliados Avenue, we had no idea where those places were, they were places in the Motherland and so they sounded very posh, my sister also liked buying Campanhã and Santa Apolónia Stations, in Monopoly you could never buy a bus station close to the sea. Even the buses look small from up here, little silver cylinders going from here to there. I will never again see the ships lost in the distance the way I see them from here. This is our last day in the hotel. We have waited for over a year but the day has finally come.

The new house has a room and a living room with no balcony. The windows are high up near the ceiling, slivers of light that hardly brighten up anything, but Mother is as happy as if we were moving to a palace. Yesterday we went to get the key and we spent a few hours there. The house was gloomy even though it was sunny outside and it smelled of mould, the same smell of our suitcases when the damp got into them. Father lowered his eyes, I promise you that one day we'll have a house like the one we had over there, Father with his eyes on the worn carpet and his promise echoing through the empty house. It was not a promise like the ones Father used to make over there, the vacuum cleaner Mother saw in a magazine, our trip to the Cambambe dam, the BaByliss to straighten out my sister's curls, it was a promise made with clenched fists, a promise that made my father raise his eyes and look at each of us, I promise you that one day we'll have a house like the one we had over there. There was such anger in Father's eyes that we were all certain this time he meant what he said, this time the promise would not be forgotten or pushed aside by some other commitment.

Mother is so happy that Father didn't even have to promise anything, there's no place like our own home, our own home is where we'll be well, Mother repeats despite the cold walls and the lack of light. I bet Mother is already going to sleep while thinking about a table for the living room and a double bed. For the time being we've found some inflatable mattresses and a camping table, now we just need a tent, says my sister, feeling pleased with herself, and we all laugh. For the time being we'll also have to make do with the glasses, plates and cutlery we stole from the hotel. It's a shame we can't steal more things from the hotel, to steal from the manager wouldn't be a sin, just as it wouldn't have been a sin to steal from the containers belonging to the dead of Sanza Pombo to take Mother and my sister to America. The containers belonging to the dead of Sanza Pombo are no longer there, someone took the whole lot in broad daylight. Pacaça says they were stolen but Senhor Acácio disagrees, the dead of Sanza Pombo had relatives here, there wasn't a single colonist who didn't have relatives here, close or distant, they all had relatives. Pacaça gets angry when Senhor Acácio says that, I know who the rats are, miserable rats, no matter how rich he becomes, someone who steals will always be miserable. Pacaça hasn't caught any thieves but he won't give up the night guards, without the night guards and without the card games the days and the nights would drag by. Anyway, stealing from the manager isn't proper stealing, the only reason I'm not taking one of the armchairs from the lounge or a table with its chairs from the dining room is that I can't carry them, but a thief who robs a thief gets a hundred years of relief.

Mother is happiest with the new house because she was the only one who never believed, not even for a second, that a room and a balcony could be a home. And she can't believe that Father will build a breezeblock factory. From time to time she says, why don't you find a job, it's less of a hassle, you could do what Senhor Orlando did, he found a job as a bus driver, he gets a pay cheque at the end of every month and no more bother. Mother says these things and Father has to say over again why he decided to find business partners and get a loan from the I.A.R.N. to build a breezeblock factory, at my age nobody would give me a job and if they did it would be a worthless job, I can't waste whatever health and strength I still have on a job that won't keep us safe when I'm old, even if my body doesn't betray me with some illness I only have some ten years of work left in it, I can't accept a pay cheque that won't even cover our daily expenses and much less allow us to save for our old age, what would happen to us when I can't work anymore, what would happen to us with a pitiful pension? But it doesn't make a difference, Mother still worries, even worse than not having anything is owing thousands of contos. If Mother still wore blue eye-powder she wouldn't look so worried, but without any make-up her eyes betray her concerns. Father repeats, the breezeblock factory is a good business, it will make us enough to pay off the loan and the interest and to have an easy old age, there's nothing wrong with asking for a loan as long as you don't throw the money away and you work hard to make things happen, the next few years will be difficult years but then it will all be well, as he tries to persuade Mother, Father is also persuading himself. Mother is always warning us, you mustn't upset your father, he's very stressed, he has a lot of work to do, but then she worries and forgets what she's just said, we won't be able to pay off such a big loan, everyone says that nobody can pay interest at those rates and that they're due to go up even more, and Father has to remind her, the worst thing about losing everything is not being here, if we don't make the most of this opportunity the worst thing will be our old age, which is just around the corner, by then there will be no more I.A.R.N. and everyone will have forgotten about us.

Father must be right, life in this hotel is bad but life out there could be much worse. Perhaps that's why Senhor Flávio did what he did, nobody knew what to think when Senhor Teixeira from reception said that Senhor Flávio's family had written to let us know about the funeral. Senhor Flávio was still a young man, the last time I saw him he was so happy about leaving the hotel, whoever has a good family has nothing to fear in this world, Senhor Flávio said, only to go and kick a chair out from under himself and die hanging from a rope. Perhaps Father is right, perhaps the worst is yet to come. But I won't think about that now, I have to think about one thing at a time, let's leave the hotel and I have to be happy about that without thinking about other things, that room and that balcony with a view of the sea were not our home, our home has one room and one living room with windows close to the ceiling, our home doesn't have a balcony and it's far from the sea but it's our home.

When I hear Father talking about the breezeblock factory I believe in everything he says but when Father is not nearby I start thinking that we should go away, that Father should have asked the I.A.R.N. for money for plane tickets the way Senhor Fernando and João the Communist did, I start thinking that Father should not have forgotten that part of the book of life that says that a man belongs to the land that feeds him, he shouldn't have forgotten that the Motherland only made him hungry, Father should not have vowed that he'd never leave the Motherland again. One morning, two or three days after his arrival, Father was sitting on the balcony smoking a cigarette, he looked out onto the sea and he vowed, nobody will ever throw me out of anywhere again, this will be my country. I understood that Father might not want to go to America, it must be difficult to make a living in America without speaking English, but I can't understand why he doesn't want to go to Brazil, which is similar to Angola, Senhor Fernando wrote a letter from Rio de Janeiro and said that it's just like Luanda, with the warm seawater and rains that gladden everyone's heart, a land as blessed as Angola was, a land where anything one plants will grow. But not even Senhor Fernando's letter made Father reconsider the vow he made on the room's balcony that morning, every time I talked to him about Brazil Father replied, nobody will ever take me away from my country. João the Communist also went to Brazil but never sent any news, I hope he's well and that he is no longer ashamed of the empire and of being Portuguese, it must be difficult to be permanently ashamed of something you can't change. Other families had left the hotel and had not sent any news either, Senhor Clemente went to the countryside to see about some land he'd inherited, he said he'd write and that he'd even send us a few sacks of potatoes but it's been months and there's been no sack of potatoes and no letters, and wasn't it Senhor Clemente who used to say we had to stick together, he always turned up at the demonstrations carrying placards, Angola is Portugal, the returnees demand justice, the returnees this, the returnees that. There are hardly any demonstrations these days, and when they happen they have fewer people, I think they've all realised it's every man for himself, no-one is buying the talk about unity anymore, no matter that they look out for number plates and honk at each other when two cars from over there come across each other. When Senhor Belchior was leaving he said to everyone in the lounge, each one of us has to get on with his life, friends don't hold friends back, Senhor Belchior didn't even say he'd write and he doubted we'd see each other again, the world is not large but it's not so small that we'll always be running into each other, whatever is God's will.

The hotel is emptier now but there are still two shifts for the restaurant and people still have to argue with the manager over every room that becomes vacant. Mourita wants to keep our room, he's tired of living with his grandmother and his parents, who knows which is worse, his grandmother praying for the war to end in Angola or Senhor Acácio groaning on top of Dona Ester. Paulo doesn't care, he spends his days giggling with his eyes heavy from the *liamba*, at least he doesn't notice the groaning. Maybe I will never see Mourita again, this year we won't even be in the same school. I had to move to a school closer to our new house but classes haven't started, they say that before the revolution everything used to start on time, I don't know if I believe that, we were always taught so many lies about the Motherland that I don't believe anything anymore. Since Mourita said that thing about Silvana and I punched him we stopped being friends like we used to be. I shouldn't have punched him, Mourita doesn't know what happened between me and Silvana and he didn't mean any harm when he said that. But I did and I can't take it back. It wasn't only Mourita talking about Silvana, many people talked about her after seeing her dance with Tobias at the New Year's Eve party, Mourita was trying to be funny and said Silvana was going to have a black baby, he didn't mean any harm, I don't know why I punched him, maybe I'll apologise before I go. Perhaps I won't see Teresa Bartolomeu ever again either. Although I won't miss Teresa Bartolomeu so much, Teresa has been very boring since she decided she wants to be a singer, she spends her days rehearsing annoying songs with the guitar her parents gave her, the worst thing isn't even that she can't sing properly, the worst thing is that now she's worried about ruining her voice, as a result she's stopped going to the rocks because she can get congested, if she has to call someone who is far away she won't shout out, she won't do anything that might ruin her voice, she won't eat ice cream, won't smoke, she's more boring than my sister, but she's prettier than ever. She should try out to be a beauty queen like Rute, but no, she wants to be in a band and travel the world singing, she is always reading music magazines that her parents bring her from England and she no longer likes America, she only likes England, people from over here are strange, what is there in England that there isn't in America, only the Queen. Rute told me that when she was a little girl she thought the Queen didn't shit or piss, because of the cloak and all of the finery, a Queen who doesn't shit or piss would be the only interesting thing about England. Rute has also left. Ngola says that he once ran into Rute's parents on a bus and they told him that Rute had left home to go and live with an older man from over here. I don't know if it's true, Ngola smokes a lot of *liamba* and is always swearing he sees things that are only happening in his head.

I thought about bringing Father up to the terrace but I never did. If I lost this hiding place I would have lost the only place where I could spend hours thinking about whatever I wanted without anyone annoying me. I don't know how nobody else discovered that it's easy to force the door open. Or if someone did discover it they didn't think it was of any interest to come up here. Silvana would sometimes come up here to be with me but she never stayed long, there was always some problem, the cold, the heat, the hard concrete, rubbish blown about, the noise. Silvana was never at ease here, she was never at ease anywhere, or she was never at ease anywhere for long. And now it must be worse, with that enormous belly she really mustn't be at ease anywhere, now she must have good reasons not to be at ease. The day I heard Pacaça congratulate Queine the porter I got on my bicycle and rode out to her house, on the way I rehearsed the questions I would ask her but when I got there the key was under the mat as always, I opened the door and Silvana was sitting at the kitchen table doing something, I think she was sewing some buttons onto a uniform, she greeted me with a kiss and asked how my day had been and I wanted to pretend that I hadn't just heard Queine the porter saying, if we don't have someone to carry on our bloodline we have nothing, Queine the porter happier than I'd ever seen him before. On the way I thought of lots of questions to ask Silvana but when I got there the key was under the mat and Silvana kissed me, everything was the same and I didn't want anything to change, I said to myself, I'll ask later. Silvana took me into the bedroom and we lay down on the bed, she kissed me and I said to myself, I'll ask later, I'll ask later. But I didn't ask and Silvana never said anything about the subject. Not even when her belly started to show. Not even when Mourita said Silvana was going to have a black baby and I punched him. Not even on the last day I went to her house.

Mourita also heard Queine the porter say, if we don't have

someone to carry on our bloodline we have nothing, and he joked, Queine the porter will find out that he happens to have black blood like Tobias, and he laughed like a madman. I told him to shut up but he only did when I punched him, what's wrong with you, Mourita looked surprised, if you don't shut up I'll give you another one, and Mourita, are you crazy or what, and me, better stop it if you don't want to get another one. I was wrong to do that. Mourita was only joking, he doesn't know what happened. But even if nothing had happened between Silvana and me, Queine the porter was also my friend. Only a friend gives you a bicycle. Or perhaps not. I think Queine the porter would not like having a black child but he wouldn't mind having a child with the blood of the Celts. I punched Mourita because I had to punch him. Friends sometimes have to do that. But it wasn't right and I should have apologised. I didn't and so much time has passed that it's not worth it now.

Silvana didn't like being up here on the terrace but I always liked it. Even when it was raining. I would huddle under the eaves and watch the rain, the rain that falls straight down, the slanting rain blown about by the wind, the tangled stormy rain, the drizzle or dunce-drencher as they call it here, I liked them all. But what I like most of all is to lie down staring at the sky, I bring up a sweatshirt to use as a pillow and I need nothing else, I stretch my legs and let my body relax. The sun is weak now but it's still enough to warm me up, there isn't a centimetre of this terrace that I don't know, there isn't a centimetre of this terrace that I haven't stepped on, if there wasn't always some new bit of rubbish on the terrace I'd say I know the terrace like the palm of my hand. But there is always some new bit of rubbish, I don't know how so much rubbish ends up here, leaves from the trees, plastic bags, broken boards with rusty nails, newspaper pages, I even found a handkerchief like Mother's and pages of sheet music. Every now and then I find dead birds, the rest of the rubbish is blown away but not the dead birds. Silvana says that dead birds are bad luck, if Silvana were here she wouldn't be able to look at the dead seagull lying over there by the television aerial. When I've been up here I've often thought about breaking the aerial to get back at the manager, but I never follow through, it won't be the manager who can't watch television, I can almost hear her, somebody ruined the aerial, once again the innocent have to pay for the sinner. Mother also says that thing about the innocent paying for the sinner when she talks about how we lost everything we had over there, the innocent paid for the sinner, there's no consolation in that, but at least we were innocent. I don't understand why the innocent have to pay and the sinners don't, what's the point in that. But Mother no longer talks as much about how we lost everything, now she is always talking about the I.A.R.N. loan, how are we going to pay back all that money, Mother asks the same question over and over again, it looks as though the demons are no longer haunting her but her mood swings are still there, neither Africa nor the Motherland are to blame for Mother's mood swings, there isn't a place

248

or a demon that can be blamed for Mother's mood swings, it's hard to believe that some things are nobody's fault but it's true.

When Father says he'll manage to pay back the I.A.R.N. loan nobody doubts him, not even Mother. If Father weren't such a good talker he would not have found five partners among the men who gather in the lounge. No matter that Dona Juvita walked past with her breasts popping out, that Pacaça interrupted, that Pernalta was chased away or that Preta Zuzú started chanting her prayers, Father never got distracted, in the lounge Father had a sole purpose, the Motherland's future will be built on concrete and whoever wants to be part of that future has to join me and my breezeblock factory. I think at first people thought he was joking, nobody believed Father despite the confident voice and the enthusiasm in every gesture, not even revolutionaries showed such enthusiasm for the revolution. Father insisted, in this country almost everything is about to be built, it is lacking in everything, houses, schools, hospitals, shops, restaurants, cafés, you can't build anything without concrete, mark my word, this country's future will be built on concrete. Father in the lounge with his idea for a breezeblock factory just like back in Luanda at the counter of Senhor Manuel's tobacco shop, with his ideas for a new nation, we'll build a new nation, all together, whites and blacks, let's build a nation more wealthy than America. But this time it was different, even the ones who disagreed with Father couldn't offer any reasons, there was no Senhor Manuel saying, steady on, man, they are going to kick us out of here, there will be a bloodbath here. Perhaps Father did well to vow that nobody would ever throw him out of anywhere. Some people said, it's not so easy to run a breezeblock factory, and Father smiled, it's not easy until someone does it, when Father talks about the breezeblock factory he's just like the father who was going to be the greatest trucking entrepreneur, the father on whose body they had not yet left any scars.

Father never talked about prison. Not a word. Perhaps that's why I can't bear to look at Father's scars when I see his naked torso. Because of Father's silence the scars say more terrible things than Father would ever have said, the scars show me the wounds being opened, Father shouting, imploring, Father must have cried, Senhor Moreira told Helder that there comes a moment when even the bravest of men cries. When I look at Father's scars it's as if I'm watching what they did to him, as if I'm watching everything and I'm still unable to move like on the day they took Father. I don't move, my body does not double over in pain like Father's but anger and hate are bursting inside me, no, it's not anger and hate, because anger and hate grow weaker with time, it's something else, something else not even I can put my finger on, what infuriates me most is not being able to understand why they took Father away, that's what infuriates and hurts me most, the pain of not being able to understand remains intact or gets even stronger, I don't know how they could have taken Father, I don't understand why, I ask myself hundreds of times, why, why, and it seems as though each time I'm further from finally understanding. Sometimes I think it wasn't them who left the marks on Father, sometimes I think that Father's body is scarred because he was fighting with the demons, like Senhor José. I like to think that demons no longer haunt Mother because Father stayed behind to fight them and he defeated them.

Father might not talk about prison but at least he could tell us about the day he was released. But not even that. When Uncle Zé passed through here on his way to the countryside, he told us that Father had been released because they had caught the Butcher of Grafanil. Father was there but didn't say a word. Uncle Zé went into the details, the Butcher of Grafanil had been caught drinking beer in a house in Maianga and when he found himself surrounded he shot himself in the head. Uncle Zé put his hand to the back of his head and pretended he was shooting himself, bang, it's over. Father wanted to smoke but his hands were so sweaty that he couldn't light the Ronson Varaflame lighter. Mother changed the subject but Uncle Zé kept talking about what had happened over there, how he had been forced to give up helping the people who had been oppressed for five centuries, it's the bloodiest war you can possibly imagine and it won't be over any time soon. Uncle Zé also talked about how difficult it had been to get a flight out after the end of the airlift, he talked about that and about the mulatto girl who came with him. From time to time it seemed as if Father were going to speak but he never said anything. We don't even know if Father came by aeroplane. Sometimes I think that Mother knows, that Father can't keep such a big secret. We don't talk about what happened to Father but it's as if it were present in every conversation. Every conversation and every silence. Lee was always reading things in magazines about black holes, they are the opposite of stars and instead of giving out light they suck in everything around them, even light itself. Father's imprisonment is the same. It's not even like Mother's illness because there is nobody to blame for Mother's illness. Or there is, but when God or the demons are doing evil things it's a whole different thing. There are real people to blame for Father's imprisonment and they are like us or almost like us and we can make them feel what we felt. Perhaps Uncle Zé is right and the war will never end. But it's hard to believe what Uncle Zé says, it's hard to believe what he says about Father's imprisonment, or about the death of the Butcher of Grafanil, or about the letters he tells us he wrote and that never reached us, or about the lengths he and Nhé Nhé supposedly went to so Father would be released. It's even hard to believe that Mena, the mulatto girl, is his real fiancée, despite having introduced her like that, this is Mena, my fiancée, and having held her hand the whole time. If we could trust Uncle Zé Father would have invited him to be a partner in the breezeblock factory, but Father said nothing even when Uncle Zé said that he would prefer to find a job here in the city than go to the countryside.

And it wasn't easy to find the partners that the I.A.R.N.

demanded in order to offer a loan. Father would go into the lounge with his talk about concrete and the future of the Motherland but there were always doubters, especially among the older men, the ones who could no longer get a loan and who would never get a job, like Pacaça, if they haven't built anything here in all this time what makes you think that they'll start building now, especially in this country where nobody knows who's in charge and where everyone can steal whatever they want, just pick up a newspaper, Prime Minister Big Cheeks is selling out the country the way he sold us out, but whatever he does sell won't be much of a loss, whatever there once was of any value is long gone and won't ever come back. Pacaça still spends his days bad-mouthing Mário Soares, Rosa Coutinho, Almeida Santos and the others who betrayed us and sold us out, and he still wears a black ribbon to mourn the end of empire. He also continues to wait for a letter from South Africa, a letter in which his son asks him to come and join him. But the letter never arrives. Pacaça goes to reception every day, he doesn't even dare to ask, as soon as Senhor Teixeira sees him coming he says, nothing's arrived, Pacaça goes back to talking about Mário Soares, Rosa Coutinho and Almeida Santos, about Otelo and the people from the Armed Forces Movement that started the revolution, the gang of traitors that sold us down the river. But hardly anyone pays any attention to him. Everyone knows that any day now the I.A.R.N. will close down the hotels and when you have no house and no food, traitors don't matter quite as much, what's done is done, even Dona Flor from room 519, who swore she would not die before spitting in the face of Rosa Coutinho, now says what's done is done.

In the beginning Senhor Miguel agreed with those who said that a breezeblock factory was a good idea but was very risky, that it would need a lot of work and above all that it would be difficult to pay the interest, Senhor Miguel asked Father, but what if you're wrong, man, and Father replied, there is no more Africa, the goose that lay the golden eggs is gone, people here can't continue standing still, someone has to do something, either we do something or we might as well jump into the sea, it's always quicker to die by drowning than from starvation. You're right about that, Senhor Miguel would say but then he would go on about his plan for getting a permit to drive a taxi, it's a bit dangerous with all those thieves out there but apart from that it's a life without too many worries, there are no strikes or unions here, even the communists will need to hail a taxi, it's a business that won't upset anyone. But the permit never came, it was one document after another, one condition after another, and one day Senhor Miguel made up his mind, let's do it your way, let the future be built on concrete. Father was so happy that he asked me to join him for a beer at the bar and then called Mother and my sister. I still remember Father saying to Vítor who was as grumpy as ever, friend, you are standing in front of the future King of the Breezeblocks, and even Vítor had to laugh because everyone in the bar laughed.

Dona Maria said, it looks like someone is celebrating his birthday, and Father replied, we're celebrating the fact that we can be born again, that's what it is, and then added, if some day you want to build a house you know where to get the concrete, I have special rates for returnees who need help, it'll only cost you twice as much as the people here. Everyone laughed again, the Judge went to his room to fetch the bottle of whisky and Senhor Acácio did the same, we stayed in the bar until the early hours telling stories and talking about the breezeblock factory and other businesses. Not every day in the hotel was bad, there were also good times like that evening at the bar. After drinking a few whiskies Father sang to Mother, *I beg your pardon, I never promised you a rose garden, along with the sunshine, there's gotta be a little rain sometime*, Mother called him my love, that evening my father carried Mother to the lift the way the neighbours used to say that he carried her the day she arrived on the *Vera Cruz*.

Nobody at the hotel knows about Father's imprisonment, everyone talks about everything but the truth is that nobody knows much about anybody else. Just as they don't know that Father's favourite whisky is Ye Monks they don't know that Father has scars all over his body either. Even in the summer Father wore long-sleeved shirts so nobody knows that when Father talked about being reborn he meant it. With those scars on his body Father had to be born again, otherwise he could not have been thinking about the breezeblock factory and about the bigger house we'll have one day. But for now this one will do, for now a room and a living room with windows close to the ceiling will do. It bothers me to have to sleep in the living room with my sister, especially now that my sister is always talking about her boyfriend, and writing letters to her boyfriend, girls can be more annoying than anything.

It was not easy for Father and Senhor Miguel to find the necessary business partners, nobody wanted to owe such large amounts of money and nobody wanted to have such hard work ahead, they said, it's certainly a good idea but don't forget that this isn't a very generous land, not like it was over there. But Mother is right, Father speaks better than a doctor, and one by one he managed to persuade five partners, I know this country isn't blessed like the country over there, I know this country will take our blood, sweat and tears in exchange for a piece of stale bread, but I also know one way in which this land is no different from any other, even the most blessed, this country won't reject whatever people build on it, I also know that, and that's why I say to you that the future will hinge on what we build on this land, houses, roads, hospitals, schools. It's almost impossible not to get excited when Father speaks with such confidence. And so it was that Father managed to find the five partners for the breezeblock factory. And so it was that Father and the five partners came to owe seven thousand nine hundred contos excluding the interest payments that nobody can anticipate yet, because money is getting more expensive every day.

I should go down to pack my suitcase but there's still some

time, this is the last time I can stay here and think about my things. This time it will be easy to pack my suitcase, there isn't much to take, the clothes I brought from over there stopped fitting me and almost all of them were thrown out. The clothes weren't warm enough anyway and since the people here don't dress in bright colours we often looked like clowns. I'm not like my sister, I'm not ashamed of being a returnee but I don't like being a clown either. This time it will be easy to pack my suitcase, it's just packing two or three sweatshirts I got from the clothes depot and that's it. It would be good if the wind calmed down a little to let me light a cigarette. It's also good to be here because I can smoke whenever I want. When I turn eighteen I'll ask Father to let me smoke in front of him, Father knows that I'm a man and that a man doesn't hide to smoke. If Father didn't consider me a man he wouldn't tell me things he doesn't tell anyone else, not even his partners. I know that the I.A.R.N. is going to rip us up with its interest rates but I have no choice, Father tells me these things but always says to me, don't tell anyone what I've told you, it's harder to work to pay for something when you think you have an unfair deal, nobody needs to know that's how it's going to be. I never said a word to anyone, we belong to the same club and members of the same club don't betray one another, and don't get angry with one another. Father had good reasons to be angry with me but he isn't, maybe I don't even have to wait until I'm eighteen to ask for his permission to smoke in front of him, Mourita and Paulo smoke in front of

Senhor Acácio and there is no problem whatsoever. I think I can ask sooner because there are some ways in which Father is different, and it's not only the marks on his body. When I told him I'd failed for bunking off I thought Father would pull out his belt and give me a good hiding. We were alone in the room, Father studying the papers for the I.A.R.N. loan and me lying in bed reading the Spider-Man book that Queine the porter had let me borrow. So, son, do you have anything to tell me, he asked, I don't know if he already suspected something. We were alone, it was a good moment to tell him that I'd failed, if Father hit me no-one would see it, it's not so hard to be whacked by Father like this but it's harder when someone sees me being whacked. I failed for bunking off, I said, that was before Carnival, I forged Mother's signature so nobody would find out and I've been pretending I go to school but I really just hang around killing time. I said everything at once and I only shut up because Father put down the I.A.R.N. loan papers. I thought he'd pull out his belt to whack me but Father didn't even raise his voice, it was the only duty you had and you weren't able to fulfil it, he said with such disappointment that it hurt more than his belt. I tried to apologise, some teachers don't even know our names, the cold froze my hands and I couldn't write, the teachers put us in the row furthest from the window, Mother's nervous attacks were getting worse, I gave all the excuses hoping that Father would understand at least one of them. Of course I didn't say that I preferred going onto the rocks with Teresa Bartolomeu and that later I preferred being with Silvana in the house with the bare breezeblocks. Nor that I went to bed with Silvana as if it were normal. Father looked at me without saying a word and I continued, I thought they had killed you and that I had to work to take care of Mother and Milucha, and in that case one year more or one year less made no difference. Still Father did not pull his belt out and did not raise his voice and when he said, you have enough time ahead of you, failing one year is nothing you can't fix, I understood that Father had learned that it is not fear that will make us do the things we have to do. And no more words were necessary for both of us to be certain that it would be just as Father said, next year you can catch up like your sister did, she got good grades and is going to university.

But my sister isn't going to university yet, they've invented a thing called civic service and that's what my sister will do this year, my sister and her boyfriend, the idiot from the Motherland who isn't at university yet but already looks like a doctor. My sister must think that if she goes out with an idiot from over here she stops being a returnee, only a girl could believe that. Gegé and Lee won't believe what my sister's boy friend is like. They'll think I'm lying when I tell them about the trip to the cinema. My sister and I had managed to get a little bit of money to go to the cinema but Mr Killjoy said, we won't go to the Casino because they show dirty films. I would never watch dirty films with my sister but Mr Killjoy got all self-righteous, they show dirty films at the Casino. Gegé and Lee won't believe that here in the Motherland families go to the matinee to watch films like "Emmanuelle", I bet that doesn't happen in Brazil or in South Africa, it must be one of the few things that are better about the Motherland. What irritates me most about Mr Killjoy is that he thinks he knows everything. Whenever I want to wind my sister up I ask her about Mr Know-it-all, she gets furious, the other day she threw a wooden clog at me, luckily it didn't hit me, it's a good thing that girls have bad aim. But my sister must like him very much because she tells him everything that happens in our lives. She has even told him about Mother's illness, and Mother's illness is not something we talk about, much less with outsiders. Mr Know-it-all's theory is that nervous conditions sometimes improve or even disappear when there are big changes in people's lives. And he might be right about that, having gone through all of what we went through may have affected us deep inside our heads. It must have messed up some people's heads, like Senhor Flávio who did what he did, but it must also have fixed other people's, like Mother's. I'd like to see what Mr Know-it-all would do during one of Mother's attacks, he would run off and my sister would never see him again.

Mr Know-it-all is like the manager, he also uses fancy words, I'm sure they could be friends. Mr Killjoy even talks about Angola as if he knew more about it than us. He's never set foot there but since he had an uncle or a cousin or someone who did his military service over there that's enough for him to say that we can't even begin to imagine the terrible things that happened. Mr Killjoy should be worried about the terrible things that are happening here and that he can't even begin to imagine. And there are lots of them because there are terrible things happening all the time here, there, everywhere.

I would like Mr Know-it-all to come up with a theory to explain how come Uncle Zé was a queer when we first came over here and now he's turned up with Mena the mulatto girl. I've not been able to come up with one no matter how much I think about it. Perhaps it's not the Motherland that changes people and people change wherever they are, perhaps what looks like a change is not a change and Uncle Zé always was the man who arrived here holding hands with Mena the mulatto girl just like he continues to be the man who paraded around with Nhé Nhé, perhaps Uncle Zé always was the man who agrees to move to the countryside with Mena the mulatto girl and continues to be the man who was eager to help the people oppressed for five centuries to create a nation. Perhaps it's me who sees change where in reality there is none, perhaps it's me who is inventing a mystery where there is no mystery, perhaps nothing changes and we only reveal ourselves in different ways. I don't feel as though I've changed but I'm certain that if the Mother who wore blue eye-powder could see me now she would say, you don't look like you. And it would not be only because my beard is growing out.

But it was strange to see Uncle Zé in reception not wearing a belt with a butterfly-shaped buckle or anything like that and on top of it all holding hands with Mena the mulatto girl. The first thing that came into my mind was that Pacaça would not be able to say, so after all there was a good reason why you were wearing that white coat like Jacques Franciú's. Uncle Zé who was standing in reception still had lips in the shape of a heart but he no longer pouted like a girl, and without the pout he was simply a man with heart-shaped lips. He could once more be the Uncle Zé who turned up unannounced at our house over there, Uncle Zé from a time before the letters from Quitexe and before Nhé Nhé, Uncle Zé who was simply Mother's baby brother and who had come from the Motherland. But he wasn't. There was the Uncle Zé who had never answered the letters I sent him. Neither mine nor Mother's. The Uncle Zé who appeared in the hotel bar did not mention my letters but said he'd answered Mother's. It's not true, so many letters could not have got lost. Uncle Zé realised we didn't believe him but he swore over and over again that he had done everything he could to get Father released. Perhaps it's true, Uncle Zé almost cried with anger when he realised that we kept saying yes of course yes of course just to make him shut up. It might be that Uncle Zé had not written to us because he had no good news to give us, and instead of a lack of love or interest on his part there may have in fact been a greater love that didn't allow him to do things differently. It doesn't matter. If he liked us he should have known how to do what we needed him to do, otherwise any love he claims to have for us is simply a nuisance. That's why, in my mind, Uncle Zé never did anything to get Father released and as soon as he had put us on an aeroplane he ran off to go and suck Nhé Nhé's cock and never wanted to hear from us again. That's what happened, end of story. I hope they're happy, him and Mena the mulatto girl, very far away from here up in the north with relatives who didn't even invite us to visit, fucking weasels, so many letters saying how much they missed us and now not a word, you can't trust people in the Motherland. Not even the ones who are nice like Silvana and Queine the porter.

I don't want to know what happened with Uncle Zé but there are many more things I'd like to know and I can't. Things that aren't as terrible as Father's scars but that also gnaw at me. Such as what happened with Silvana and Queine the porter. I can't remember much of the last day I went to see Silvana. She had been refusing for some time to sit on the handlebars like Etta, the Sundance Kid's girlfriend, used to do on Butch Cassidy's bicycle. I had heard Pacaça congratulate Queine the porter and I knew the reason but Silvana could have told me, I'm afraid of falling and losing the baby. I think I would have preferred that. But who knows. It's always easier to say these things after the event. Silvana was making a cake, sometimes Silvana made cakes on her day off, she even put cream and silver sprinkles on them. Summer was near and the fields around the house were not so ugly, they weren't pretty either, the fields were streaked with purple and yellow. Mother would also make a cake for our birthdays. The cake would never rise, I opened the oven door too soon, she'd say, I didn't beat the egg whites, I forgot to sift the flour. There was always a reason and it was never Mother's lack of skills. Mother would take the cake out of the cake tin and cover it in cream that was not any good either, a thick paste that was difficult to spread, she sprinkled it with grated coconut, like snow. The grated coconut would fly all over the place when we blew out the candles and Mother would promise never to use coconut again, but come the next birthday she'd do the same. In our new house Mother will make cakes for our birthdays and it won't matter if they don't rise or if Mother covers them in grated coconut. We'll blow out the candles and everything will be well. Even if Father takes a while to fulfil his promise of getting us a better house, everything will be well.

Queine the porter's shift finished at six in the morning and we still had a lot of time to be together. I was looking forward to going into the bedroom, to Silvana undressing me, to feeling her hair touching my chest, her hair tickling my chest always made me laugh, it was good to be with Silvana, I liked seeing her fall asleep holding on to me. But that day Silvana was making a cake and was talking about unimportant things, about Senhor Maurício who had moved out of the hotel and had left his room smelling of the meat he grilled on the balcony, no matter how much they cleaned nothing could get that smell out. She didn't mean to criticise, and it was nothing against the returnees, she was just telling me for the sake of telling me. The manager had threatened to expel him many times but Senhor Maurício would say, the manager can go fuck herself. Senhor Maurício was like that, he was always swearing, he didn't mind if there were women or children nearby. A lot of people didn't like him because of that. That and his permanently blackened fingernails, it's from his old profession, said his wife, Dona Isabel, a mechanic can never deny his trade. Senhor Maurício found a job in a town on the other side of the river, Pacaça used to say it was a town so full of commies that even the statue of Christ the King turned its back on it. But hardly anyone laughs at Pacaça's jokes anymore.

Silvana ran her finger along the rim of the bowl with the remains of the cake mix and licked it. She handed me the bowl and I did the same. For some time we stood beside one another licking the cake mix out of the bowl with our fingers. Then out of the blue Silvana said, it's better if you don't come again. I didn't know what to say. I should have said anything but I didn't know what to say. Instead of leaving I sat at the kitchen table on one of the kitchen stools. Silvana sat on the stool opposite, the empty cake bowl between us. It's better if you don't come again. Just like months earlier she had said, you know the way to my house. I looked around, the kitchen was as ugly as the one in our new house. I was about to ask, who'll take care of me when I have a fever. But Silvana smiled and I didn't ask. I didn't even think of asking later. I know the way to your house and I know how not to come again. Since then, whenever we run into each other at the hotel we say hello and nothing else. We're not angry at each other. At least I'm not. And I'm sure Silvana isn't either.

I continue lying on the terrace. The heat from the floor warms my body more than this tepid autumn sun. I have to shake this sluggishness from my body, get up, look out for a last time at the sea and go and pack my bag. The sea still telling me that despite Father's breezeblock factory the future can be anywhere I want. Before, whenever the sea was unsettled, in every little white speck I saw Pirata running towards me. Pirata with the determined air of a dog who knows that she would catch up with me if she didn't stop running. I can't see Pirata in the sea's white specks anymore and I no longer believe that Pirata finally realised that she would never catch up with Uncle Zé's car and is still resting in the shade of a tree.

Tomorrow I will no longer be here. It seems impossible. It seems impossible that the day to leave the hotel has arrived and that I'm scared of us being a family with a house again. I'm scared of us no longer being one family among many families of returnees in the same hotel and of becoming a family of returnees among families from over here. I realise I won't ever be able to think and feel one thing at a time. I'll have to get used to that until it no longer bothers me. I can't stop certain thoughts from summoning new thoughts or from making others disappear. There's no harm in it. It won't do me any harm. Just as it won't do me any harm not to know what happened to Father in prison, what happened to Mother's demons, to Silvana or to Uncle Zé. There's no harm in not knowing any of those things as long as there are things I do know for sure.

An aeroplane streaks the sky. Silent. Like a lazy chalk scrawl in God's invisible hands. In earlier days I would have replied from down here. Perhaps I'll still reply. In earlier days I would have written something, perhaps I'll still write, in very large letters spread across the terrace so that he'll see me, I was here.

I was here.

The things that die
should not be touched.

DULCE MARÍA LOYNAZ

DULCE MARIA CARDOSO spent her childhood in Luanda, Angola, after her parents moved there when she was an infant. Her family returned to Portugal following the Angolan War of Independence in 1975. She studied law at the University of Lisbon and worked as a lawyer before becoming a full-time writer. Her first novel, *Campo de sangue*, won the Grand Prize Acontece de Romance, *Os meus sentimentos* won the E.U. Prize for Literature and *O chão dos pardais* won the Portuguese Pen Club Award. *The Return* is her fourth novel and the first to appear in English translation.

ÁNGEL GURRÍA-QUINTANA is a translator, historian and journalist. He has reviewed extensively for the *Financial Times* and continues to write for various newspapers and magazines, alongside his work as a literary translator from Spanish and Portuguese. He is co-curator of FlipSide Literary Festival, in Suffolk.